Praise for ARMSTRONG

"The world has a new hero—actually an old hero reimagined—George Armstrong Custer, in this delightfully funny alternative history that's better, or at least happier, than the real thing."
  —**WINSTON GROOM**, bestselling author of *Forrest Gump* and *El Paso*

"Droll satire, this is the West as it might have been if the Sioux hadn't saved us."
  —**STEPHEN COONTS**, bestselling author of *Flight of the Intruder* and *Liberty's Last Stand*

"If Custer died for our sins, *Armstrong* resurrects him for our delight. Not just the funniest book ever written about an Indian massacre, but laugh-out-loud funny, period. The best historical comic adventure since George MacDonald Fraser's *Flashman*."
  —**PHILLIP JENNINGS**, author of *Nam-A-Rama* and *Goodbye Mexico*

"Crocker has created a hilarious hero for the ages. *Armstrong* rides through the Old West setting right the wrongs, and setting wrong the rights, in a very funny cascade of satire, history, and even patriotism."
  —**ROB LONG**, Emmy- and Golden Globes-nominated screenwriter and co-executive producer of *Cheers*

Armstrong

THE CUSTER OF THE WEST SERIES

ARMSTRONG

H.W. CROCKER III

REGNERY FICTION

Regnery Fiction™ is a trademark of Salem Communications Holding Corporation;
Regnery® is a registered trademark of Salem Communications Holding Corporation

Cataloging-in-Publication data on file with the Library of Congress

ISBN 978-1-62157-711-9
e-book ISBN 978-1-62157-712-6

Published in the United States by
Regnery Fiction
An Imprint of Regnery Publishing
A Division of Salem Media Group
300 New Jersey Ave NW
Washington, DC 20001
www.RegneryFiction.com

Manufactured in the United States of America

10 9 8 7 6 5 4 3 2 1

Books are available in quantity for promotional or premium use. For information on discounts and terms, please visit our website: www. Regnery.com.

For Sally, my own Libbie Custer

Invictus Maneo

CHAPTER ONE

In Which I Reveal How I Was Born to Ride

D ear Libbie,
   I realize it must be quite a shock to learn that I am not dead, but by these tokens you will know that it is true. First, the bearer of this packet will be a man over six feet tall, well-groomed, dark of hair, with a pleasing countenance and Southern manner and eyepatch embroidered with the rebel flag (it could be over either eye; he doesn't actually need it but uses it as a signaling device: on the left eye it means Indians or desperadoes to the west; on the right eye, to the east; one if by land, two if by sea).

   He should answer to the name of Beauregard Gillette. When it comes to cards he is sharp as a razor. Don't let your friends play with him. With women he is as smooth as a bar of soap but a moral man all the same. I trust him implicitly.

   Besides the manuscript you hold in your hands, he will give you a curl of my golden hair, a clipping from my moustache, and a tintype of me disguised as a Chinaman (though you, Libbie, will no doubt see through the disguise).

I cannot come back to you myself, my dearest, though I long to do so, until I can show that the massacre at the Little Bighorn River was through no fault of my own. We were betrayed, as surely as the Spartans at Thermopylae. But I must be able to prove it. And I am in the process of doing so, though I don't know how many weeks, or months, or even years it may take. I will restore the name of your husband to the ranks of military glory.

How did I survive? I will write more about that later, but for now suffice it to say that I grieve for the loss of my men, my brothers Tom and Boston, young Autie and Lieutenant Calhoun, and even my gallant horse Vic. (I assume he perished, though Dandy was kept back and is likely safe. If you have my staghounds Bleuch and Tuck—I left them behind; the Army may have returned them to you—I'd appreciate it if you'd send them to me through Beauregard. As you know, it can be lonely out here in the vast expanses of the West.)

One moment I was in the center of an ever-receding circle of my Seventh Cavalry, amidst the crack of gunfire, the stench of gun smoke, the shouting of the men, the crazed yelping of the Indians, the stinking sweat of our men and theirs, and then one massive Indian crashed into me like an enraged bear, and I rolled on the ground with him—he clubbing and missing with his stone-headed ax, me striking his snarling primeval face with my gloved left fist while my right hand, holding a revolver, was pinned to the ground in his vicious grip.

Then a sudden darkness.

When I awoke, I saw a striking pair of brown eyes, the classical features of a beautiful woman—only the bottom half of her face was that of a skull, a bone-white jaw and sugar-cube white teeth in a rictus grin. As my bleary eyes cleared, I realized the skull was the design on a neckerchief that she wore over her nose like a cowboy does on a dusty trail.

She removed the neckerchief, revealing the fullness of her beauty, and said in a variant of the Sioux language that I could understand because, I later realized, it was Sioux-accented English, "Your hair is as radiant as the sun, your eyes as blue as the dawn of a happy day, a son of the morning star"—the usual thing. But then she added, "An Apollo, an Adonis in his prime." I'd never reckoned a Sioux to know Greek mythology. So, I tried my luck.

"Begging your pardon, ma'am, but are you white?"

"Why, yes, of course. Are you delirious?"

"But you speak Sioux, or at least a Sioux dialect."

"Yes, Boyanama Sioux."

My head, neck, and shoulders ached with a dull throbbing pain, and I stared at her, my mind still somewhat hazy, as though she were a ministering angel and felt for my Indian medicine pouch, the gift of a Ree scout that hung from a thong around my neck. There was no superstition attached to it—it held a small supply of salt and a foldable toothbrush for circumstances such as this. I extracted the toothbrush, snapped it open, licked its bristles wet, applied some salt, and busily scrubbed my teeth as she went on.

"They kidnapped me—long ago, it seems, but it wasn't. You're safe now. Don't worry. But... but what are you doing?"

I spat out blood-tinged salt and said, "Just freshening my breath, ma'am. Never want to offend a lady." She looked at me quizzically, so I decided to change the subject. "Begging your pardon, ma'am, but where am I? Last thing I remember, I was grappling with an enormous enraged Indian covered in nightmarish tattoos. I suppose I must have killed him." I flexed my gloved fists. They felt strong as ever.

"You did—and then I rescued you."

"Well, much obliged, ma'am."

"He was my husband—my *Indian* husband. By their law, I claimed you as my slave."

Now it was my turn to be surprised. "Your slave, ma'am?"

"Yes, and you should be glad; only I can kill you now—or a warrior on my behalf. They call me Scalp-Not-My-Woman, but you can call me Rachel. That was my name before... before I was taken by Bearstalker."

"Well, thank you very much. And about your husband..."

"That, thank goodness, is over. You have freed me."

I reached to tip my hat, but it wasn't there—lost on the battlefield, I reckoned. I also wondered how my right glove, tucked into my belt during the battle, had been restored to my right hand. I said, "Well, ma'am, happy to be of service."

"I do have a question, though."

"About your new slave, I suppose."

"Actually, yes: the Cheyenne women say you belong to them—that you are married to Monahsetah."

I nearly swore under my breath. Will I never be rid of this wretched rumor? It was an embarrassing and painful subject, of course, and I shook my head and sighed.

It is true, Libbie, as I've told you, that Monahsetah had the grace and dignity of a chief's daughter and that for an Indian she was exceedingly comely, with a well-shaped head, a luxuriant growth of the most beautiful silken tresses, rivaling in color the blackness of the raven and extending, when allowed to fall loosely over her shoulders, to below her waist. It is also true that she was a spirited woman who shot her first husband before she divorced him—and you know how I love a spirited woman.

She was, as well, very useful to me as a translator negotiating peace with the Plains Indians. It is even true, however shameful it is to relate, that campaigning soldiers sometimes take on squaws as companions. But I was not one of them. And Cheyenne women, especially *noble* Cheyenne women, are noted among the Indians for their chastity. Granted, there is some reason, perhaps, to fault Monahsetah on those grounds—but not, I hasten to add, to indict me. It is true that she bore two children of unknown provenance. But the first was conceived before I had even met her. The second was named Yellow Bird, and while gossips wagged their tongues about that name and pointed to supposed blond tints in the child's hair, I was not the child's father; and if that child was named after me—something I do not know for a fact—it is no doubt a tribute to Monahsetah's admiration for my commanding presence, strength, courage, and dash—qualities that, as you know, Indians value highly, perhaps more so than people do back East. But I need hardly say, dearest Libbie, that my vows bind me to you alone, and despite Monah-setah's charming manners, girlish figure, cascading inky black tresses, and natural affection for me, you know that your Autie would never be tempted.

So, I quickly set my rescuer aright. "No, by any white man's law, I have only one wife, and that is my darling Libbie. I can have no other."

"You might need me," she said. "Your men are dead; the Sioux are celebrating."

I hadn't heard them before—but I heard them now, a distant howl-ing; dull drumbeats prodding them on.

"They'll force you to take an oath. It will make you a Boyanama Sioux. It will be protection of a sort, but it will come at a high price. You will be their prisoner, as I am."

She motioned to two, giant, aboriginal red men I hadn't noticed earlier. They were standing far enough behind her that I had to raise my neck, painfully, to see them. They were ugly and brutish, ritually scarred, tattooed, and painted. They had rifles at the ready, and their dark eyes gleamed with hatred. I'd have returned their spite if I'd had the energy, but I felt sick and filthy, winded and battered. I had scraped the blood from my teeth, but it still caked my nostrils and stuck in my throat, and I could feel it dried like thin red clay around my ears.

She nodded at the Indian guards, and they slung their rifles and lifted me, roughly, to my feet. Normally I would have shrugged them off, but I couldn't—each one had a hand clasped beneath my armpits, like the top of a crutch. Rachel led the way, and, supported by the red men, I staggered after her. Ahead of me, across a gentle rising meadow, maybe only forty yards away, I saw dozens of tepees, smoke rising from fires, and small dark figures—children, I reckoned—darting under the illu-mination of the slowly rising sun. There was a wikiup set off from the tepees and nearer to us. An animal hide flapped at its entrance. The Indians gripped me hard and shoved me through.

The interior of the wattled wikiup was dark and smelt of horse dung and wood smoke. Through the dusk I saw the leering smile of a crazy-eyed, grey-haired, old Indian, his hair mostly tied in two long braids, but with wisps tangled on his skull like a nest of spider webs. Before him was something like an inkstand, made out of a bear claw with a knitting needle stuck in it.

Most Indians wear warpaint, but these Indians, like Bearstalker, whom I had slain, and the belligerent guards who stood behind me, had tattoos running over their faces and arms and everywhere. Except for the tasteful, dutiful rendition of his initials, the flag of the Republic, and Lady Liberty on the arm of my impetuous brother Tom, I had rarely seen a tattoo before, even on sailors, and you can imagine my dismay when Scalp-Not-My-Woman (who was unmarked herself) told me that this was part of my induction: I was to be tattooed as a Boyanama Sioux.

At least I was given a choice of my defacement. The crazy old man handed me a stick, dripping with blood, apparently, and asked me to draw my preferred design—my Indian coat of arms, as it were—on the back of an elk hide, which served as a sketchpad. For a moment I was at a loss; then, inspired, I reached to find my muse, and it was gone. In a frenzy I patted the shreds of my uniform trying to find it.

"Looking for this?" Scalp-Not-My-Woman held out my locket compass—the one with your portrait. It swung gently from its chain. "I should have left it behind, when we pulled you from the battlefield, but every woman has a heart."

I took it gratefully, stared wistfully at your image, and on that hide I drew the only escutcheon for me. I handed the marked-up hide to the old man, along with the locket so that he could see what I was driving at. He nodded, examined the compass carefully, and then shook it, trying to make the needle shift. He tapped your portrait. I nodded in turn. He eructed a dry laugh, and a hideous, bestial grin played across his features.

He pointed to my face. I shook my head and tapped my arm. He said something to Scalp-Not-My-Woman. They exchanged guttural remarks, which seemed slightly heated, and then he chuckled again like a dog choking on its dinner, and she helped me, gingerly, out of my shirt. I was as sore as if I had gone twenty rounds with Gypsy Jem Mace; my ribs ached with every movement of my arms. The Indian motioned for me to place my hands together. I did and he bound them tightly with rawhide strips, his sneering grin growing as he did so. He examined my left arm—as an artist, I suppose, might examine his canvas.

"Golden Hair?" said Scalp-Not-My-Woman.

"Yes, I do have golden hair. What of it?"

But it was merely a ruse to get my mouth open. She drove a large stick horizontally between my parted teeth and against my protesting tongue. The stick was too big for my teeth to crunch or my tongue to dislodge. Then the crazy old man went to work, plunging that needle into my skin like a lunatic woodpecker doing its worst to a pine, and applying his dyes or whatever they were. I tried to scream in protest—not just at the mutilation of my arm but also because it was being done entirely at odds with the image I had given him. It took hours of low-grade torment before he had turned my entire left arm into what I assume was some Indian depiction of flames shooting down from my shoulder to my wrist.

The old codger had stamina—I'll give him that. Without a break he moved to my right arm. To ensure my cooperation, he tapped the locket with your picture and pointed at my upper arm. He had me flex it so that the muscle grew large, and on it now imprinted is your sacred name: *Libbie*; your portrait too, as if a mad Indian Michelangelo had engraved it there, which I suppose he had, in a way; and *Feb 9*, our wedding date. Circling it like an aura is my new motto, the only motto for a cavalryman: *Born to Ride*.

When we meet again, my dearest, it will be another way for you to know it is truly I, George Armstrong Custer. For when we meet again, I may be in disguise.

One thing I hope you will not mistake me for is a red man, despite my being inducted into the ranks of the Boyanama Sioux.

That ceremony was an astonishing thing. The two dull-eyed warriors who were my guards frogmarched me into a scene of primitive frenzy— drums throbbing, braves dancing, their guttural voices joining the ululating of the squaws. To me it sounded as if they were chanting a dirge from their primeval past, when the earth was inhabited only by people like themselves... or like me, now that I was to become one of them.

I was still stripped to the waist—which inevitably caused a little flutter among the squaws—with the stick jammed in my mouth and my hands bound. I was hatless under the hot sun, and my tattooed arms dripped blood. A warrior stepped forward with a knife in his hand. The blade was dirty and stained but sharp enough, and he severed the rawhide tethers from my hands. It was freedom, but only for a moment, as other warriors grabbed me and shoved me against a six-foot-high stake. My arms were pulled behind me, and new rawhide bands bound me to it, while warriors gathered round, thrusting spears and lances and stone-headed clubs. The drums pounded harder, and the warriors came closer. They slapped their chests and snarled. Brave girl that she was, Scalp-Not-My-Woman strode up to me and pulled the stick from my mouth. Involuntarily I coughed up a wad of blood. It rested for a vile moment on my tongue, and I spat it on the ground.

"*Awahuh!*" the Indians shouted as one. The drums silenced. The warriors drew back a step. Their dark, menacing faces grew darker. They sensed an insult. A spear was flung directly between my feet. A tall man—built big and strong, but old now, his back slightly bent, his gait stiff—emerged from the mass. Around his neck, like a chain-mail collar that seemed to weigh him down, was a necklace of what appeared to be linked coins. Even with that accoutrement, he was an ugly brute—grey-black hair hanging lank; a pugilist's nose; a pessimist's frown; exhausted-looking eyes; his face dotted and dashed with either warpaint or tattoos—and arrogant. No doubt he had been a mighty warrior once, but I reckoned a feral challenger could take him now, if he dared.

He pointed to Scalp-Not-My-Woman and barked at her in a Sioux dialect I couldn't understand. She came between us, our translator.

His voice was not just guttural, like the others', but gravelly.

"Chief Linewalker asks why you do not fear him. His men slaughtered your pony soldiers. He could slaughter you now. But you look, he says, like the cougar—golden hair and ready to fight."

"You can tell him," I said, looking the old man straight in the eye, "that I fear no man—least of all those who fear their own bodies, their own faces, and have to desecrate them with the designs of a crazy old man with a knitting needle."

"I can't tell him that—he won't understand."

"I think he will."

"*Awahuh!*" It was exhalation from the crowd.

The chief eyed me steadily, then his gravelly voice vomited up a thought for Scalp-Not-My-Woman to translate.

"He says, 'Why did you allow it then on your own arm, the arm that wields the gun and the saber?'"

"Because I do not fear his silly medicine; I have turned it to my own uses. This"—I flexed my right arm and nodded towards it, trying to highlight your portrait and name—"is the great white queen I serve. This"—I nodded again, trying to indicate my motto—"will tell every white man that I am, proudly, a pony soldier, no matter what you do to the rest of my body."

"He asks about your great white queen. You are Golden Hair, a pony soldier. You are not a warrior of the red jacket. *He means a Canadian.*"

"Yes, I know what he means. You can tell him that the red jackets and I are blood brothers, brothers of the sword."

The chief held out a savage knife, like a primitive Bowie knife, handle forward. With my hands still bound, I couldn't take it, but that seemed to be the idea.

"He says that while the Boyanama Sioux celebrate a great victory, they also mourn for the loss of their braves, including my...my former husband. He says that, as my slave, you must assist in my mourning. You must take this knife and cut a top knuckle from one of my fingers."

A feeling of revulsion shot through my body like a sudden wave of fever; every sinew of manliness within me was aroused against this outrage; and I glared at the chief as I had glared at few men in my life. For I knew exactly what he meant; I had seen Indians in mourning before: they scarify their faces, arms, and bodies with knives, dull knives, wielded not with the skill of a surgeon but with the brute stupidity of a savage. It is not uncommon for a widowed spouse to lop off the first joint of her little finger. When the wound heals, the skin retracts and the remaining bone protrudes in a most revolting way. I would not let that happen to Scalp-Not-My-Woman.

"You fiendish dog of hell," I said. "I will not—and you will not—touch one hair of that woman. If you need some sacrifice, take it not from the hands of she-who-should-remain-unblemished, take it from…*my moustache*!"

"But Golden Hair…"

"*Tell him!*"

"*Awahuh!*" All the Indians were astonished—except for Linewalker. He showed no emotion but eyed me beadily.

"He says you find Boyanama Sioux customs bestial."

"Yes, I do."

"He says, 'But you will soon be one of us.'"

"If that is so, tell him, it is by compulsion—and I can only hope that I can make him and his people the better for it."

"He says you are arrogant—but brave."

"I fear no man."

The chief came towards me, flipped the knife around so that its blade faced me, and, with a sudden violence I didn't expect, raked it across my left shoulder. I couldn't help but recoil when he pressed his rubbery lips to the wound, sucked blood, and spat it at the spear point between my feet.

Then he shouted something and the knife was above my nose, as though he intended to plunge it between my eyes. But instead he paused, made the slightest incision in my forehead and another on his palm, and clasped that hand to my brow, chanting some words as he did so.

He barked another order and a brave cut me loose from the stake. The chief slit his own forearm. He motioned for me to extend mine. He slit it and we shook hands in the manner of the ancient Romans, forearm to forearm.

"He says he will spare my finger as a courtesy to you, as you are now a blood brother of the Boyanama Sioux. He says you will kill the Indians no more forever."

"Tell him that I am a man of my word, and if those are the terms of my parole, I accept them."

The chief shouted at me and gave me a ceremonial punch to the chest. I gulped hard to keep from spitting blood. Then he turned to his braves, gave them a one-minute hellfire sermon (at least that's what it sounded like), and as they gathered round, yippying like dancing devils, he passed through them, broken nose held high.

"It is done," Scalp-Not-My-Woman said. "Thank goodness that's over. There is already a tepee set aside for us."

"For *us?*"

"Remember, you are my slave."

"Oh, yes, yes of course, ma'am."

You can imagine how discomfited I was to become the slave of a beautiful woman—even if she had saved my life. Still, I had no choice but to follow her into her relatively charming little tepee—much nicer than that filthy wikiup of the tattooist. There were even two bearskin rugs laid upon the earth. We reclined on them. Her Indian husband must have been a man of prominence.

"He was," she said. "He was the son of Chief Linewalker."

Well, that threw me. I couldn't image such an accommodation in the white world. You kill a man's son, you become a slave to his daughter-in-law, and you get inducted as the old man's blood brother. No one can deny the Indians have their points.

"What now?" I asked.

"Now you do as I say."

"What happens when the Army comes looking for me?"

"They won't. We put another golden hair in your place. Those are his buckskins." She pointed to a neatly laid out uniform behind the bear rug. "They are now yours. You will wear them. His hair was cut short, like yours."

"There's more to me than hair and clothes."

She gave me a baleful glare. "You've seen an Indian battlefield—not just the scalps but the bellies ripped open, the unspeakable things they do. Bodies full of arrows, lining them like porcupine quills. Heads, arms, hands, and legs chopped off. Knives plunged into eyes. Tongues ripped out. That didn't happen to this man; we guarded him. He was shot in two places, but his body wasn't desecrated. They only plunged awls in his ears to aid his hearing in the afterlife—or that's what the Indians think. Your scouts will mark it as a sign of respect. He wasn't mutilated—so he can be identified as you."

"But they'll know it's not me."

"He fooled the Cheyenne women; he'll fool your army. I knew him well—he was a slave too."

"Now hold on there, Scalp-Not-My-Woman…"

"Call me Rachel."

"I'm not calling anyone who keeps white men as slaves Rachel."

"He was captured and spared on my word. He was another soldier, or a former one, maybe a deserter. They found him riding in the Black Hills."

"So, you're the Pocahontas of the Plains. Any other white slaves around here?"

"No—unless you consider me; and I wish you would."

"There was no initiation for you?"

"Not the kind you had. Another of my names is Tattoo-Not-My-Woman-On-Her-Face-On-Her-Arms-On-Her-Legs-On-Her…"

"I get the idea. You were too valuable as is."

"I think you'll find me very valuable too. I can help you escape. We can escape together. They trust me. They still don't trust you."

"Well, that makes us even, because I don't trust them—not even as blood brothers. And I'm not sure I trust you—though I am indebted to you, ma'am. If it's not an indelicate question, how many white slaves have you had?"

"Only two—including you."

"And you had my predecessor killed."

"I learned how to be cold-hearted from the Indians. It was his life or yours; and he could do nothing for me. You are General Custer. I saw you on the battlefield. I saw you kill Bearstalker. I saw you fight as bravely as any man has ever fought. You can rescue me."

"And what about my look-alike?"

"He had hair like yours. But he didn't have your spirit, your strength. Oh, physically he was close enough—close enough to fool a Cheyenne.

And anyone who looks for bodies on that horrible battlefield will take him as you; his body was arranged to make it seem so. But really he was not at all like you. He was weak. He was afraid. He was no companion, no leader for an escape. But you are General Custer. You can get me out of this horrible place, away from these horrible Indians."

High praise indeed, camped, as we were, among hundreds if not thousands of them; but warranted, I had to grant. "It'll take some thinking," I said.

"But you," she repeated, "are General Custer. You will find a way."

Yes, I thought, I better.

⚮

She was a clever one. Scalp-Not-My-Woman had already secured us two excellent mounts—abandoned cavalry horses that, for my money, were better than the best Indian pony. I inspected the horses while giving the impression to any spying Indians of merely doing my mistress's bidding, rubbing the horses down and cleaning their hooves. They would do fine.

The Boyanama Sioux, many of them, were still drunk, literally or figuratively, on their massacre of my troops—dancing and chanting and drumming—and I hated them for it. But the soberer ones, like Linewalker, were preparing to move—they had apparently moved once already, immediately after the battle; I'd slept through it, unconscious, dragged on a travois. They were expecting vengeance from the U.S. Cavalry, and I hoped that vengeance would soon make its appearance.

In the meantime, I was busy too. Scalp-Not-My-Woman bossed me like the slave I allegedly was—and I played my part. I had a big audience. Plenty of braves, I noticed, kept an eagle eye on me—whether because they didn't trust me, or because they wanted to kill me and claim Scalp-Not-My-Woman as their own, or merely out of admiration, I do not know. I wasn't much interested in making conversation with them. And I doubt that talk was much on their minds either. That's not the Indian way.

"Linewalker intends to leave at first light tomorrow," said Scalp-Not-My-Woman. "Do you have a plan?"

Sure enough, by now I did. I figured that the worst thing we could do was bolt quickly. Better would be to withdraw with Linewalker and lull him and his braves into thinking I had accepted my lot. When their eyes were less keen, we would slip away on the trail. The Great Sioux Reservation was to our east—and though plenty of vaguely peaceable Sioux would cover for him, I reckoned Linewalker had no intention of going in that direction. Most likely he would head north, maybe all the way to the Canadian border. I didn't have a map, but I thought our best route of escape was along the Yellowstone River heading west. My goal was Bloody Dick Creek, near Red Butte and Coyote Flats, a place that I had seen on a map before and that I reckoned would put us beyond the reach of the retreating Boyanama Sioux. But our chances depended on how much Linewalker valued his daughter-in-law—and on that point, I was worried.

The more I got to know her, the whiter Scalp-Not-My-Woman became. She was olive-skinned, whether from the sun or from some Indian dye or because of a tincture of Indian or Spanish blood, I couldn't say. But I can say that her father had been, of all things, a judge—or so she told me. He had come, idealistically, to bring law to the West and been an itinerant magistrate. A widower, he traveled with his daughter. While riding from one small-town court to another, they were ambushed by a Sioux war party. Bearstalker captured Rachel—a mere girl of sixteen, as she then was—and took her for his squaw.

Being a judge's daughter, she was educated and refined, which had made her imprisonment among the Sioux all the more horrible. Still, all in all, they had treated her relatively well, and as Bearstalker's woman she held authority and respect in the tribe. I had to assume she inspired a mite bit of jealousy as well. And she was as cunning as an Indian. When I told her how we might melt away with the retreat, she nodded and added a touch of her own.

The morning of our departure, I was awake before the Indians, or most of them. Scalp-Not-My-Woman had brought me breakfast—jerky

and a pancake washed down with water—and we were packed and ready
to ride. Linewalker, I noticed, kept a beady father-in-law's eye on us. It
was pretty clear my blood brother thought I had tainted blood. From his
perspective, he was right.

The Indian caravan set out at dawn. Their belongings were few and
easily transportable. And they kept a sorry camp. They had no concern
for good order or cleanliness—and if you don't care about cleaning up
and burying your waste, you can move a lot faster.

As I predicted, the path went north—and it was only us, the Boyanama Sioux. I had no idea where the other tribes were headed—indeed
I saw no other tribes. Our encampment must have been set some ways
off from the mass of Sioux and Cheyenne we had battled. I reckoned we
had more than two hundred braves and at least as many women and
children among us. Scalp-Not-My-Woman and I had started near the
vanguard, but slowly—I hoped imperceptibly—we fell back along the
trail, until we were near the rear guard by dusk. As dark settled in, Scalp-
Not-My-Woman pulled away into a spinney set in a gulley. A brave
guarding the tribe's small remuda rode over to question me.

I had pledged to kill no more Indians; but I had said nothing about
knocking them senseless. So, while he was in mid-guttural interrogation,
I struck him full-on with a gloved fist that sent him reeling. He was a
young brave, not yet fully grown, and I caught him with my other hand
and lifted him onto my horse. I herded his horse and another, cut from
the remuda, down to where Scalp-Not-My-Woman was waiting with
our little surprise for the Boyanama Sioux.

She gagged the young brave with her skull-decorated neckerchief and
bound his wrists and ankles with strips of rawhide. Then she unloaded
the bear rugs she had draped over her horse.

Stuffed within the rugs were cleverly packaged bundles of clothes
and sticks and grass that she quickly fashioned into a dummy woman
and a dummy man. We tied the dummies to the two Indian ponies I had
brought with me.

I led the horses back up to the trail and sent them trotting after the
remuda. If the Indians were looking for us, and didn't look too closely

in the dark, they might be fooled—or so she thought, and I reckoned she knew the Boyanama Sioux better than I did.

We remounted our cavalry horses and rode west, riding quietly at first and then at a full gallop in what I guessed was the direction of the Yellowstone River, beyond which was the Idaho Territory. I reached for my locket compass—I wanted to calculate how long it would take us—only to find that, once again, it was missing. And then I realized that I hadn't seen it since I had been tattooed. I reined up next to Scalp-Not-My-Woman and said, I confess a bit roughly, "Where's my compass?"

"Don't worry; I took care of it."

"What do you mean, you took care of it?"

She looked me straight in the eye and said, "I left it with the old man, the Indian who tattooed you."

"You what?"

"I should have left it on the corpse of the man impersonating you. But as I said, every woman has a heart."

"And so you gave it to that lunatic Indian who defaced me for life?"

"If someone saw it, it would betray your identity."

"And I suppose this tattoo doesn't."

"Not in the same way. You can explain that. The tattoo is not as exact. And how many people are going to see it? Anyway, I had to let him keep the locket—or he would have tattooed her face on yours; he wanted to make Golden Hair a woman."

Now, Libbie, no couple has ever been more devoted than we are, but it was horrible to contemplate you smeared across my face in whatever ashy dye that mad Indian had used on my arms. The idea was like something out of an Edgar Allan Poe story—eerie, horrifying, a transformation most foul—though of course you are wonderful with your own face on your own body.

"You did right," I finally said to Scalp-Not-My-Woman. "Still, I will miss it—the locket, that is—and my wife's picture."

"It's closer to you now than it's ever been," she said, and there was no doubting that.

We rode through the night, pressing our horses as hard as we reasonably could. Summers in Montana are hot, naturally, though the nights are cool; and as it can snow in the mountains as late as June, finding streams to keep the horses watered was no great trouble. We stopped around noon in a pleasant grove of trees to rest the horses and ourselves. I told Scalp-Not-My-Woman to sleep while I kept watch, but she insisted on keeping watch with me.

"You cannot know, General Custer, how long, how desperately long, I have waited for this moment. I'm not going to let anything go wrong now."

I appreciated the sentiment but had to say, "You do realize, my good woman, that I am a trained officer of the United States Army and can spot enemy cavalry as well as any man alive."

"Then look there," she said.

Sure enough, there was a war party on the horizon, perhaps as many as a dozen braves. We had no weapons to speak of—they had allowed me a small knife—and the Indians had my word not to kill them. As good as our horses were, they were near spent. The Indian ponies, though, couldn't be much rested either. I scanned the ground west. There was a ravine just beneath us that would keep us screened from the Indians, at least until they ran into it themselves, or unless they had spotted us already. I took our horses and guided them down.

"All right," I said, patting my horse's mane, "don't die on me, old boy, but let's go as fast as you can."

We shot through that ravine like a storm shower down a drainpipe, and we kept riding until our horses were so soaked in sweat that patting their sides was like slapping a sodden sponge. We rode out the opposite side of the ravine and kept riding until we found a hillock topped by a cluster of trees and lined by a trickling stream—a perfect position to rest our horses and spot the enemy, if he was still after us. Scalp-Not-My-Woman and I watched for pursuit, resting the horses for a good two hours. Then I turned to her and said, "I can't bring myself to call you Rachel yet, but I'm willing to call you Scout—you've earned it."

She batted her eyelashes, as you women do, and said in reply, "All right, you can call me Scout—if I can call you Scalp-Not-My-Man."

It seemed a fair trade. She had saved my scalp once already. She might be in a position to do it again.

We remounted and moved farther along, finally making camp at dusk in a copse of sweet-smelling pines and firs. There was a rocky outcrop that served as my watchtower over the land behind us. I felt pretty confident now. Much as they wanted to recover Scalp-Not-My-Woman and her slave, the warriors were likely on a tight leash. I'm sure in his dastardly Indian heart, Linewalker would have enjoyed torturing us; I'm sure he valued Scalp-Not-My-Woman as a possession; but Indians aren't romantics, and he had a tribe to save—and maybe cavalry on his heels, or so I hoped—and his braves, I expected, had orders to return if they didn't capture us quickly.

The next morning we led our horses down a gentle slope onto a long flat plain. Smack in the middle of it was salvation—a town of fairish size, a church steeple prominent at the far end. Our cavalry horses knew immediately that it was their salvation too and picked up their pace. The townsfolk thought we made a sight—a sunburnt, buckskinned hero (or so they seemed to regard me, but I'm used to that, and I didn't pay it any mind) and his beautiful half-breed squaw.

We rode to the livery stables to get our horses settled.

"Looks like you rode these critters pretty hard."

"They're sturdy mounts. Indians made us ride faster."

"That they shorley do. How long will you be stayin', mister?"

"Oh, I reckon maybe a week."

"Them's cavalry mounts, ain't they?"

"Used to be a soldier myself. Bought 'em on my way out."

"I see. You got bills of sale for 'em?"

"Used to, but they're long gone. Been trappin' in the hills; got no use for paper. Still wear my gauntlets, though, and my cavalry boots—kinda grew attached to those."

"Fair enough. All righty, then. You just sign the ledger. Payment's half in advance; half when you collect your horses."

I wasn't about to sign the ledger "Colonel Custer," and I suddenly realized that I hadn't a penny to my name. But as you know, in a crisis I'm a quick thinker.

"Name's Armstrong," I said, flourishing that signature on the paper. "And I'm a little short of money right now. Trapping ain't what it used to be. But I tell you what. I've got two bearskin rugs on that horse there. You can take 'em both as payment in full."

"Well, there now, I reckon that's a fair shake. Thank ye kindly, Mr. Armstrong."

"How do I find the hotel?"

"That'd be the Applejack Hotel, right over there. And if you and the Misses are looking for some entrytainment, there's a show in town."

"Wonderful. I do love a good show."

"We've got a fancy stage with a curtain and all at the saloon. Sallie Saint-Jean's Showgirls and Follies, they call it. Some trick shootin' too, they say. If you want to wet your whistle and get a quick peek, saloon's right over there—the Branch Creek Saloon, best in town, just across the street. Assumin' the Misses don't mind."

"No, I'm sure she doesn't."

Scout smiled like the white woman she was but stayed as quiet as an Indian.

As we walked out of the stables, she grasped my arm—the one with your name on it. "General, how are we going to pay for the hotel?" She gripped my arm harder. "I'd forgotten about hotels, clean sheets, real food, dresses—we're free, General Custer, we're free!"

"And we're broke," I added. "And from now on call me Armstrong; and yes, I'll call you Rachel; and truth be told, I'm a colonel, thanks to that ape Grant—a dead colonel as far as the world knows."

"But you were a general..."

"Yes, and will be again, if there's any justice in this world. In the meantime, I'll make us some money. Before I took the vow, I knew something about taverns and games of chance." I espied a general store. "Now you go on over there and make a mental list of all the things you'd like to buy, and I'll be around in a little while."

She did as she was bidden, practically skipping down the street—she was more girlish and white by the minute—and I set my boots on the floorboards of the saloon. No shortage of men at tables. I saw the quiet, curtained stage to my right. Normally, as you know, I drink milk, but I figured I wouldn't find that here. "Sarsaparilla," I told the bartender.

"Sarsaparilla?"

"Or plain branch water if you don't have it."

"Naw, I got the sarsaparilla."

I turned around, leaned against the bar, and said, "I've been up in the hills for months. Looking for a game. Anyone oblige me?"

"Well, surely, mister," rang from several tables. I winked at the bartender. "I'll be back with your shekels in a few minutes." I tipped my fingers to my brow in acknowledgement to all and settled at a table where the men looked most well-to-do.

"Don't have any pocket change, but if you'll stake me, have some furs tucked away at the livery stable. They should be worth a tidy sum."

"Reckon we can get you started. Where you from?"

"Oh, been traveling for so long, it's almost hard to recollect. Ohio, originally, but been out West for quite a spell. Was in the cavalry for a while; trappin' now mostly."

"Did you hear that, boys?" said a rough-looking customer from another table. "Cavalry— down to the boots and drinkin' sarsaparilla, don't it figure—and on credit. How's men like that supposed to protect us from them Indians? They couldn't protect themselves from a doe-eyed mule."

I looked this ruffian square in the face. He was at a table full of bravos like himself: big, rangy cowboys whose idea of a good time was a drink and a fight. I knew their type.

"You hear what happened at the Rosebud, soldier boy? Some idiot general named Crook got bushwhacked by the Indians. Then that feller Custer led a bunch of sarsaparilla sissies like you smack into the Sioux and got massacred. When you get your boots, don't they teach you how to fight, or do you just wear 'em to ride away?"

I stood up. "If you weren't such an ignorant excuse for a human being, I'd try to teach you something."

"You think so, soldier boy?" He stood. "You really think so?"

"You take off that holster and I'm sure of it. I don't need a gun."

"You reckon not, eh? Well, maybe I can oblige you with that." He unstrapped his gun belt and dropped it on the table. Then he reached into his boot, drew a knife, and flung it into the table like an Indian challenge. "And look at that. Even takin' off my blade. Fair's fair, right, soldier boy? They teach you how to fight fair, don't they?"

I brought up my fists. "You'll soon find out."

"Yes, you surely will."

He closed on me like a tornado, but I parried and blocked his blows with forearm, elbow, and palm before pivoting so that I hit him flush on the jaw, full force, and sent him sprawling into hastily deserted chairs behind him.

"Why you..." I saw him reach beneath his vest and pull out a pea-shooter, but before he could draw a bead on me, I was at the table where he'd dropped his holster. I heard the pop of his little gun, and, as I was still alive, yanked out his revolver and fired back.

He wouldn't be shooting again.

"He's dead!" the cowboys shouted. Then their eyes pivoted to me. "Get him!"

I was out the saloon doors and cutting down side streets, figuring a straight line meant a dead Custer. I beat my way around to an alley behind the hotel and into a camp of big, garish wagons—theatrical wagons, each with four walls, a roof, and a door. I flung open the door on one, slammed it behind me, and leapt into the arms of a woman seated just inside. She had flaming red hair and a welcoming smile, and I instinctively felt to see that my Indian medicine bag with salt and a toothbrush was still tied around my neck.

"Well, make yourself at home, why don't you?"

"Excuse me, ma'am, but I'm an innocent man running for his life."

"Well, aren't you unique? I've never met an innocent man. Go in there, honey," she motioned to three full-length closets behind her, partially hidden by an oriental partition. "You'll find plenty of disguises. And you can trust me to distract them."

It was only then I noticed that she was dressed in the manner of a certain type of woman of the theater: garters and stockings, the highest of heels, and an outfit that looked more like a colorful corset than a proper dress.

"Thank you, kindly, ma'am—and please pardon the intrusion."

"No trouble at all. But you better get going." I bolted into a closet, cast off my cavalry boots (not easy in that confined space), slipped out of my buckskins, and grabbed what felt like the largest and least feminine thing I could find—something like a robe.

I heard shouting outside and then boots on the floorboards.

"Pardon us, ma'am, we're looking for a desperate killer. Have you seen a tall man: cavalry boots, big blond moustache, short-cut blond hair, wearin' buckskin?"

"Oh, honey, did you hear that?"

I couldn't believe it! She was calling to me! I tried to make my voice as high-pitched as possible, "Oh, no, dear; I saw no one at all."

"That's a funny soundin' voice."

"He's just a Chinaman," she said reassuringly. "Part of our act. A trick shooter. I'm sure he can protect me in the meantime. Toodle-de-doo."

I'll be darned if they didn't leave.

"You can come out now," she said. "And perhaps you can tell me your name."

"Armstrong," says I, and as I stepped from the wardrobe I could see that I was indeed dressed in what I took for the robes of a Chinaman.

"Seems a pity," she said, "but the moustache will have to go, and we'll have to bootblack your hair."

"What?"

"I reckon you know how to handle a gun. Our Chinese trick shooter was lynched a few towns ago. He wasn't much good anyway."

"I can't be a Chinaman."

"Better than being a dead man. I can arrange that too, if you'd like."

"Who in heaven's name would mistake me for a Chinaman?"

"You leave that to me."

"I guess I have to."

"I'm guessin' so. You'll find bootblack in the first wardrobe in the left-hand corner. And there'll be a shavin' kit in the third wardrobe in the right-hand corner. You get started; then I'll help."

In the course of thirty minutes I had my head blackened, my face shaved and powdered, my eyes framed with mascara into some semblance of a Chinaman's, my feet encased in silk slippers, and my manly form draped in a red Chinese robe with black dragons roaring across it. I must say, I cut a figure—as I saw in a full-length mirror that was affixed inside one of the closet doors, and as you can see in the tintype provided by Beauregard.

My first performance, it turned out, would be that very night; and the tintype was made that very day, to promote it. Miss Sallie Saint-Jean—for that was the name of my protectress—instructed me in the essentials of my routine, which seemed simple enough—mostly popping balloons held out by the showgirls. Easy shots that weren't likely to impress hardened men from Montana, I thought. But I could always come up with a few new tricks. My old Ree scout, Bloody Knife—likely dead now and mutilated by the Sioux—always joshed me about my marksmanship, and while I grant you I'm no Wild Bill Hickok, I'm no near-sighted Chinaman either. When it comes to shooting, I can handle my own.

My colleagues were a dozen dancing girls (the main attraction) and a small Chinese contingent: five acrobats, a strong man, a magician, and me, a trick shooter. A San Francisco shipping baron had apparently seen these Chinamen performing in a camp, hired them on the spot, and backed them in a series of shows until he lost interest. When the flame-haired Miss Saint-Jean rediscovered them, they were on hard times and willing to work for pennies. We Chinamen were the interval acts between the ladies' cancans and were also charged with guard duty if the cowboys got rowdy.

My delightful female assistant, Bernadette, walked me through my role, though we had precious little time to rehearse before taking the stage. Behind the curtain we could hear the audience assembling, the raucous cries for whiskey and beer, the scraping of chair legs on the plank floor, the cries of "where's the entrytainment?" and "bring on them girls!" I felt a pang that no one said, "We want the Chinaman trick shooter!"

But my time on stage would come soon enough, and I vowed I would make my mark. My hands were shaking as they had never done on the battlefield. This was the theatre, after all; this was the stage; this was a chance to do my part to lift the souls of these wiry, dirty, tobacco-stained cowboys to those heights reachable only in a dramatic performance. Granted, my role was not Shakespearean, or anything remotely like it, but in my red and black dragon robes, with my hair dyed, my face powdered, and my eyes highlighted and slanted with mascara; with my long-barreled revolver, my assistant in her dancing costume and tights, and my target balloons arrayed before me; I felt as though I was performing in a sort of drama these men could understand, a test of skill as dramatic, in its own way, as a soliloquy. I was playing a role—and intended to play it to the hilt.

The curtain opened. Catcalls and whistles greeted my assistant, and Miss Saint-Jean stepped to center stage to introduce us. "Gentlemen and ladies, I introduce Bernadette LaBelle"—storms of foot-stomping and applause—"and the world famous Chinese marksman and master trick shooter, Li Wing Yu, or, as we call him, Master Wing."

"I'll wing him one," guffawed some drunken cowboy, and I suspected I knew why the last Master Wing had had a short life.

But I also knew what to do. I blew a hole in the ceiling. "Excuse me, honorable cow farmers." That got them riled up and paying attention. I nodded to Bernadette, who plucked two inflated balloons from sacks she had full of them and held them at arm's length in front of a foot-thick target board, about as high and wide as a coffin. The bullets were of low caliber, much lower than our cavalry revolvers, and the wood was supposed to absorb them. I spun the revolvers in my hand and in one catlike motion fell to a knee and popped the balloons: Bang! Bang!

Behind me there was another coffin slab of wood with feathers stuck on it. I swiftly pivoted and blasted off two of them. I reloaded and did that sequence twice. But I knew what the cowboys really wanted. I had Bernadette take two balloons in either hand and cartwheel down the stage, never stopping, and every time she came upright I fired and popped a balloon. That got them hollering, and I figured it was best to quit while I was ahead. But then through all the commotion I heard a woman's voice cry out, "Get your hands off me!"

"You cain't be so particular; ain't you part Injun squaw?"

"You tell us where that buckskin dude is," said another, "or you'll get worse than Jasper."

I looked past the footlights into the crowd and saw Scalp-Not-My-Woman sitting at a table of ruffians. I decided to extend my act.

I fired at the ceiling again. "Humble cow farmers, my next trick requires the assistance of several gentlemen and a lady. You men there—and you, young lady—I humbly pray that you might join me on the stage."

"What the heck for?" said one. "I came here *for* entrytainment—not to *be* the entrytainment."

"You couldn't entertain a flea off a dog's backside," said another.

"It will be a test of your skill and mine," I said. "And there's a prize."

"Skill? You mean with pistoleros? Chinaman, you wouldn't stand a chance. What's the prize?"

"A bag of gold—straight from the Black Hills." I patted my robes where a pocket should have been.

"Well, hell's bells. I'm willin', if y'all are," said one.

"You ain't goin' to get that prize from me."

"And you, Miss? Will you join my humble display?"

"I will not."

"Perhaps these men," I motioned to our audience, "will encourage you."

The encouragement took two forms—cheers and whistles and boot-stomping from the crowd, and meaningful hard looks, with hands drifting to holsters, from her harassers. Rachel got the idea and sidled her way up the steps to the stage with the ruffians as an escort.

"For this trick I will ask our lovely assistants to hand each man two balloons, which he will hold with his arms upright. I will take two as well. At a count of three—given by our two most gracious assistants—we will release the balloons and each man will attempt to shoot as many as possible. Accept humble challenge?"

"Why sure, but you got two revolvers there."

"But only one humble servant; it is you four men against me: four guns to two."

"All righty, I'm ready," said one.

"About that prize, mister…" said another.

I nodded meaningfully.

"Okay," said bright-eyed Bernadette.

"Gentlemen," I said, "I will raise the odds. I will put my life in the bargain. You can shoot at the balloons—or you can shoot at me, as I will be shooting at you."

They looked suspicious and perplexed as I motioned to Bernadette and she chanted, "One…two…THREE!"

I let go of the balloons and dropped to one knee, as I had done on my previous trick shot, and waited for them to draw, as honor demanded. They squinted at me in confusion, or maybe partial recognition, their hands lunging for their sidearms, but I was faster, and with both guns blazing I blasted the blackguards to heaven, or, more likely, hell—taking the first two before they could fire a shot, and the last two in quick succession even as they fired at me and missed, their bullets blasting holes the size of wine corks in the floor of the stage. I emptied my revolvers, taking no chances.

"Oh! So sorry," I said.

The audience was stunned, but I knew they wouldn't be for long.

"Quick! Come with me!" I grabbed Scalp-Not-My-Woman's wrist and ran backstage and out of the saloon and into one of the wagons. I already had a plan. I shoved her into a costume closet, threw my robe and slippers in another, and scrubbed my face in the washbasin. I could hear shouts and chaos outside, but when in battle—and that's what this was—one's mind has to stay cool and focused. I knew what I had to do—hat, breeches, boots, shirt, star, a mighty handy costume that I knew was in here.

"Don't move; don't make a sound," I said to Scalp-Not-My-Woman, hidden in her closet. Then I bounded out of the wagon. "He's not here," I shouted. "Blast him!"

I joined in the chase. Someone noted the glittering tin on my chest. "You a marshal?"

"Yes, been tracking this varmint for weeks. He's killed more men than… Well, let's leave it at that. You men keep looking for him. I'm going back to search the saloon."

I passed through the swinging doors and saw that the Chinamen were onstage trying to hold back the hostile mob, while Miss Saint-Jean was shouting the cowboys into silence.

"Now listen here," she said. "That man was an imposter. He was not our Chinaman—and I don't know where our Chinaman is; he may be dead for all I know; and that impersonator was as much a risk to my girls *and* our Chinamen as anyone. So, simmer on down. He picked these men on sight—there was bad blood somewhere."

"Yeah, *his!*"

"For all we know, he's waiting just outside of town to pick us off— and I mean *us*, not you. If you cowhands had any manhood in you, you'd volunteer to be our escort out of town tomorrow mornin'!"

"We need to hang these Chinamen first!"

I boomed out, "You'll do no such thing. I'm a U.S. Marshal. I've been tracking that man for months. He isn't any Chinaman. He's a plumb no-good killer, the worst this side of the Mississippi. That woman's right, we ought to give her an escort out of town. And if it wouldn't trouble you, ma'am, I'd like to ride alongside for a spell, in case he's tracking you like I'm tracking him."

"Well, thank you, Marshal, that would be most kind."

"Good: now some of you men—bury these boys. Whoever runs this saloon—get it cleaned up. The rest of you—go to bed. Ma'am—you and your troupe be packed and ready to leave at sunup."

"Yes, Marshal, we surely will."

I stepped between the cowboys dragging the dead desperados away and said to Miss Saint-Jean, "Ma'am, I would appreciate it if I could see you privately. I need to ask you a few questions."

"Of course, Marshal." Miss Saint-Jean led me outside to her wagon. I sat across from her.

"You know it's me."

"Yes, of course, I know it's you," she said.

"And the woman is in your closet back there."

"I hope she can dance."

"I reckon I owe you an explanation."

"That would be nice—especially as our engagement here has ended now and I don't have another."

"Any town would be happy to have you."

"Aren't you a romantic? There are no towns around here—and if there were, they'd happily hang my Chinamen."

"You protect me—I'll protect them."

"You're handy with those revolvers, I'll give you that. And you're a big, strong, handsome brute. But how can you protect anyone? You're one word away from a hanging."

"Ma'am, those men were out to kill me. One of them, at least, wanted to disgrace that woman. And, ma'am, I can assure you that I'm here to do what's right. I'm seeking justice as surely as any man ever has. The woman in the closet knows who I am—and I guess that's a secret I'll have to share with you as well. Maybe it'll make you trust me: I am Colonel George Armstrong Custer, late of the Seventh Cavalry. My men were massacred at the Little Bighorn River. We were betrayed. But that woman in the closet—the white captive of an Indian warrior—rescued me, and I rescued her, helping her escape the Sioux. Now I need you to help me—and her—escape these men."

Miss Saint-Jean is not a woman easily shocked, but she regarded me with wide-eyed wonder. "*Custer*, General George Armstrong Custer?"

"Colonel now, ma'am, thanks to that jackanapes Grant. But yes, Custer of the West, that's what I am now—or actually, I'd rather you call me Armstrong. I have to travel incognito."

"But why?"

"I have my reasons, ma'am. The world thinks I'm dead. If I came out now, alive, they would think me a coward or a fool. Before I return, I need to find the man who betrayed us into the slaughter. I need to have proof. I intend to do that."

After a moment she said, "Why don't you tell your girl to come out."

I walked to the closet, opened the door, took Scalp-Not-My-Woman by the hand, and helped her up.

"Miss Saint-Jean, I have the honor of presenting…" I paused, thinking about exactly what I should call her. Scout wouldn't do. Scalp-Not-My-Woman did not fit her circumstances. There was nothing else for it: "I have the honor of presenting, Rachel, Rachel Armstrong, my ward."

CHAPTER TWO

In Which I Discover a Company Town

Disguising Rachel was not so very hard. She was, after all, white to begin with, and not an unprepossessing woman. The ladies of our troupe dressed her and powdered her nose and rouged her lips so that she looked as they did, which meant like a dancing nymph. As for me, I was safe behind my star, my absence of Oriental features, and my hair being now neither bootblacked nor fully gold but a sort of murky brown after I had scrubbed my scalp with water.

We were quite a wonderful sight that morning: our wagons formed up; Chinamen at the reins; honorable cowboys ranged up on either side of us; and I riding to the front. "Forward ho!"

Needless to say, we were in no danger from a mythical Chinese sharpshooter, so after a few miles I told the fine men of Applejack (for such was the name of the town) that they need see us no farther and waved them farewell.

Our course wasn't aimless. Ever the businesswoman, Miss Saint-Jean had pinpointed what she assumed would be the next—and safest—entertainment-starved town, the bustling metropolis of Bloody Gulch, population unknown but smaller, she assumed, than Applejack because there were no sizeable settlements this side of Bozeman. Rachel had recommended it; there was an Indian trading post nearby, which she had visited as a member of the Boyanama Sioux, who would surely *not* be headed back that way; and while Applejack was full of drifting cowhands and prospectors and the like, Bloody Gulch was trying to establish itself as a town of settlers and small businesses, or so she'd heard. That sounded safer, perhaps, but to my novice ears less commercial as well. A cowboy and his money are soon parted—not so much a small-town businessman.

Still, it was a pleasant several days' ride. The country was ramblingly beautiful, the food as good as anything that old Eliza used to make, and my evenings were spent playing cards with the Chinamen (the magician was a tricky one) and watching the girls teach Rachel the art of the can-can (which, as I can attest from close study of their rehearsals, is most definitely an art).

The showgirls' performances were wonderful, evocative reminders of civilization, and I valued them highly. But as we rode along I couldn't help but think: if I weren't a white man, with all the benefits of civilization before me, I would happily opt to be an Indian. I know I've said this many times before, Libbie, but how wonderful life would be as a Crow scout or a Ree scout for the U.S. Cavalry, living on the open plains, serving the cause of civilization, but living like the savage that I essentially am. The only penalty would be that you could not be part of such a life—and that is a penalty too severe to be contemplated. I remind myself of that now as I write, glancing down at your image on my arm, while Rachel brings me a welcome cup of coffee.

Our wagon-borne troupe ambled along the lonesome Montana prairie until the outline of Bloody Gulch was etched on the horizon. There were the buildings—and sure enough, there was the gulch set around the town, a muddy reddish-brown stream serving as an ineffectual moat, easily fordable, and even if it hadn't been, there was a rickety bridge directly ahead of us and another visible on the eastern bend. We chanced our wagons to the bridge, which creaked and swayed a bit but met the challenge, and we rolled along the dusty approach into town.

Rachel and I had drawn stares in Applejack, but nothing like the yawps of amazement that greeted Marshal Armstrong and the wagons of Sallie Saint-Jean's Showgirls and Follies. I led the wagons up to the front of the Bloody Gulch Hotel and Spa, a euphonious name if ever I heard one.

"I'll deal with the hotel," Miss Saint-Jean said as I helped her from the wagon. "You go to the saloon and drum up some business."

I did as I was bidden and sauntered down the street. Bloody Gulch looked like a town yearning for commerce but with no customers, just cowboys who wandered like bored, undisciplined sentries. They looked me over and said nothing. At the clapperboard shops the proprietors, wide-eyed at our arrival, now lounged about, listless—like a people beaten down by vanquished dreams. Even the saloon was quiet as I passed through the swinging doors, though it did have a few customers whisperingly minding their own business. In one corner, sitting alone, playing solitaire was the man I now know as Beauregard Gillette. He winked at me in a most peculiar manner and tapped his whiskey glass rhythmically on the table. It was only later that I learned he was winking and tapping in Morse code, trying to warn me of danger. I spotted it anyway—a cocky-looking good-for-nothing peckerwood in a stained sweaty shirt with beer-wet stubble, sitting at a table with a group of four Indians who despite the summer heat were wrapped in blankets. I saw why: the butt of a rifle rested between each pair of moccasins on the planks of the saloon floor.

"Howdy-do, Marshal," said the white man. "Looking for some-one?"

"Matter of fact I am—a vicious killer; been tracking him for days."

"You always travel with a circus like that? Don't seem so incon-spicuous."

"Something to drink, mister?" interrupted the bartender.

Much as I could have used a glass of milk, I asked him for a shot of water, given what trouble sarsaparilla had gotten me into last time. "Riding shotgun. The killer is a Chinese sharpshooter."

"A what?"

"He might have an accomplice. The other man I'm looking for is bearded, disheveled, likes a drink and a cigar, and could use a bath."

"That describes most everyone here."

"Name is Hiram Grant."

"Never heard of him."

"Count yourself fortunate."

"What makes you think he's around here—or that Chiner feller?"

"The Chinaman killed a passel of men southeast of here; and he threatened the folks in those wagons."

"Well, there ain't no trouble here, Marshal. Never had none; never will. And before you came into town we ain't had no Chinermen neither. Maybe you should pack 'em off back to China so that they don't go hurtin' folks."

I took the shot of water and downed it after swishing it around to wash the grit from my teeth.

"These Indians work for you?" I said finally.

"Yes, indeedy. I guess you never heard of the Largo Trading Company? We got ourselves a government contract. We work with the Injuns and the people of Bloody Gulch; keep everybody happy. You stick around here, you'll see plenty of us. But I reckon you'll be headin' on. No need for a marshal here."

"Oh, I figure I'll stick around for a short spell; until I know those theatre people are safe."

"Oh, they're safe all right. Largo Trading Company will see to that—trouble's bad for business. We don't want no trouble; and we take precautions to make sure there ain't none. That's why we hired these redskins—and a bunch more besides. They keep the tribes happy; me and my boys, we keep the white folks happy. You won't find a more contented town than Bloody Gulch. Buy you another drink, Marshal? I reckon I heard it was water—I can pony up for that."

"Not just now, thank you. I think I'll stroll around the town and stretch my legs."

"Suit yourself. Anything you need, look me up. Tim Dern's the name. I'm usually here."

I nodded to him and passed through the swinging doors. I expected I'd have trouble with him soon enough, and with those Indians too. In the meantime, I thought I'd reconnoiter and see what intelligence I could gather. I didn't like the look of this town or of Tim Dern or of those Indians with rifles under their blankets, and I didn't like the sound of the Largo Trading Company.

I strolled casually, but not so casually that I didn't notice the three men who followed me out of the saloon. I decided to lead them on a merry chase, but maybe not the one they expected. A short way down the street was a telegraph office. I strode up to the counter and tapped the service bell, and a little man, bald, or mostly so, and perspiring as though he'd run a mile rather than just emerged from his glassed-in partition, hurried to my service. He wore a green eyeshade, and pencils poked out from behind his ears. He looked like a midget Hermes with a winged helmet.

"Yes, sir, what can I do for you?"

"I'd like to send a message to Washington, D.C., office of the president, the White House."

"Office of the president? Why, yes, sir—you're a U.S. Marshal!"

He licked his pencil and applied it to the paper.

"Dear, Mr. President, No man here named Hiram Grant. Expect he doesn't exist. A bogeyman to frighten children. Have met representative of Largo Trading Company. Will report later."

At the words "Largo Trading Company" the clerk shivered visibly. "Yes, sir, will that be all, sir?"

"Yes, make sure that gets off right away—official government business."

He would have tugged his forelock, if he had one. My three shadow companions were waiting for me outside. One of them ducked into the telegraph office.

"Anything we can help you with, Marshal? We heard you were look-ing for someone."

"You'd like to be deputized?"

"No, nothin' like that. It's just that we know the town real well, and if you're lookin' for someone, or somethin' in particular, we can help."

"Thank you, gentlemen, I'll let you know. I might be onto something but need to ruminate. I'll be at the hotel."

"To rummynate?"

"Yes, exactly."

"And you wouldn't want us rummynating with ya?"

"*I don't know how to rummynate*," one of them whispered.

"Gentleman, no need to trouble yourselves; I'm content to ruminate alone."

"Suit yourself, mister—I mean, Marshal. We'll be around if you need us."

I winked. "I betchya will, and it's a great comfort."

I strolled down to the hotel where I found that the ever-practical Miss Saint-Jean had booked our rooms, tucked our wagons behind the estab-lishment, and seen our horses to the livery stable.

"Drum up any business, Marshal?"

"Let's talk inside," I said. We walked into the hotel parlor, which was appointed rather well, I thought. The wallpaper looked new, the chairs plush. We were alone and took adjoining seats.

"Well, was I right?" she asked. "Are we going to draw a crowd?"

"Oh, I'm sure you'll draw customers—of a sort, anyway; but not the sort who will fully appreciate the balletic art."

"They don't need to; if they've got the money, we'll learn 'em."

"Not sure I like this place. Armed Indians at the saloon—I take that as a bad sign."

"I take this hotel as a good a sign. There's money behind this place. And as for your Indians, fair's fair: if they buy tickets and stow their guns, they're fine by me. That's a lesson you could learn, by the way—don't shoot the customers."

"Happy to oblige, ma'am—if they'll let me."

"Oh, they'll let you, all right. You're an educated man, Armstrong, even if you were a soldier. Not everything has to be settled by violence.

"We'll see about that."

"Yes, we will—and don't you go shooting off those guns again without my permission. Look, I'm no blushing daisy. I know the value of a strong man. But gunplay is bad for business. And if you get antsy for trouble, just remember: I'm the one woman standing between you and a noose. You're a wanted man—wanted in Applejack and maybe wanted in Washington. If they knew you were alive, you'd have some awkward questions to answer, wouldn't you?"

I felt my face flame red at her impudence. And when I heard a cough at the entry to the parlor, I inwardly cursed her recklessness. Standing there was the man with a rebel-battle-flag eyepatch.

"Beggin' your pardon, ma'am; pardon the intrusion: Beauregard Gillette, at your service. I could not help but notice your wagons as they came into town, a wonderful display. I take it you are Miss Sallie Saint-Jean, the proprietress?"

She cast an appraising eye upon him. "Yes."

"And you, Mr. Marshal, sir, I saw you in the saloon. I might be of service to you both."

"Well, Mr. Gillette," I said, "a man who can serve both a U.S. Marshal *and* Miss Sallie Saint-Jean's Showgirls and Follies must be a man of many talents."

"And so must you, sir, to be riding with them."

"That's my affair, Mr. Gillette."

"Oh, no offense meant, sir. I can assure you, if I meant any offense you'd know it. I believe in staying on the right side of the law."

Miss Saint-Jean intervened. "State your business, Mr. Gillette."

"If you're in need of another attraction, ma'am, I am a master of card tricks. Also, I have a keen eye for figures—by which I mean, I could keep your accounts."

"I'll take that under advisement. Now, Mr. Gillette, how might you be of service to the marshal?"

He adjusted his eyepatch slightly, and his exposed blue eye bore in on me with an intensity I did not expect. He handed me a card, which read, BEAUREGARD GILLETTE, *Gentleman of Cards, Richmond, Virginia.* "I'm an itinerant card player, Marshal. After the war, a deck of cards was about all I had left. That's how I make my living, and I don't complain. When my winnings exceed my welcome, I mosey on. I'm pretty observant. I have to be, in my business—and I get the impression you are too. Those Indians with the rifles—you noticed the rifles—they don't live on a reservation. The real reservation is this town. The people here are trapped. I don't know how; I don't know why. I do know they're scared—too scared to even play cards. Dern—you met him at the saloon—he'll play, and so will his Largo Trading Company friends, but no one else. The Largo boys walk around the town like they own it—and I reckon in some way they do. You've noticed how awful quiet it is around here. Wouldn't a wagon show like yours attract children? Seen any? Ever seen a town where the school's boarded up—and the church? There are homesteads north of here, but you rarely see the homesteaders, and then it's only women who scamper away when you spot them. This is a town of shopkeepers—but only proprietors, no help. And nine times out of ten, their only customers are from the Largo Trading Company. I'd call that mighty peculiar, wouldn't you?"

I went to stroke my moustache, only to be reminded it wasn't there. "Mighty peculiar indeed, Mr. Gillette, but you've not pinpointed any crime, and as I'm already in pursuit of a killer..."

"Marshal, beggin' you pardon, but that killer's just one man—an evil man for sure, but one who'll find his own grave pretty fast; they always do. This is bigger, big enough for me to trouble a U.S. Marshal."

"It seems to me my duty's clear—and that's to stick with the job I have." I turned to Miss Saint-Jean and said, "Sounds like this town isn't the best commercial prospect for us."

"You, Marshal, in business with the lady?"

"No, no, no—just advising her. It sounds like she should move along."

"And you?"

"Let me ask you a question, Mr. Gillette. Why are you still here?"

"The Largo Trading Company boys are free and easy with their money."

"I see."

"And there's something else, Mr. Marshal. You look and sound like a gentleman, and you know as well as I do that a gentleman has certain obligations, including helping those in distress. I figured the odds were a bit high for one man to make a difference here. But two?"

"Two you think is plenty."

"Never have fought on a battlefield where I wasn't outnumbered—not in the war; not in the West. I'm used to it."

"Well, Mr. Gillette, I was a soldier too, and sometimes the odds are worse than you think."

"Fair enough, Marshal. You'll be leavin' then?"

"That depends on Miss Saint-Jean. Like you, Mr. Gillette, I have a weakness for ladies in distress."

"In this case, sir, it is not just the ladies, it is the children." He bowed slightly, turned to leave, and then added, "And of course there's the Delingpole treasure—and the murder. I thought, Marshal, you might be investigating that, but apparently not."

"No, I'm not. I confess, I hadn't heard about it."

"That's too bad. Someone should look into it. Justice is a fine word, but too rarely found in this life—or that's been my experience. Good day, then, Marshal, Miss Saint-Jean." He tipped his fingers to his hat and closed the door behind him.

I confess, the treasure interested me but little; and the same was true of the alleged murder—that was business for a real marshal. It was what he said about the women and children that stuck. Miss Saint-Jean and I sat in a rather anguished silence.

Finally, Miss Saint-Jean said, "First time a professional gambler has made me feel small."

"There's more to him than gambling."

"Treasure, for one thing."

"Montana's full of stories like that."

"Not quite like that—not a town with a boarded-up school and church; no children; women frightened on the farms; no women in town."

"This is the West, Miss Saint-Jean: men without women—nothing to write home about. Not every place is civilized."

"Don't tell me about the West, Armstrong. I know it as well as you do. There's something wrong here; you know it and I know it."

"Maybe so, but I don't know what we can do about it."

"And I'm responsible for all those girls—even those Chinamen…"

"I understand. I'll get the horses."

"No, you don't understand. This is my future—and most likely yours—and theirs. To you that badge is a stage prop; to the gambler, you're the law."

"But I'm not the law."

"Yes, you are. You wear a different uniform now, but you're pursuing justice—isn't that what you said?"

"Well, yes, but…"

"Don't my girls deserve justice?"

"But they have nothing to do with this."

"Oh, yes they surely do. There's not a one of my girls who doesn't dream of giving up the cancan and settling down with a man and raising children. Anyone in this territory who would rob them of that dream, I take that as a personal affront. And as an officer of the U.S. Cavalry, even in disguise, I expect you should too. And isn't that what's happening here?"

"Is it?"

"That's what he said—no children, no families, no women in town, no men at the homesteads; all because of this Largo Trading Company. That's not right."

"Miss Saint-Jean, even if I had a troop of cavalry under my command, what would you expect me to do about it? All we have is the word of a one-eyed Southern card sharp who thinks there's something peculiar going on—and maybe there is, but that gives me no authority to go charging into battle. There would have to be a proper investigation."

"So investigate."

"Investigate what?"

"Well, that treasure for one thing—and he said there was a murder. And what about those Indians with guns? You're an Indian fighter—isn't there something there?"

"I was an Indian fighter; I am no longer; I have never been a treasure hunter; nor am I a real marshal."

"The people of this town don't know that; the Largo Trading Company doesn't know that; Beauregard Gillette doesn't know that; and if they don't know it, why do you have to know it?"

I paused for a moment. "That, madam, is an excellent point."

I confess, Libbie, that I found her logic convincing. You know me: I need duty, a challenge, action to feel alive, and here it was offered to me in the smudged business card of a one-eyed Southern gambler. By Jove, I thought, I would be a fool not to take it: women to rescue; children to save; a treasure to find; a murder to solve.

"Miss Saint-Jean, no commanding officer ever gave me a more justified rebuke. You're right, you're absolutely right. And I'm going to do something about it."

I bolted from the parlor and through the front doors—and stopped short on the hotel's stoop, for there sitting as cool as you please on a bench was Beauregard Gillette.

I burst out, "My dear man, I have come to my senses. I will of course join you in trying to rid this town of whatever evil has accursed it. And I hasten to add that we are more than two men. I have an entire team of Chinese acrobats at my disposal—including a strong man and a magician. I feel that little can stand in our way."

"Well, that's mighty fine, Marshal. I thought I could count on you. And I reckon with that star you should command."

I slapped him on the back. "Beauregard, my good man, I know you said you were a soldier—what was your rank?"

"Major, First Virginia Cavalry."

"The First Virginia—my, my; we may have met on the field of strife—at Gettysburg, perhaps."

"And you, sir, a colonel?"

I winked. "Let's just say higher than a major."

"I assume, sir, that you'll be wanting to organize your command—your, uh, acrobats and all."

"Plenty of time for that later. Let's fetch our horses and do a little scouting."

"My pleasure, sir. I've already done a little myself, but tried to be inconspicuous. I've ridden up north, past the homesteads. You might find it instructive."

"I'm sure I will."

Frankly, what comes next is an embarrassment. Beauregard was silent most of the way, riding slightly ahead of me, and I was so mesmerized by the beautiful, blue, Montana sky, the waving yellow grasslands of the prairie, the lolling stroll of my horse, and the ominous silence of the surprisingly well-maintained homesteads that it took my Confederate comrade to ride up beside me and say soft and low, "Begging your pardon, Marshal; but those Indians following us—they look mighty hostile."

"By thunder," I said, looking around desperately before spotting them several hundred yards to the southeast, "so they do."

"They've been picking up braves along the way—I reckon that's bad. If they were Yankee cavalry, they'd charge; expect they might, any minute. Your orders, sir?"

"My orders, Major, are to hightail it west. Let's go!"

Our horses sprinted like greyhounds. Emboldened, the Indians lunged after us, yelping their war cries. I espied a muddy stream bending south. We pounded for it; it surely led back to the homesteads; and if there were lonely women there, they'd desperately need our help, with a war party on the loose.

We kept up a pell-mell sprint for at least a mile; a farmhouse appeared to our southwest. Beauregard glanced back. "Looks like they're easin' up, sir. Can't imagine their horses are blowed; must think we're not worth it."

"Cowards."

The farmhouse had a fenced courtyard. Our horses slowed to a walk and ambled through the open gate. The house looked tidy and quite respectable, with a large red barn set off behind. We tied our horses to a hitching rail and mounted the steps to the front door. We didn't have to knock. Our boots announced us and a woman, blonde and handsome, her hair in a bun and hands concealed in a towel, faced us from the doorway. We removed our hats.

"He's not here," she said.

"Now who might that be?" I replied with a smile. "Your husband?"

"You know very well who I mean."

"My dear lady, I don't know you from Eve. Perhaps you know my friend here."

"You aren't any friends of mine, I know that much." The towel fell from her hands. She had them gripped around a revolver.

"Now, madam, I want to be plain as day. Neither my friend nor I mean you any harm. In fact, we were pursued here by Indians. Now, don't fret, they seem to have drawn off. But we thought we ought to warn you."

"You came to warn me about Indians? As if they don't follow your orders."

"These Indians, madam, surely don't. I've commanded Crow and Ree scouts before in the army, but..."

"Pardon, me, ma'am, my name is Beauregard Gillette, at your service, and I think I know how to clear up this little misunderstanding. I'm supposing you think we're affiliated with the Largo Trading Company. But here, ma'am, is my card. And you'll notice that my companion here is a U.S. Marshal. That's a marshal's star he's wearing."

"A marshal?"

"Yes, ma'am," Beauregard continued. "He's been trailing a wanted man up through these parts. I told him there might be something bigger, more worthy of his attention here. I've been in Bloody Gulch just a short while, but it seems to me there's something not right."

"Come in, gentlemen," she said, lowering the gun. "I'll get you some coffee."

"I can help you with that, ma'am," I said. "Beauregard, you keep a look out for Indians. Don't let that eyepatch worry you, ma'am. He can see better with one eye than the rest of us can with two."

"I'm also quite handy with a coffee pot," he said. "Marshal, maybe you should keep a lookout. I wouldn't recognize that man you've been hunting."

"You both stay here," she said. "It's made. I'll just be a moment."

Reckless men that we are, we followed her into the kitchen. It wasn't coffee that was waiting for us (at least not immediately) but three Indians, dressed in flat-brimmed, large-domed black hats, black pants, and black vests over red-and-white check shirts, open at the neck, though their attire wasn't the first thing we noticed—that would be their rifles, held waist high, and pointed at us.

Our hostess gasped and jumped back a little and I caught her, despite Beauregard trying to jostle me aside to do the honors. I wrapped my arms around her for a moment—knowing the comfort you always take from a good strong hug, Libbie—and then with the masculine mastery you so admire I lifted her up and moved her out of the line of fire, which was no small task, because she was rather tall and long-legged, if thin and shaped like an hourglass. I let her gaze into my eyes, thinking it might calm her and give her confidence. I noticed her eyes were as wonderfully sparkling blue as my own.

"Marshal," said Beauregard, "I think you should attend to these Indians."

With a wistful touch of sadness, I nodded at our hostess and turned my attention to the savages. "Put those rifles down and your hands up," I said.

They didn't move. I got a good look at them. They were big ugly brutes, with craggy red faces better suited to gargoyles. The biggest, oldest, and ugliest said, "No marshals in Bloody Gulch. We handle law here. Give us wanted poster. Provide bounty. We deliver."

"I see: bounty hunters. And how did you track me here?"

"Uh, begging your pardon, Marshal, I think we know the answer to that." Beauregard nudged me to look out the kitchen window where five mounted Indian warriors, Cheyenne, I thought, were sitting their horses. "Looks like we didn't lose those Indians after all."

The spokesman for the black-clad Indians repeated, "We handle law here. Give us wanted poster. Provide bounty. We deliver."

"All right," I said. "That's a fair deal, but I don't have the poster. It'll be sent to me from Washington. That might take a while. But when I have it, I'll find you men."

"We handle law here. Give us wanted poster. Provide bounty. We deliver."

"I'm not sure they understand me."

"Wait. I've got something that might help," our hostess said. When she returned, it was with a small portrait of Sam Grant.

"Why the devil do you have this?"

"My husband bought it. He was a Union officer."

"Well, so was I, and I confess I've got one too, but..." I handed it to the chief gargoyle. "Here—find that man, and you can keep him."

"Bounty?"

"A thousand dollars—dead or alive."

He nodded, clutched the portrait, and led his black-hatted men outside, where they joined their painted comrades and rode off.

Our hostess said, "I thought you could explain that you are in the service of President Grant. I didn't mean..."

"Well, ma'am, I know of no better use for Sam Grant than as wampum for Indians. That was quite resourceful of you."

"Ma'am, I do not believe we've had the pleasure of learning your name," said my one-eyed, molasses-tongued Confederate.

"Isabel, Isabel Johnson," she said.

"Miss Johnson, is it?"

"Yes."

"So, it's your father then, ma'am, who is missing."

"Well," she said, and then paused. "Let me get you that coffee." She extracted two white cups, nice porcelain ones, from the cupboard and handed them to us. She took the coffee pot from the hob and poured.

"Your father, ma'am?" repeated Beauregard. "Missing?"

"It depends what you mean by missing. I would call him free."

"Begging your pardon, ma'am," I said, stepping between that Southern Lothario and Miss Johnson, "but 'free' in what way?"

"It's only a rumor," she said, "but apparently he has escaped the foundry. But I haven't seen him."

"And 'the foundry' would be?"

"I'm sorry, Marshal, I forget that you're not from these parts. It's part of the Largo Trading Company. Everyone here knows about it. Most of the menfolk—fathers, husbands—work there. But none of us knows exactly what they do. The men don't come back."

"And the children, ma'am," said Beauregard, casually elbowing me aside, "we haven't noticed any children."

"They're at the mine. Everyone knows it exists too, but no one knows exactly what they're mining, though I reckon it isn't gold—at least they don't go splashing gold around the town."

"No ma'am, they don't. Plenty of greenbacks, though."

I tapped Beauregard on the shoulder and pointed out the window. With him thus distracted, I was able to sidestep in front of him and resume my interrogation. "So, ma'am, do you mean to say that the Largo Trading Company has the men and children of Bloody Gulch in slave labor?"

"I'm afraid so, Marshal. Oh, there's a few shopkeepers they've let stay. But mostly yes, we're all under their thumb."

"But how can that be? I mean, surely you didn't all just submit."

"It was submit or die. The Largo Trading Company has its own army—those Indians are part of it. Between the Indians and the company's white gunmen, peaceable citizens don't stand a chance."

"And you women?"

"Well, I guess you could say we're part of 'the deal.' The company told our menfolk that we'd be left alone if they didn't resist. And it's the boys who are at the mine. The girls are kept as hostages at the old Blake homestead to the west to make sure we don't try to free our men. They're used as farmhands, slopping hogs and tending chickens and crops. That's what we do too—those of us who are full-grown women—we work our farms as best we can. They pay us for the hogs and the apples and all; I guess they think that'll keep us quiet."

I know, Libbie, that most women, like yourself, take pride in your milky white complexions—and with good reason—but to look upon this statuesque golden-haired woman, browned radiantly by the sun, with her blue eyes glimmering like pools of fresh cool water, was to see yet another model of womanly perfection, though lesser of course than your own.

I was taking a mental note of all this when that blackguard Beauregard again cut in front of me. We had backed Miss Johnson into a corner, and she suggested that we take seats at the dining table.

"Well, Marshal," said Beauregard, "I don't think we can let this stand. Do you?"

"Miss Johnson, I pledge to you my confederate here—who is actually a real Confederate—and I will not let this stand. Together with my troop of Chinese acrobats we will end the tyranny of the Largo Trading Company."

She stared at me as if this was an astonishing assertion, so I continued, "Ma'am, I assure you not only of my sincerity but of my capability. Mr. Gillette was a major in the Confederate service, and I, ma'am..." I shot a commanding glance at Beauregard's exposed eye, "I was a general in the Union service. You could have no finer champions than we." And then, I'm afraid, I so forgot myself in my passion for justice that I rolled up my right sleeve, exposed my Indian-engraved escutcheon, and flexed my arm so that the words stood out. "You see, Miss Johnson, I was born to ride—ride at the head of a troop of cavalry!"

"Who is Libbie?"

Realizing that I was in danger of exposing your identity—and mine— I had to respond quickly. I said: "A mere spelling error, ma'am. A Chinaman did it. It's meant to say 'Liberty'—the Liberty that Major Gillette and I will soon restore to Bloody Gulch. And that woman—that woman is a representation of the Roman goddess *Libertas*."

Beauregard, the fool, said, "Well, what do you know? Would never have guessed that, Marshal. Never seen the like. I thought only convicts and sailors were tattooed. But mighty handsome all the same." He raised his cup. "To liberty, ma'am."

"But what will you do?" she asked me, wisely ignoring that Southern card sharp, her pleading eyes tapping my every reservoir of sympathy.

"All military campaigns," I said, asserting my commanding presence over Beauregard, "depend in the first part on the gathering of information about the enemy, his strength, his dispositions, the surrounding terrain. You, Miss Johnson, have an important role to play in this. Reporting directly to me, you will be my Indian scout, advising me on everything I need to know about the Largo Trading Company, its operations, its men, its location—and the location of its foundry and mine. Everything you tell me I will use to make a battle plan. And, ma'am, with one grievous exception, where I was betrayed, I have never lost a battle, and I will assuredly not fail you in this one."

She ran her fingers over my "Born to Ride" tattoo, and then looking directly into my eyes she said, "No, general, I don't believe you will fail me. You will have my full cooperation."

"Thank you most kindly, ma'am. Our first consideration should be your own safety. I am presently booked in rooms at the Bloody Gulch Hotel and Spa, but if you would prefer, I could stay here as your guardian."

"Beggin' your pardon, general," said Beauregard, "it might be better if I stayed here. I won't be missed from the town. People expect card players to drift. But you, sir, as a marshal—they have their eye on you. And there's your troop, sir. They'll be needing you for training and instruction. And I assume you'll have to make arrangements with Miss Saint-Jean."

"Who is Miss Saint-Jean?"

"Another lady in distress, ma'am," I said, forthright and honest.

"One of many, ma'am, who are in the custody of the good general," added Beauregard.

"Yes, thank you, Major."

"Not at all, sir."

"Perhaps, Miss Johnson, you could billet Major Gillette in your barn with the other animals."

"Yes, of course, my father often slept in the barn loft."

"Well, then, Major Gillette, I will leave Miss Johnson in your good care. I will come in disguise, when I am able, to receive your reports. Major, get your horse out of sight—and if you need to reach me, you know where I am."

He saluted. "Yes, sir, Yankee General, sir."

I returned my hat to my head, tipped its brim, and said, "Farewell, Miss Johnson. I trust you'll be safe with the major."

I rode away with that thought much in mind.

CHAPTER THREE

In Which I Find Myself at War Again

The Chinamen had little grasp of English, Miss Saint-Jean had no grasp at all of Chinese (she simply had a gift for making her wishes—or demands—known), and my own knowledge of Chinese dialects was limited. Nevertheless, I thought the strongman would make an impressive sergeant major, the acrobats passable "foot cavalry" in the manner of Stonewall Jackson's Brigade, and the magician a second lieutenant, as he seemed a man of some intellect, and perhaps cunning.

As in Applejack, the saloon at Bloody Gulch featured a more than serviceable stage. Using my authority as marshal, I commandeered it, when the saloon wasn't otherwise in use, to train my deputies. In the wee hours of the morning, when the barkeeper had closed up shop and the drunks had been swept out the swinging doors, we conducted rehearsals for the Chinamen's new martial role. I had no rifles or carbines to distribute, but they did have long single-edged swords they called *dao*s, which they used as part of their act and which looked quite fearsome,

51

especially as they swung them with the speed and facility of jugglers. It wasn't anything like the saber drill we have in the Army, but it was quite impressive in its own way and was sure to befuddle, if not perhaps affright, our adversaries.

And I did get the Chinamen lined up in formation and marched them around the stage a bit. Since verbal communication was difficult, we learned to work together silently, via hand signals. At one point, the strongman got my attention by grabbing me respectfully by the neck and placing me in position to watch a demonstration of Chinese hand fighting—another skill at which the acrobats were adept. They did not actually strike each other, but went cartwheeling around the stage ducking and dodging as they kicked and punched the air—the punches very different from boxing as we know it. Whether it could be effective as a means of self-defense, I had no notion. But again, it might easily befuddle an enemy shocked at the spectacle.

The uses of the strongman, whom I took to calling Hercules, were potentially manifold. More of a mystery was what I could do with the magician, whose specialty seemed to be making fans appear and disappear. But a man's a man for all that, as I read once somewhere, and I figured that he would be of use to us in some way.

Miss Saint-Jean, meanwhile, kept her dancers in tip-top condition; and while she had not yet announced a date for our first performance, it was clear that we would have an avid audience from the male employees of the Largo Trading Company. I was regularly accosted on the street by them with the question, "Pardon me, Marshal; do you know when them showgirls is going to be kicking up their legs?" These men did not have regular access to the theatre, as we do when we're in New York, so you can imagine their anticipation. When I finally could tell them, "Why, the posters are going up now, boys. The first show will be this Thursday night," they pumped my arm with a gratitude that was both rare and gratifying.

Even though I no longer had a formal role in the performance, I had opening-night jitters just the same—perhaps particularly acute because I now considered Rachel something of a protégé. It is true that I could teach her nothing of the cancan—though she seemed to have mastered that quite well without me—but I did try to pass along to her, during breaks in rehearsals, my own insights into stage presence and posture, and the importance of enunciation and projection when she sang in a chorus, *"Buffalo gals, won't you come out tonight, come out tonight, come out tonight,"* etc. She was an apt pupil, and we often practiced late into the night after formal rehearsals. She also often watched as I drilled the acrobats. She had picked up a bit of their lingo and could advise them on Indian fighting methods—at least those of the Boyanama Sioux.

The day of the performance, I went to the town barber for a shave and haircut—the price of which was two bits—and settled down to one of man's simple pleasures. The lather had been applied and the first delicate scraping had been done, when the doorbell jingled and the shop door opened. I smelled them before I saw them. It was the Indian bounty hunters. There were three of them this time.

"This man not wanted."

"You're right about that," I said.

"Give us real poster."

"Don't have it yet."

Three rifle barrels were pointed at me. "You lie."

"You think so?"

"Give us poster."

"Or what? You'd shoot a U.S. Marshal?"

"Plenty more of us—not so many marshals."

"Should I take that as a threat, I'm a trifle confused."

"Poster!"

The barber had stopped his shaving and, trembling a little, said, "Marshal, these men help the Largo Trading Company enforce the law. I think you'll find them quite useful. I'd definitely cooperate with them."

"Is that so?"

"Oh, yes, sir."

I stood up suddenly, yanked the barber's cape off me, and in one swift motion threw it in the faces of the Indians. I slammed my boot into the knee of the nearest one, and he fell like a leveled tree. I wrenched the rifle from the second and smashed its butt into his face; and as he fell, I was in a perfect position to pivot and smack the barrel into the face of his companion, who likewise fell backwards. I dropped the rifle and then spun out my revolvers, cocking the hammers so that they heard them click.

"Now listen here, I represent the law; and if you don't like it, you can take it up with the U.S. Government. In the meantime, I suggest you leave these rifles in my care, drop those ammunition belts, and hightail it back to the Largo Trading Company. You tell your boss that there's a new law in town, and if he'd like to powwow with me, I'm more than ready to meet with him. Shoo out of here now—and leave that picture of Grant if you don't mind."

The one whose knee I had kicked was hobbling. The fellow who had been rifle-butted was still groggy. And the third had a cut over his eye but was stoic about it all the same. They did as I told them and stumbled out into the street.

"Oh, dear, sir, oh, dear, I wouldn't have done that, sir, no, I wouldn't have done that."

"Of course you wouldn't have. You're not Marshal Armstrong of the West." I picked the barber cape off the floor and tied it around my neck. "Let's finish my shave, shall we?"

"Do you think it's wise, sir?"

"I think it's wiser than going half shaved." I had my revolvers back in their holsters. I patted them. "Two guns against three disarmed Indians isn't bad odds. Come on now; there's a show tonight. That's a reason for a man to look his best, isn't it?"

"Yes, sir."

"Not to mention that we've got President Sam Grant looking up at us. I'm sure he'd like to see the job done right."

"Yes, sir."

His shaking hand had me more worried than the Indians, but he did a decent job. I gave him another two bits for his trouble and a spray of cologne (Miss Saint-Jean had put me on an allowance, but, as you know, Libbie, money doesn't rest easy in my pockets) and then picked up Sam

Grant's picture. I decided I ought to return it. But I needed to do something else first. If the Largo Trading Company thought I could be bullied by three Indian bounty hunters, they needed to be set right—and a trip to the telegraph office and another "message to Washington" might establish that I had more power and perseverance than they imagined.

I gathered up the rifles and ammunition belts and carried them like a clerk in a dry goods store to the telegraph office. Somehow I wasn't surprised to see Dern sitting behind the counter, leaning back in a chair, boots propped up on a desk.

"Well, howdy, Marshal. What can I do for you?"

"You can handle a telegraph?"

"Well, actually, no, sir, but don't have much use for a telegraph anyway—not here in Bloody Gulch."

"Where's the funny little man, the clerk?"

"Homer? Oh, I reckon he's off for a spell. Wasn't sure he liked it here."

"So, you're sitting in for him?"

"Somebody's got to, and I like to be useful. Say, Marshal, you looking for a posse? That's quite a load you're carrying; I can handle a gun right well myself."

"Winchester repeaters; I got them off some Indians. They're not supposed to have them, are they?"

"Indians with Winchesters? In town? I do declare that sure is plumb peculiar. I mean, I know they're allowed for huntin', but..."

"You wouldn't know how they got them?"

"No, sir, I surely wouldn't."

"The Largo Trading Company trades with Indians, don't they?"

"Well, yes, sir, we have a government contract, but we surely wouldn't be selling Injuns repeatin' rifles unless they was authorized—as I say, for huntin' and whatnot. No, sir, that wouldn't be right at all."

"They didn't act like it was a secret around here."

"Well you know Injuns, Marshal—peculiar, ain't they? They got their own way of doin' things. Me, I'm kinder a live and let live feller, if you know what I mean. I never look for no trouble, Marshal, not with

Injuns, not with anyone. I reckon there's a lot of people like that around here in Bloody Gulch."

"Yes, it appears so," I said and stepped out the door.

Riding up the street in my direction on a painted pony was an Indian dressed in buckskin and moccasins and a bowler hat. He was young, strong, and handsome in that impassive Indian way, as though carved from red rock. His horse pulled a drag sled with a trunk on it—like a shipping trunk—just the right size for smuggling rifles, I thought. He stopped when he drew even with me. He was no more abashed at staring than I was. Finally he nodded and pointed up the street. Walking towards me were the three Indians I had disarmed at the barber shop. They had knives and hatchets tucked in their belts. In their hands, aimed in my direction, were old single-shot pistols. The door of the telegraph office opened and Dern leaned against the jamb. He looked at the Indian on the horse, seemingly puzzled; then he looked down the street.

"Them the Indians you took the guns from?"

"Yes."

"Looks like they want 'em back."

Indians are bad shots, and they'd have to reload after they missed, so you might think the odds weren't so bad. But Dern wore a gun belt; so did the Indian in the bowler hat. I wasn't sure which side they were on.

The Indians hadn't broken stride. They were close. They'd be firing soon. I trusted my instincts.

I tossed a Winchester to the Indian with the bowler hat, dropped to one knee, let Grant, the ammunition belts, and one rifle fall to the floor-boards, and spun the other rifle around in my hands to cover Dern. Three pistol shots pinged and ricocheted off the floorboards and the wood railing; three rapid rifle shots answered. I looked down the street; the Indians were dead.

Dern snickered. "Why you pointing that at me, Marshal? I ain't done nothin'. And who's that Injun? Friend of yours? I thought they weren't supposed to have repeaters."

"There's a time and a place for everything," I said. I picked up my gear—the rifle, the ammunition belts, Grant—and said to Dern, "You like to be useful. Make sure those men get buried." Then I walked out onto the dusty street. The Indian with the bowler hat dropped the rifle into the stack on my arms.

"Nice weapon," he said.

"Awful nice. Good shooting too. What's your name?"

"Guillaume, Guillaume Jacques."

"Guillaume?"

"It is a French name. Do you speak French?"

"No, not really; I had to study it at West Point, but..."

"Spanish?"

"No."

"Latin?"

"Latin?"

"Yes, Latin, the language of the ancient Romans."

"Yes, I know what it is, but no."

"A priest gave me that name; he made me a Christian. He was an educated man. You speak English, at least."

"Yes, yes, of course I do."

"In English, Guillaume is William, Bill, Billy; Jacques is Jack."

"I don't care about that. You're a Crow, aren't you?"

"Yes, I am a Crow."

"And you recognized them as Sioux."

"Yes, enemy of the Crow. Your enemy too, I see."

I paused and silently cursed myself for mentioning West Point. "What's in the chest?"

"Books. I'm educating myself. The priest who made me a Christian introduced me to books. I have much to learn, but I have learned much already."

"Like how to fire a Winchester."

"I prefer fighting with my hands—and my feet. My Crow name is Pony-that-Kicks. As a boy I liked to fight. I have ridden with the pony soldiers too."

"Why are you here?"

"I look for you. Your enemies," he nodded at the dead Sioux, "are my enemies. I come to help, as one pony soldier to another."

I wasn't sure whether I wanted to pursue this line of questioning. I couldn't tell how much he knew, and I wondered whether ignorance was bliss.

He dismounted and we walked together down the street to the stables, he leading his horse.

"You know about Greasy Grass," he said, "Little Bighorn? A massacre—pony soldiers, more than 250, and Custer, dead."

I nodded.

"Sioux and Cheyenne—thousands of warriors; some are here too."

"Not the same?"

"Still Sioux; still Cheyenne."

We stepped into the livery stable. The manager looked as perplexed as Dern had been, eying the bowler-hatted Indian and the trunk on the travois. "He with the Largo Trading Company?"

"Not exactly," I said, "but his stable fees can go on their tab."

"You think that wise?" said the Indian.

"From the point of view of my wallet, yes; and yours?"

He nodded, and it was done. We removed the travois and stuck it in the corner of a stall. We each grabbed a side handle on the trunk and brought it to the hotel. The clerk at the counter stopped us.

"Uh, Mr. Armstrong, isn't it? Is that Indian gentleman a friend of yours?"

We put the trunk down and I drew myself up to my full height, chest out, chin down. "It's *Marshal* Armstrong, and this man here, Guillaume Jacques—that's William Jack to you—is my deputy."

"Do you intend on him staying here…uh, Marshal? The hotel is completely full, what with all these showgirls and Chinamen and everything, I don't know how we can possibly…"

"He'll stay with me."

"I don't mean to be a problem, Marshal, but you and Miss Saint-Jean have put the reputation of this hotel at risk."

"More likely we've made your reputation, Mr…."

"Smithers, Smithers, sir, and your friend will still have to sign his name on the ledger—he can write, can't he?—and pay for half a room."

"Miss Saint-Jean booked me a full room—that should cover it." I nodded at the trunk. "Any additional charges can go to the Largo Trading Company."

"Oh, oh, oh," he said, suddenly flustered, "is that so? Well, I suppose there shouldn't be a problem then. We've always been on very good terms with the Trading Company. If you'll just sign the ledger, sir," he said, dipping a pen in ink.

"What language?" said the Indian. "In French, Guillaume Jacques; in Spanish, Guillermo Jack; in English…"

"English is fine, if you please."

I looked over his shoulder and saw him sign *Billy Jack Crow*. He saw me and said, "My name with the pony soldiers. We are at war again, are we not?"

I told you I liked Crow scouts.

We carried his trunk up to my room and had a proper military discussion. Billy Jack had apparently come to Bloody Gulch along the same route we had. He had seen sentries high on the hills. He had waved to them and they had waved back. We both reckoned they thought he was coming with guns for the Largo Trading Company, which he said had a powerful name among the Indians, especially the Sioux and the Cheyenne; he considered it an enemy.

"Well, Billy Jack, I'm forming an army, as I guess you've reckoned. We're taking on the Largo Trading Company. You're in, if you want to be."

"I am prepared for war."

"Good. I'm making you a sergeant of scouts. From now on, you're Sergeant Bill Crow. You'll meet our troops in due course."

He picked up the picture of Grant. I had placed it face down on the dresser, but I guess he was curious.

"You work for President Grant?"

"I have, worse luck—but not now. His son was on my staff—or Sheridan's actually—and served under me. I liked the boy. As for his father…"

"Good man," he said, "good Republican."

"Well, sorry to separate you two," I said, plucking the picture from his hands, "but he's not mine, thank goodness. I need to return him. I'll be back later. You stand guard here."

"Yes. Stand guard—and read." He reached into the trunk, extracting a book.

"What's that?"

"Catechism. Everything I need to know is here—or so the priest says."

"There, and in Army regulations," I said, closing the door behind me.

⁂

I rode to Isabel Johnson's farm and knocked on the door. It opened to a smile as white as the stripe on a skunk's tail, only the scent was distinctly that of blueberries.

"Why, Marshal," Isabel said, wiping her hands on her apron, "this is a pleasant surprise. Why, I was just baking a blueberry pie. Major Gillette is quite partial to blueberries."

"I'm sure that's not the only thing he's quite partial to. I just thought, ma'am, that I ought to return your picture of Sam Grant. Those Indian bounty hunters kindly returned it to me."

"Well that's very thoughtful of you, Marshal. Would you like some coffee?"

"I'd love some, ma'am, if it's no trouble. Also, I have an invitation for you. There's a show in town tonight. If you'd like to see it, I'd gladly escort you."

"A show? Oh, you mean the dancing girls."

"Not just dancing girls, ma'am—a magician, a strongman…though maybe not as strong as some," I said, winking, "and acrobats, sword-wielding Chinese acrobats. I've helped train them with sabers, having been in the cavalry and all."

"Well, Marshal, I don't know…"

"Come now, there's nothing like the theatre to lift one's spirits. And anyway, you deserve it for billeting Beauregard."

"Oh, he's earning his keep, Marshal. He's out there now repairing some fences for me."

"Wonderful, then let's have coffee. I've got some matters I'd like to discuss with you."

We sat at her breakfast table, with its red and white checkerboard tablecloth, fresh butter in a dish, and fine porcelain cups with strong black coffee fit for a soldier.

"So, ma'am, I hate to trouble you with questions, but those Indians who were here, the ones who claimed to be bounty hunters..."

"They're not bounty hunters—not like you think of them."

"I know—they work for the Largo Trading Company—but who commands them?"

"Well, I don't know for sure, but it could be Seth Larsen; he runs the company, and he's a cruel, vicious man."

"Where's he from?"

"Oh, I don't know. He's been here for as long as I can remember. The company too. But at first it didn't seem so bad."

"You cook good coffee, ma'am," I said. I didn't mean to be distracted by it, but it really was powerfully good; maybe not as good as yours, Libbie, or the coffee that old Eliza used to make for us, but second best. Then I added, "What changed—about the company, I mean?"

"It was sudden—or maybe I just didn't notice until they forced me to notice; until they started taking the men and the children, and closed the church and the school."

"And how long ago was that?"

"Almost a year ago; right after the harvest. Before that there was some trouble too. There was a big landowner, an Englishman with a funny name, Jack Delingpole; he was sort of a town benefactor. He paid for the building of the school, though he had no kids of his own, and of the church, where he acted as a lay preacher. He had a big spread north of here. The foundry and the mine are up there too. The Trading Company said he had no right to the land, that the government had set it aside for the Indians. There was a big to-do because the Englishman claimed to have a title and all that. The Company said the title was a fraud. The Englishman said he was going to get the law on his side, but before he could do that, the Indians strung him up by his heels, skinned him alive, and burned him to death. Some folks claim they heard his screams—they were that loud and horrible—but they were too frightened to help. Then the Company took the land and gave it to the Indians—or so they say. I've heard tell that Larsen often lives there—Delingpole built a sort of mansion. I've never seen it, but that's the rumor; and of course Larsen runs the foundry and the mine."

"So, Delingpull was murdered and his property stolen?"

"Delingpole, Marshal; but yes, there should have been a trial; the Englishman was murdered. The Trading Company said the Englishman got what he deserved; that he stole that property from the Indians. There were always Indians here, it being a trading post and all, but more arrived all the time; and they got organized by the Company. Some people got worried right away. I guess they were the smart ones."

Her skin, usually sun-kissed a rosy brown, was looking a little whiter with despair, and I decided to change the subject to something happier. "About my invitation for tonight?"

"But it'll be full of Largo Trading Company men, won't it?"

"I guess that's the way things are around here—but I'll be there; no need to fret, Isabel—I can call you Isabel, can't I?"

"Oh, yes, surely."

"They'll be no trouble, ma'am; not with me as your escort."

"All right, then. I'll come."

"Good."

"And Major Gillette?"

"At your service, ma'am." That Southron was as crafty as Mosby. He had an uncanny way of turning up unbidden, leaning on a door jamb, exerting his self-regarding charm. "Fence is nailed solid. Thought I smelled coffee—and blueberries—and the marshal."

"Marshal Armstrong has just invited me to the show in town tonight. Would you like to come?"

"Well that's right neighborly of you, Miss Johnson; and I accept. You might need a guardian in a crowd like that."

"Marshal Armstrong assures me it's quite theatrical."

"Oh, I'm sure it is—quite theatrical. Honored to attend in your company, ma'am."

"I'll be escorting Isabel."

"That so, Marshal; is that what brings you here?"

"Just returning Miss Johnson's property," I motioned to Grant, who was back on the mantelpiece.

"I heard tell he had a rough time, old General Grant—mighty rough time with some Indians."

"He's been promoted to president, you know."

"Ah, well, Yankee General, sir, there are some political developments best left ignored."

"Where'd you hear about the Indians?"

"I've got an instinct for self-preservation—and even in a town as locked down as this one, word travels plenty fast. Way I heard it, you and an Indian in a bowler hat shot down three Indians of the Largo Trading Company. You should know, people here are mighty scared about what happens next."

"And how would you know that?"

"I've been extending my card, as a gentleman should, to the neighboring farm folk."

"I see: a regular knight errant to ladies in distress."

"Why of course, sir."

I was about to say something more when I glanced in Isabel's direction—as I often did when she was near—and saw fear in her big blue eyes. I knew I needed to comfort her.

"Beauregard, you're a soldier. You know that fear is an enemy—and that boldness in the face of the enemy is a strength. The Largo Trading Company has now seen strength—strength it hasn't seen in a very long time; strength behind a badge. The people shouldn't be scared; the Company should be."

"Yup, I reckon I'd be quaking in my boots if I had a big business, big money, a big army, and a little town under my thumb, and I had to face you. I'd be plumb scared, wouldn't I?"

"You, Beauregard, are a special case. You're used to trouble; they're not; they try to avoid it."

"Yankee General, sir, anybody who does what they do—whatever it is—isn't afraid of trouble. Take it from me, bad 'uns don't think that way. I've seen too many of 'em."

"Beauregard, I'm trying to reassure Isabel that she has nothing to fear."

"Well, she doesn't—as long as I'm around; I know how to deal with the bad 'uns. Good thing you'll have me along tonight." He shifted his eyepatch for emphasis.

"Major Gillette, I've forgotten myself, would you like some coffee?"

"Would love some, ma'am; and since we're all getting down to a first-name basis, why don't you call me Beauregard."

I'll be darned if she didn't smile at that. "Major," I said, subtly shifting the tone, "I think perhaps we should have a council of war tonight, before the evening's performance."

"Yankee General, sir, you give the orders, and I obey."

"Let's meet at the hotel at six. The show is at eight. That will give us plenty of time to dine and to talk."

"Well, since Miss Isabel will be our guest—I defer to you, ma'am; would six o'clock be agreeable with you?"

"That's fine by me—and you, uh, Beauregard?"

"As you wish, ma'am." He turned to me. "And, Yankee General, sir, will you be escorting Miss Saint-Jean to dinner, or Miss, uh, or Miss, uh, well, there are *so* many I hardly know all their names."

"No, thank you, Major, I shall have the honor of dining with Miss Johnson, Isabel—and you—alone."

"We are honored, sir."

"Well, then," I said, tipping my hat to Miss Johnson, and looking again at how those white teeth lit up her sun-kissed face. It was such a dazzling display—though nothing on your own gleaming smile, Libbie—that it almost kept me from scowling at Major Gillette. "I shall see you tonight, Isabel. Until then," I took Miss Johnson's hand and kissed it in the gallant French fashion. Then I nodded at Gillette. "Major."

"Oh, no kisses necessary for me, General, sir," said the blackguard, saluting.

I returned the salute and strode out of the breakfast parlor, out the front door, and silently cursed that Southern Lothario. I untied my horse and he nuzzled me. Horses and dogs I can always count on—and you, of course, Libbie dear.

⟡

Our plates were gone and we were polishing off the coffee.

As the three of us were alone in the hotel dining room—the Company men took their meals in the saloon when they were in town—Beauregard, though all charm and flattery with Miss Johnson, did not hesitate to pass along intelligence as well.

"I've made a few rides out from the farm."

"Yes, I know, Major. You mentioned the local ladies in distress."

"Yankee General, sir, I mean no disrespect to the ladies when I say those visits were in the service of a greater cause. It surely looked less suspicious if, when I surveyed our general environs, my rides were punctuated with calls on the fair sex."

"I see; very clever, Major."

"I'm surprised your wagons made it here in the first place—or that I did, for that matter. They've got Indian patrols covering the most likely entrances into town. I located the so-called foundry—it's northeast of here—and the mine is northwest; they bracket the canyon where Delingpole lived. They both look like mines to me; the foundry just has a 12-inch Napoleon parked outside. I reckon I know what they're digging for too: 'Delingpole's treasure.' That's the rumor anyway."

"Dueling Pool's treasure?"

"Delingpole, sir; Miss Isabel mentioned him—the town benefactor. He used to mint his own coins—gold, so nobody complained. Interesting hobby. I reckon they're looking for where he got that gold. As Miss Isabel said, Largo Trading Company's not throwin' gold around. They trade in greenbacks."

"Find anything else?"

"The Blake homestead where the young girls are held is due west, not far. I didn't spot any guards. The Company men just seemed to doze on the terrace. A commander like you, with Chinese acrobats at his disposal, could take it in a trice."

"*Sword-wielding* Chinese acrobats."

"To be sure. But before we free the children, we'll need a safe place for them."

"The acrobats?"

"No, I was thinking of the children, sir."

"Oh, yes, of course. I have an idea for that. But for now the primary issue is how to hit each position—the Blake homestead, the mine, and the foundry—with thunderclap surprise. Once we know how to liberate the hostages, we can formulate escape plans, probably to Fort Ellis or Fort Shaw."

"You know, General, if we could get word to the cavalry—I expect those forts have cavalry—it would even up the odds somethin' fierce."

"And what would we tell them: children in mines; men in a foundry that might really be a mine; a private army; people living in fear. Would you believe that story?"

"Wouldn't need to—just ride in with your marshal's badge and tell 'em what you've seen: Indians armed with Winchesters, apparently from the Largo Trading Company. Don't you think they'd come running mighty fast to investigate? I reckon they would."

"I do too," said Miss Johnson; and such is my devotion to duty that I have to confess that I had nearly forgotten she was there. But now that I was reminded, I looked into those glittering blue eyes of hers and saw such tremendous depth and understanding that I paused for a long while to reflect on what she had said.

Beauregard broke the silence by saying, "Uh, begging the general's pardon…"

"Yes, what is it? I'm thinking."

"About getting word to the Yankee cavalry?"

"No, no, no, I can't do that; I can't leave Isabel in danger."

"I'll be here, Yankee General, sir."

"Precisely—and look here, I'm no messenger boy."

"No, sir, but as a marshal…"

"As a marshal, I should send my deputy."

"You're not referring to me, sir?"

"No, I'll send Billy Jack Crow; they'll trust him."

Beauregard shifted his eyepatch from one eye to the other, and Miss Johnson said, "Who is Billy Jack Crow?"

"Oh, sorry—forgot I hadn't mentioned him. He's an Indian, guarding my room against inquisitive Largo men; former Army scout; saved my life today in a gunfight."

"The secrets you keep, General. So that's the Indian I heard tell about," said Beauregard.

"Yes: hates the Sioux, hates the Cheyenne, distrusts the Largo Trading Company; could be a good man. I reckon we're done here—let's go upstairs. I'll introduce you before the show."

I led them up the red-carpeted stairs, which matched the red, velvet, flocked wallpaper of the stairwell, to the third floor and my room. I knocked on the door. "Sergeant Bill Crow? It's me, Marshal Armstrong, open the door."

We heard the key twist in the lock, and the door drifted open. Billy didn't even look up; he was reading a book.

"Catechism?" I said.

"Caesar, *Conquest of Gaul*. Three roads lead into Gaul, much like Bloody Gulch, leading to the Belgae, Aquitani, and the Celts—the three Gallic tribes; much like the Sioux, Cheyenne, and Crow."

"Quite so. Sergeant, I'd like you to meet my second in command, Major Gillette, and Miss Isabel Johnson." Scouts don't salute much, but Billy Jack saluted the major, who returned his salute, and he bowed to Miss Johnson. I put that to his credit

"We're going to see our army on stage," I said. "I think it prudent, however, to keep you here on guard duty."

"Yes, sir: read Caesar; keep watch; learn more."

"Can't complain about a sergeant reading Caesar, can we, Major?"

"No, sir, I reckon not."

"Might help you on a mission we have in mind; we'd like to get a message out to the pony soldiers."

Billy Jack looked dubious. "Largo Company guards let me in; might not let me out; they have a noose around this town; if I try to leave, the noose will tighten; they know I'm with you."

"Cavalry can break a noose."

"A noose can break a man's neck before that happens."

"You're not afraid, Sergeant?"

"No, sir, only informed. From your hotel window I can see the street. Largo Trading Company men were excited today. Someone or something is coming. Also, this," he said, picking up an envelope that lay on his trunk. "I found it slipped under your door. Can only be bad news: smells of skunk."

I held it to my nose. "That would be perfume, Sergeant."

"Reckon it must be for you then, General," said that hound Beauregard.

The envelope was addressed, "To: Marshal Armstrong." I grunted and ripped it open. It read, "Must see you after show. You are in danger. Sallie Saint-Jean."

I didn't want to worry Isabel so I said, "It's merely a reminder about the show. We should be off." And I slipped the note into my pocket.

"Shall I ride for pony soldiers or stand guard? I follow orders, but there is great danger everywhere. We need to be ready."

"We'll be ready, Sergeant. And I take your point. Stand guard for now."

I realized he was a marked man—and so were we all.

⚜

The saloon was packed like a jar full of pickles—luckily, we had a table reserved for us, front row on the right. I noticed Dern sitting at a front-row table on the left with a couple of other cowboys and a large man, tall and wide but not exactly fat, grey-haired but not old, boisterous in conversation with the cowboys but obviously set apart by his self-important manner and more formal dress (a vest, a ruffled shirt, a string tie, and a pale cream jacket that matched his pants and felt hat). He was the man in charge, all right. I put him down as a politician, and you know how badly I've always done with them. Miss Johnson told me that was Seth Larsen.

When the curtains went up, I gave him no more mind. The room thundered with applause and boot stomping and yahooing—and with good reason. The show was a masterclass in the theatrical art—from the perplexing drama of the magician and his tricks, to the Samson-like demonstrations of force by the strongman (whose performance silenced the early catcalls from the local Goliaths), to the awe-inspiring feats of the Chinese acrobats who seemed nearly capable of flight, to the stunning array of high-kicking dancers, among whom—as Beauregard was quick to point out to Miss Johnson—I had many good friends, including Rachel, who in skill was now indistinguishable from her colleagues, all of whom drilled with a perfection I have rarely if ever seen in a military formation. I was, I must say, greatly moved.

When the show was over and I was still basking in its reflected glory, a sudden cloud seemed to settle over me and I looked up to see the large form of Seth Larsen. "Well, Miss Johnson, glad you could come into town and see the show. Things are certainly livening up here in Bloody Gulch, aren't they? And you must be the marshal I've heard so much about. If there is anything I can do to help you in any way, Marshal, just let me know. The Largo Trading Company is a proud recipient of contracts from the federal government, and we are proud to support all lawmen who come our way. In fact, I heard that my man Dern was able to assist you in a gunfight with some troublesome Indians. Don't usually have trouble in Bloody Gulch. In fact, that's the first trouble I can remember."

"Funny," I said, "I seem to recall something about an Englishman, Delingfield or something, killed by Indians about a year ago."

"Oh, him, Delingpole—deserved a pole up his backside if you ask me. He was an effete scoundrel—one of those snooty types who thought we were still a colony. Fought with the rebels during the war, thinking it would be fun. Later came out here thinking he could lord it over us. The Indians did us a favor. That was their land he had—or actually ours, under a government contract to manage it for them—not his. Whatever the Indians did to him, he deserved. So that wasn't trouble; that was just cleaning up a mess. You know our ways out here, Marshal; in the West, law might not always be sure, but it is certainly swift. And Dern is usually pretty good at keeping the peace. We want every Bloody Gulch visitor to leave with happy memories. And you, Marshal, when will you be moving on?"

"Oh, soon enough; I've become this traveling troupe's sort of guardian. We'll move out together."

"Shame to see them showgirls go, but they might need some protection after all—even though this is a quiet, peaceful community, as I'm sure Miss Johnson can attest."

In her silence, Beauregard piped in, "I can surely confirm that. Beauregard, Beauregard Gillette's the name. Trying to raise a card game around here is like trying to raise the dead—excerpt for a few daring bodies like Dern."

Larsen looked like he'd stepped on a cow pie and couldn't get the stench from his nostrils or shake the manure from his boots. "We don't have much use for gamblers here. You might want to mosey along to another less respectable town."

"Yes, my profession is an itinerant one. I won't be staying long."

"Miss Johnson, would you care to join me for dinner?" Larsen asked. She looked down and was silent.

I quickly defused the situation. "As I'm sure you have recognized, Miss Johnson has the most admirable figure—why, she could have been on that stage tonight, and not had to blush at all. But like those talented young women, she needs to train, to keep in tip-top shape, and as she dined, delicately as a bird, with us earlier, I cannot imagine she would be inclined to dine again, however polite she might be."

I thought that put matters rather succinctly and diplomatically, but Larsen looked at me as if I had just passed wind.

"What the hell are you talkin' about?" he said.

"What the Yankee Marshal is saying, is that the young lady has no need of your hospitality; she has ours."

I saw red fire flash in Larsen's eyes for a moment; he looked at me and then at Beauregard.

"I could take that as an insult, mister."

"You can take it as you please. I believe the Yankee Marshal and I are going to see Miss Johnson safely home. We've heard there are Indians about."

"Yes, Indians," said Larsen, and his eyes turned on me. "I've heard the same. One is with you, isn't he, Marshal?"

"That'd be a fact," I said. "On official government business; acting as my deputy now. I assume your men will extend him every courtesy."

"We're used to dealing with Indians. We run a trading post. The government knows we treat them well. You'll find no complaints here from anyone—will he, Miss Johnson?"

"I guess the only complaint would have come from Delingfield," I said.

"Delingpole," he scowled.

"Well, she did tell me," said Beauregard, "that for a young charming lady like herself, there is a terrible shortage of equally charming young men, balls, and dances—the sort of thing that livened many an evening in Richmond before the war."

"I was never in Richmond before the war..."

"I could see that; but it was something..."

"But I was there after, teaching you damn rebels a thing or two about respect."

"Why, respect is something that is earned."

"I demand it—and I can't stand you fake gentlemen. Your darkies did all the work, while you sipped bourbon and talked treason. In this land, *every* man needs to work. Nothing is inherited; nothing is given."

"And poor Miss Johnson has no social life."

"If Miss Johnson would like a more active social life, I'm sure that can be arranged; and if you need help packing your bags—that can be arranged too. Goodnight, Miss Johnson; goodnight, *gentlemen*; and watch yourselves; as you noted, there are Indians about." He stepped away and his praetorian guard of cowhands went with him.

"He's a Yankee as sure as Sherman."

"Major, I'm a Yankee too."

"I'm aware of that, sir, but beggin' the general's pardon, there are Yankees and there are Yankees—and that one's a *Yankee*. If he isn't an arrogant, scheming scoundrel who'd sell his mother to a glue factory, what is he?"

"Well, apparently the sort who would lock up a town, imprison its men, make hostages of its women, and enslave its children. That sounds bad enough to me. Yankee or no Yankee—that doesn't much matter; the question is, can Billy Jack Crow break through their lines?"

"I wouldn't bet my life on it. Not now. If we bolt—your Indian or any of us—they'll just shoot us down and bury us; no witnesses. That's what they want. Too bad he knew about your Indian."

"That's all right. We'll have surprises for him later."

"He might surprise us sooner—I reckon we should skedaddle before he figures a way to bushwhack us."

I thought about Miss Saint-Jean's letter.

"I was rather hoping to congratulate Miss Saint-Jean on the evening's performance."

"I'm sure you were, General, but personally, I mean to congratulate myself on seeing Miss Isabel safely home. So, if you'll excuse us..."

"Hold your horses. I'll come with you, Major—safety in numbers. And I'll grab Billy Jack Crow—we could use an Indian's eyes and ears."

∽

We rode out together—Billy Jack and I and Beauregard and Isabel. I reckoned we were reasonably safe, but of course every hooting owl, every critter scurrying in a bush, kept us alert. My wager, though, was that Larsen wouldn't want to kill us in front of Miss Johnson—even a villain likes to look respectable to a woman.

The Indians? Well, that might be another story. He could always explain that away as a renegade attack.

We rode in silence—or nearly so. Billy Jack and I led the way. Beauregard rode alongside Isabel. I knew that was a risk. There was a big shiny moon in the sky, and I could hear his soft molasses whispers and her stifled flutterings, but I tried to ignore them; duty is my mistress—whose only rival is you, darling Libbie.

We made it back to Isabel's farm without incident and stabled our horses in the barn. Then we had a brief council of war. I thought it best to post guards.

"Sergeant, take cover behind the water trough by the front gate. Major, resume your billet here in the barn and keep your eyes open; you're our rearguard. I'll guard the parlor of the house. No one will get by me."

"No, Yankee General, sir, I reckon they won't, no matter how hard they try."

It was good to hear his vote of confidence—not that I needed it.

Beauregard rolled up his sleeves and shifted hay bales to the barn door. He'd take his position behind them. Billy Jack trotted in a low crouch to the water trough. Indian scouts tend to be cautious like that.

I walked boldly as you please through the moonlit night, the crook of my arm offered as a comfort to Isabel and accepted as such. I knew she valued it because she gripped it tightly, admiring its strength, I reckoned, as I patted her hand.

She opened the front door and lit a kerosene lamp. I accompanied her on a tour of the house, just to make sure no intruders lay hidden. When she was assured we were quite alone, she said, "Well, Marshal, thank you for everything—for a lovely evening, and for your protection."

"No need, ma'am. Pleasure was all mine. That's what marshals are for. I'll camp out here in the parlor. You'll be safe."

"Good night, Marshal."

When she bade me adieu, I again smelled blueberries and scented coffee, even if it was only a fond memory.

I was awake most of the night, attentive to the creakings of the house. But there were no alarums from Billy Jack Crow or Beauregard; no feathered flaming arrows crashing into the walls; and I did eventually find myself catching brief snatches of sleep. Still, my mind stayed active, and dawn was swiftly upon us. I got up and looked out the windows. I saw nothing but the natural beauty of Montana. My eyes took it in, the vast panorama, the glowing rising sun, and I found myself daydreaming about coffee—and then a cup was gently placed in my hand.

"Good morning, Marshal. Did you sleep?"

"Too well, ma'am, didn't mean to. You're as silent as an Indian."

"I heard you rustling. I was already awake. I had the coffee made."

I sipped it gratefully and we moved together into the kitchen.

"It's good to have a man about the house again. It does get lonely, Marshal."

"Call me Armstrong."

"Is that your Christian name?"

"Er, yes, ma'am."

"And your last name?"

"Uh, Armstrong."

"Your name is Armstrong Armstrong?"

"Yes, ma'am. If you'd rather call me Marshal that's fine. I'm afraid my parents weren't very creative."

We stood there, awkwardly, looking at each other for a moment—admiration (I for her coffee making; she for my manly form, I assumed) competing with perplexity. There was a knocking on the front door, but it wasn't insistent or threatening and neither of us moved. Needless to say, Beauregard appeared.

"You told me to keep an eye on things, General. Noticed movement in the kitchen—wasn't likely to ignore that."

Isabel shook her head as if dispelling a dream. The spell broken, she said politely, "Coffee, Major?"

"Beauregard, ma'am, Beauregard, and bless your soul, yes; and if you have any more of those blueberry biscuits and that delightful honeyed butter, well, ma'am, I reckon I'd stay awhile."

"No doubt of that," I said.

Inevitably there was another knock at the door and Billy Jack Crow slipped inside in his stealthy Indian way. "They're watching the house," he said. "Sioux. All around."

"How many?"

"Small war party: maybe a dozen men; here to make sure no one leaves."

"Another noose," I said.

"Another noose," he repeated.

"Maybe we should invite 'em in," Beauregard said. "Let 'em know they don't have the drop on us."

"They apparently had the drop on you, Major. You didn't see them?"

"No, Yankee General, sir, I was keeping an eye on the house; I figured that's where the greatest danger was."

"Well, you got here safely—that's something. But I can't remain—noose or no noose. I must return to Miss Saint-Jean and her showgirls."

"I thought you'd say that," said Beauregard, smiling at Isabel as she handed him a cup of coffee and a hot buttered biscuit wrapped in a napkin.

"It's our army, Major; that's what I'm thinking about."

"No doubt, sir—lost without their commanding officer."

"Well, they do have Miss Saint-Jean—but I had intended to discuss strategy and tactics with her after the show."

"Of course, sir."

"But there was no time—not after Larsen's threats."

"No, I reckon there wasn't. No time to chat with Miss Sallie, or with Miss, uh, and the other one, Miss, uh…"

"Sergeant, you think they'll attack us if we leave?"

"Cannot say; they might just report back to the Largo Trading Company. But they have guns."

"So do we; if it's a dozen, we can take 'em."

"Uh, Yankee General, sir, if they have repeaters—that's an awful lot of lead flyin' around."

"A trained man with a revolver is better than a wild Indian with a Winchester."

"Twelve Indians, twelve Winchesters; I'm not scared, mind you, sir; just want to make sure you've got the math figured nice and proper. Now, if I was planning the attack—"

"Theirs or ours?"

"Ours, naturally—I'd see two scenarios, maybe three. One, you go—with Billy Jack as your interpreter—nice and cordial; and try to powwow a safe passage."

"And the other?"

"We surprise 'em: hit 'em from three directions; drive 'em off; make our way out."

"I take your point, Major. Safest option: smash 'em with a surprise attack."

"Actually, sir, safest option is scenario three, you and Billy Jack ride out fast as you can, forcing your way with pistoleros, as necessary, and I stay here, guarding Miss Isabel."

"I see."

"Her safety is our priority, sir."

"No doubt, Major."

My baleful scowl shifted from that Southern chancer to Miss Johnson, and immediately my manly heart was overwhelmed by the periwinkle glow of her big blue eyes; the shining radiance of her long blonde hair; the rosy tints rising in her sun-kissed cheeks. I sensed a woman in distress, and I tried to set her at ease. "Don't be alarmed, ma'am. I doubt you're in danger here—or at least not much." I shot another baleful glance at Beauregard. "But I'll gladly take you into town; you can stay at the hotel."

"Might be danger there, too, Yankee General, sir."

"Major, there can be no greater safety for Miss Johnson than on the cancan line of Miss Sallie Saint-Jean's Showgirls and Follies—of that I can assure you—and you, ma'am."

Isabel moved her lips, but no words came out. Beauregard filled the gap.

"Yankee General, sir, I mean no disrespect when I say your general idea of strategy seems to consist of having everyone you know join a traveling circus."

"Do you have a better plan, Major?"

"No, sir, I don't reckon I do. I hope to join that circus myself. You're not the only one who wants another conversation with Miss Sallie."

"Miss Saint-Jean," I insisted.

"Marshal Armstrong," said Billy Jack. "Three by the fence posts; one by the trough."

"Major, check that window behind us. I'll check the one in the kitchen." I kept low and as I raised my head to peek over the sill, a satanic Indian face, looking like a human gargoyle, baring its teeth, eyes enraged with bloodlust, rose directly in front of me on the other side of the window.

A hatchet came crashing through the glass; his arm with it. The blade missed, and I seized his wrist and elbow. Applying all my weight and leverage, I brought him smashing through the window and onto the kitchen floor. Before he could recover himself, I had the knife pulled from my belt and was about to ram it into his chest when I remembered my pledge to kill no more Indians forever. I turned the blade away and, clenching my fist around the knife handle, punched him in the face, once, twice, three times. I stood up and backed away. "Major Gillette!"

He skidded into the room like a horse pulling up at a cliff—stopped by the sight of the Indian, who breathed heavy as a bull, blood foaming from his nose and mouth. The red man roared his defiance, pulled out his own knife, and leapt to his feet. He lunged for me and I dodged. Then he saw Beauregard and stabbed for him. Beauregard shot him twice, which was enough to put him down permanently.

"You all right, sir?"

"Fine. Major, I must tell you: I could have taken him myself, but I made a vow to kill no Indians."

"A vow to kill no Indians—not even if they're trying to kill you?"

"That was not specified."

"But for heaven's sake why?"

"I'd rather not say."

"What sort of vow is that? I mean to say, Yankee General, sir, a woman's life is at stake. Perhaps we make a codicil to the arrangement."

"Back to your position, Major."

I confess, his words gave me pause. I pivoted to the window, knelt, knife clenched in my fist, and waited for the next brave to show himself. Even with danger directly in front of me, I had to answer a deep philosophical question. A vow is a vow, but a woman is a woman—and, as I mentioned before, a man's a man for all that.

I had to decide where my duty lay. I looked at the dead Indian, a giant of a man, laid out on the floor. I thought of Isabel and what she might have endured. I looked at my fists—strong as iron, but against armed Indians, how many could they handle?

We were surrounded by howling war cries—and then gunfire: theirs, Beauregard's, and Billy Jack's.

"Isabel, stay down. Beauregard, Billy Jack—make your shots count!"

Our gun belts were the limit of our ammunition. I felt the bullets lined up along the leather. I could strip my belt and give it to Beauregard, or I could take the revolver from its holster—regard it as a tool like any other—and put it to its most noble purpose, defending a woman. I shifted the knife to my left hand, pulled the gun, and felt its weight, heavier now with decision. You know, Libbie, I am a man of my word.

As if competing for my allegiance, I heard the coyote yells of the Indians and Isabel crying out, "Major, over there!" Another shot.

I peered over the shattered glass. "All clear here," I announced. "Billy Jack, do you need help?"

"Three dead at the posts; one's at the trough." Bang. "He's dead too."

That was at least five. "Major?"

"Got two, sir. Don't see any t'others. But they're sure as heck raisin' a ruckus."

That was true enough. They were still yelping like hounds of hell and bullets were blasting and chipping away at the house.

"Beauregard, Billy Jack, be sure of your targets."

We had ammunition enough—if we were disciplined. I'm careful about that: always save a bullet for another day, especially when you've got no quartermaster.

"Isabel, stay down, but crawl to the kitchen; it's safer here."

She was my responsibility; I wanted her close; and I'd made my decision: I would kill no Indian—unless it was to save her.

Her blonde head appeared in the doorway. She pulled back and gasped when she saw the Indian carcass.

"Don't worry, he's dead."

She crawled around him, keeping her distance, as though he were a giant snake that might rise and strike again.

Knife in one fist, revolver in the other, I reckoned I looked like a buccaneer. I tried to ease her mind. "I'm sorry about the window, Isabel. But we'll repair it—and I promise you, if they put a hole in your coffee pot, I'll wreak a terrible vengeance—a vengeance such as they have never known. No woman will ever suffer on my account—and that pledge," I said, thinking aloud, "takes precedence over any promise wrested from me under the compulsion of the Boyanama Sioux."

Isabel looked deeply into my eyes. "Marshal, are you wounded?"

"No, ma'am."

"Have a fever?"

"No, ma'am."

"You're quite sure? You're all right?"

"Ma'am, with the new clarity in my thinking, I'm as right as a wolverine with a treed squirrel." She seemed confused and I tried to reassure her. "Everything will be fine, Isabel, everything will be fine," and I patted her hand with my fist that still gripped the knife. "Oh, sorry."

I looked over the window sill. Twenty yards away, the barrel of a Winchester rifle seemed to have propped itself on a fence rail; behind it, unseen, was a hostile. Thought and action were suddenly one. Trusting my speed and marksmanship over his, I fired, ducked, and shoved Isabel flat on the ground. I peered over the sill again. The Winchester had fallen like a stick through the railing; its owner's hands hung there like brown mittens on a wash line.

I heard more gunshots and Beauregard shouted, "Dropped another—for sheer impertinence: tried to use my hay bales for cover."

A mounted Indian sped across my line of sight. "Billy Jack—can you get him: Indian on horseback."

There was a shot, and an answer: "Yes."

The yelping ended; the shooting too; the survivors were slipping away. I couldn't let that happen. They'd go to Larsen. I knew that meant more danger for Isabel.

"Beauregard—to the kitchen. Guard Miss Johnson."

"Thank you, Yankee General, sir. Thought you'd never ask."

"Billy Jack, come with me!"

The two of us stepped out the front door: he cautious, crouched like a panther; I bold, tall, revolver drawn, knife held low, ready for a fight. We stepped off the porch and onto the dirt. Billy Jack swung round, checking the rooftop and rear approaches. I strode for the front gate, brash as can be, hoping to draw enemy fire, flush them out. I reached my hand for the fence post. Winchester rounds cracked the air, splintering wood, erupting plumes of dust. Billy Jack and I flopped on our bellies, rolled from the gate, and three mounted howling Indians burst from a small copse, snapping off rounds. Billy Jack and I returned fire—and so did Beauregard from the shattered kitchen window. One hostile dropped immediately. The other two came on fast with bullets singing over our heads. Billy Jack I think got one; whether I got the other I cannot rightly say, but he came hurling off his horse at such a velocity that his corpse rolled right into the barrel of my revolver. I prodded him; he didn't move; and there was silence again.

I tried to do a quick sum in my head. "I think that's thirteen, Sergeant."

"Still could be others."

"Could be, but I reckon not. If there were, they would have charged together."

I stood and dusted myself off. Billy Jack followed my lead.

"Well, Sergeant, it looks like we're in a war after all."

CHAPTER FOUR

In Which I Am Reminded
of My Duty

We had another swift council of war in the parlor, where we decided it would be best if Beauregard and Billy Jack stayed behind with Isabel and I went into town on my own. If we had in fact killed every Indian meant to spy on us and keep us captive at the Johnson farm, it would be quite a shock for Seth Larsen and his gang to see me sauntering down the street. I thought I'd relish that.

But it wasn't mere vanity that called me away. It was that harsh drillmaster: duty. There was a high-kicking line of women counting on me for protection. There were Chinese acrobats who needed my military leadership. There was Rachel to whom I was still indebted for my life and Miss Saint-Jean to whom I was still indebted for my disguise. And there was duty, always duty: I had an army to train; and from what Isabel had told us, a cause that was just.

I have always been a master at reconnaissance, assessing an enemy's disposition, recognizing gaps in his line. Those talents, along with dash, courage, and stamina are what made your Autie the youngest major-general in the Army, Libbie. So, I tried, on my ride into town, to regain that mental acuity, maintain a sharper lookout, and hone my scout's eye for skulking Indians. But I saw none, and my mind drifted to those in my care. I thought of Miss Saint-Jean and our first meeting; she in her theatrical apparel, I in my buckskins, and how welcoming she had been to a tall, handsome, strong, fair-haired stranger—for that was all she knew about me at the time. I thought of Miss Rachel, how she had rescued me, how attractive she had been as an Indian (even with that half-skull neckerchief), and how she had become even more attractive as a white cancan dancer, revealing talent that I had never before fully realized she possessed. I thought of Isabel at the farm—a blonde blossom of Montana, tall and radiant as a sunflower, and as needful of protection as a palomino threatened by wolves.

For a while, these three women, these three grave responsibilities weighed upon me, as only duty can, and then my mind roamed to thoughts of freedom, of escape from burdensome duty, if not as a Ree scout, perhaps the freedom of an actor whose responsibility lay not in saving lives but in elevating hearts and minds, bringing people to new insights about humanity, and putting me in regular professional contact with women like Miss Saint-Jean.

Could I have been an actor? No, as attractive as it was, I pushed that silly thought away, and again recollected that more likely, if I hadn't been a soldier, I would have been a scout with nary a care in the world other than riding after the enemy. No worries about paperwork or politicians; none of the weight of command; merely the joy of life in the open air and the satisfaction of duty well rendered, of an enemy found so that he could be destroyed. Yes, I should have liked to have been an Indian scout.

I think that was the thought foremost in my mind when I rode into Bloody Gulch and tied my horse to the hitching rail outside the Bloody Gulch Hotel and Spa. I pushed open the front door and approached the clerk. "Any messages for me?"

"Why, no, sir. Were you expecting something?"

"Maybe from Washington. I'll check at the telegraph office."

I walked down the plank boards past the saloon and the General Store, and I do believe that every soul in town who heard my boots, could see out a window, or was passing me by on the dusty street turned to stare. When I swung open the door of the telegraph office, I had my first reward. Dern, leaning back, boots on the table, nearly fell out of his chair.

"Why, Marshal, I thought you were at the Johnson place."

"Was. Here now."

"No trouble? No Indians and such, I mean. I heard you was worried about Indians—you know, after what happened here with the gunfight and all. We're not used to that sort of thing."

"No, no trouble. Nothing I couldn't handle anyway. Just came by to see if there was a message for me from Washington."

"Well, I tell you, Marshal, I gotta confess. I still don't know how that dang thing works. 'Fraid I can't be of any use to you at all on that score. But if it does go clickety-clack, and you're at the hotel, I could always let you know. Can't tell you what it says, but I can let you know it's workin'."

"Much obliged, but that won't be necessary. If they want me, they'll find me—even if it means sending a troop of cavalry."

"Are you really all that important, Marshal? I mean, no offense, but it ain't quite expected, is it, that a marshal is so darned important to the United States Government that they'd send a troop of cavalry to find him?"

"This one is," I said, smiling. I winked. "And some day you'll know why." I moseyed on back, the floorboards creaking beneath my boots, past the saloon, down to the hotel. Miss Saint-Jean was standing just outside.

"I heard you were in town."

"Just got back."

"You got my message."

"I did, but I couldn't keep the appointment."

"You had a better offer."

"I wouldn't say that. It was a matter of duty."

"Yes, you soldiers are very keen on your *duty*, aren't you? Shall we step inside? Coffee and a chat? Dining room's empty; just the two of us."

"I'd like that," I said. Speaking low, I added, "My duty, by the way, included killing a dozen Indians. My deputy should have scalped and buried them by now. But no worries, they weren't customers."

Miss Saint-Jean is not easily shocked—I mean no dishonor to her when I say that—but my news gave her pause.

We sat down, a bored waiter (who doubled as cook and bellboy, I'd noticed) brought us coffee, and Miss Saint-Jean said, "Well, Mr. Marshal, Mr. Indian-fighter, I suppose it won't come as news to you, but all these young gunmen slouching around town, looking for trouble, have finally found some—*you*. They've got *you* in their sights. They can hardly wait to pull the trigger.

"You mean men like Dern? They don't bother me."

"They've hired new gunmen."

"Why would they do that?"

"To kill you—the new ones have a reputation apparently."

"So, do I."

"For being dead."

"Anyway, Larsen wouldn't be so foolish."

"The hiring's supposed to be secret, but they were so cocky and excited, they were spouting off at the saloon. If you get killed by known outlaws, the blame will fall on them, won't it, not on the Largo Trading Company? The cowboys thought that was pretty funny."

"Strange sense of humor, don't you think?"

"My point, *Marshal*, is that on *your* account, *we're* not safe here. Gun battles—I've seen too many—can get out of hand. They might start by shooting you, and then…"

"There won't be an 'and then,' Miss Saint-Jean. They're not getting me—or you or your showgirls either. In fact, I'm giving you another one."

"Another what?"

"Another showgirl—Miss Johnson, with whom I dined last night. And I'll give you: Beauregard and his card tricks; and an Indian who is a human dictionary capable of translating any word into Spanish, French, Latin—you name it. No one has an act like that."

"No one would want it."

"It's a matter of theatrical vision; I can see him now..."

"I've seen him already."

"Then you know."

"I know, Marshal, that my show is not an orphans' home; it is a business, a business to which you have already done a great deal of financial harm."

"But surely yesterday's performance was successful?"

"How can you talk about success? Gunmen are coming to kill you."

"They won't..."

"Those cowboys I heard were talking loose; they didn't care who heard them. They said that you're a dead man; a dead marshal; they said these hired guns are bad men, *really bad* men; they're betting on who gets the honor."

"Of killing me?"

"Yes."

"Well, no one's collected so far—and their Indians lost."

"From what I heard, they're not the last."

"Miss Saint-Jean, the fact is: we can't turn tail, even if we wanted. Larsen's men have us penned in."

"He's after you—not us."

"I wouldn't count on it. You know too much. He enslaved a town; why have mercy on a handful of Chinamen and cancan dancers?"

"All right—so leaving town is a risk; so is staying here with you."

"Miss Saint-Jean, you once reminded me of my duty, and I'm grateful. Now I remind you of yours. We've got these girls to protect and we've got the future of Montana and the West to defend. We can't let the Largo Trading Company destroy these people's families and farms when just beyond here, if we can break the company's noose, is the U.S. Cavalry who can set things aright. And you, ma'am, should have more faith than anyone in our mission, because you know who is actually leading it, and if I may remind you, ma'am, I was the youngest general in the war..."

"…and the man responsible for leading a troop of cavalry into a massacre…"

"Redemption, Miss Saint-Jean, I seek redemption, and I shall find it in leading you and your girls, and the Chinese acrobats, and Beauregard, and Isabel, and Billy Jack—that's the Indian, the walking dictionary…"

"And Isabel—that's the woman you were with last night?"

"Yes, but the point is, I'm going to lead you all to safety—do you understand?"

"I understand, General—or Marshal—that I don't have much of a choice, thanks to you. I only ask that you remember your duty extends to *every* one of my girls."

"Madam, they are never far from my mind—and the Chinamen, Miss Saint-Jean, I never forget the Chinamen."

"The Chinamen can take care of themselves."

"Even better when I'm done with them. Our regular routine will be saber drills and skirmish practice. The Largo Trading Company will regret they tangled with us."

⟋⟍

To ensure they would, I needed to cogitate on strategy and tactics. I retired to my room and there envisioned the disposition of our forces and the enemy's. Larsen had an overwhelming superiority in numbers, and he had us surrounded. We held the hotel, which was not easily defensible, and Miss Johnson's farm. Considering how precarious both positions were, I reckoned that consolidating our forces at the Bloody Gulch Hotel and Spa was the right and proper choice. Not only were there rooms for all of us, and a restaurant, and of course the stage (our drilling field) at the saloon, but the hot springs behind the hotel offered ample bathing facilities for Miss Saint-Jean and her terpsichoreans—and proper hygiene could prove crucial if we faced a prolonged siege. Strategy, tactics, and duty demanded, then, that I return to the Johnson farm for Isabel and encourage her to return to town with me. It was by far the safest course.

If Larsen compelled us to fight a pitched battle, I would be content to fight it here, at the hotel, at the center of Bloody Gulch, with the shopkeepers as witnesses to our courage. Perhaps it might fan whatever embers of manliness remained in them.

Though I am a man to keep my own counsel in matters of strategy, I informed Miss Saint-Jean of my intentions and asked her to set Hercules and the acrobats as guards around the hotel. I also asked that, as a temporary matter, the magician, Fu Yu, be assigned to me as an aide.

"A lone rider, even as gallant a one as myself," I explained, "might be easily ambushed. But a two-man patrol, combining a cavalryman's dash and daring with a fan-wielding magician's talent for mystification, would doubtless be unstoppable."

"Oh, yes," she said, "I can see that," and she gave the appropriate orders to Fu Yu, who bowed in response, flashed open a fan, and said, with expectation, "*Mah?*"

"He's asking for his mother?"

"No, Marshal, that's what he calls a horse. He usually rides in one of the wagons. He'd rather ride a horse."

"*That* I can understand. Assure him that he shall have his *mah*."

We rode to the farm without serious incident—and Fu Yu, though he spoke not a word to me, proved an interesting companion. Every so often he set a bird loose from his billowing sleeves. It flew some distance and then returned at the beckoning of his singsong Chinese voice. I was put in mind of Noah and the doves aboard the ark. I assumed Fu Yu was using the bird as an avian scout, and I marked the magician as a man of initiative, if not an Old Testament prophet.

I introduced Fu Yu to Isabel. He bowed and when he came upright reached out and pulled an ace of hearts from behind her ear and handed it to her as a gift. He bowed to Beauregard as well and then waved his palm before the major's face, lifted his eyepatch, and said (the first English words I'd heard him speak), "You see, yes?"

"Yes, much obliged," Beauregard replied, flipping the eyepatch down.

To Billy Jack, he bowed, then waved his palm in front of the sergeant's bowler hat and said: "Lift hat." Billy Jack did, revealing a cooing dove.

"Wrong bird; I am Crow."

We stepped inside the parlor, and our council of war was brief. Miss Johnson's soft blue eyes practically caressed me with her concern for our mutual well-being as I laid out our situation, the grave dangers that confronted us, and the necessity of bringing our command together. I promised her that she would receive expert training from Miss Saint-Jean in the intricacies of the cancan and that I would assist in any way I could.

Throughout my presentation Fu Yu impressed everyone with the wide variety of colored fans that appeared and reappeared with startling rapidity in his hands, as though he was somehow shuffling decks of them up his sleeve. I regretted his distracting from my remarks, but his act seemed to calm the others, so I took it in good grace. Billy Jack was especially impressed: "That magician, that Chinaman—fantastic," he said. "In French, *fantastique Chinois*. In Spanish, *Chinaman fantástico*!"

Beauregard raised an important question: "Begging the Yankee General's pardon, but it's one thing to consolidate our force; it's another thing to supply it. If the Largo Trading Company shuts down supplies to the hotel, we'll be in worse shape than Marse Robert trudging to Danville before Appomattox; no supplies and no room to maneuver."

"Hadn't thought of that, Major."

"But, sir, a Confederate officer does not raise a difficulty without offering a solution, and my solution, sir, is this farm. Miss Isabel, while short of cattle, has a couple of dairy cows, a mess of chickens and pigs, and a large smattering of vegetables—not enough to sustain us indefinitely, but enough to help. We might also encourage the hotel proprietor to stock up—perhaps we could book rooms for an entire month and advise him to take on appropriate provisions, as we intend to dine regularly at the hotel."

"By Jove, Major, that's a splendid thought."

"To avoid arousing suspicion, Miss Isabel, the sergeant, and the two of us should gradually and subtly assemble our food and supplies. Miss

Isabel and I should come into town only after the hotel is nearly fully stocked—something I reckon you'd want to see to yourself, sir. Then, Yankee General, sir, fine horseman that you are, you could return here and lead us in the chicken drive."

A *chicken drive*—there was a thought to inspire the inner cowboy in my heart; less dangerous than cattle, I grant you, but skittish animals all the same, and it would require tremendous skill, I reckoned, to herd them in an effective way. And would not the Largo Trading Company men be taken aback, as we drove the cackling yellow-and-brown hens and strutting red-and-white roosters down the main street to the Bloody Gulch Hotel and Spa? I could imagine no more inspiring a scene.

I clapped Beauregard on the shoulder. "My good man, that is strategic genius. So many of you Southerners had it; so glad we're on the same side now. And you, Isabel, you'd be willing to part with your chickens…"

"…and pigs…" interjected Beauregard, who I suspected was partial to bacon.

"…to the cause?"

Isabel came towards me and we held each other's arms with an emotion that can scarce be imagined outside of wartime. She said, "Yes, Armstrong Armstrong, for the cause; I will do anything for the cause—and I will do anything to keep my chickens and my pigs and my cows and my asparagus and everything else I have from feeding the Largo Trading Company!"

"There's a girl!" I proclaimed, and I knew, dear one, that your image engraved on my arm smiled in approval at this joyous union of thought (Beauregard's) and action (Isabel's) and my own role in helping to carry it out. It was a moment to savor, and as our eyes locked I could think only of the rapture you would have felt if you could have been a part of it.

But as is so often the case, duty bade me to depart—this time, in the service of quartermastery—and on my ride back to town it was hard for me to focus on my surroundings, hard not to imagine the Montana plain swarming with chickens—Beauregard and Billy Jack and I waving our hats and shouting: "Yahoo, ride that chickee in!"—and Isabel, perched on a buckboard laden with asparagus and other comestibles casting her brave blue eyes on the far horizon, seeing in our chicken drive the looming freedom we hoped to deliver to the honest citizens of Bloody Gulch.

Given how distracted my mind was, I later felt fortunate that I had not been bushwhacked by one of the Company's Indian raiding parties. That thought, however, came much later. My immediate challenge was convincing Miss Saint-Jean to extend her deposit on the rooms so that we could pull off Beauregard's strategy. I explained everything to her in detail. We were sitting in her room. She was in her business attire, one of her many matching outfits of spangled corsets. This one was purple with frills and black silk stockings, and she wore a feathered bonnet. Canny businesswoman that she was, she was reluctant to part with her capital—either on excess fabric for her corsets apparently, or, more to the point, to extend our stay at the hotel, even when I pointed out that it could be that or starvation.

"You, Armstrong, are trying my patience. Our lives are at risk; our earnings are at risk; everything we have is at risk because you had to ride in from the hills, chased by Indians, kill someone in Applejack, and then jump into my lap, from which point, out of the kindness of my heart, I have saved you by making you, in turn, a Chinese sharpshooter and a marshal, and in both capacities you have seen fit to cause me endless trouble."

"Miss Saint-Jean, as you surely know, the trouble is not of my making. I am a man pursued by enemies."

She stared me down hard. There was none of that vibrant compelling warmth of Isabel's gaze, none of that magnetic attraction between two noble souls—no, this was the hard, dark hue of a blue-steeled revolver, but I liked it and respected it just the same. "Armstrong, this only works as an investment. If I'm going to book it for a month, I'm going to buy it for forever—make it a permanent showplace when we're not touring; I'll need it *and* the saloon. We could even establish homesteads for the girls. This could become *our* town." She envisioned the sign welcoming weary travelers: *The Bloody Gulch Hotel, Spa, and Saloon, Featuring Sallie Saint-Jean's Showgirls and Follies.*

I have—as you know, Libbie—talked to the titans of industry, but I have never talked to a financier more blessed with commercial vision than Miss Sallie Saint-Jean of the eponymous showgirls and follies. Discussing business with her was different from discussing "the cause" with Isabel, but it was thoroughly engaging and mesmerizing all the same, and I am deeply honored to have known two such wonderful women—and you, dear Libbie, most of all. The deal was struck—with me at least—and Miss Saint-Jean and I talked long into the night about a negotiating strategy to acquire the hotel and saloon, until I came up with the perfect stratagem.

I employed it the following morning by sticking my revolver up the nose of Mr. Smithers, the clerk at the front desk who also happened to be the owner of the Bloody Gulch Hotel and Spa. The deal was swiftly made. I promised him a fair market price for the hotel, to be paid in reasonable monthly installments from our earnings after we overthrew the tyranny of the Largo Trading Company. I also promised him his full weight in chickens to compensate him for his trouble. He seemed nervous, dubious, and unwilling at first; then I cocked the hammer on my revolver and he became much more agreeable. I drafted appropriate papers; we rode out to Billy Jack to have him copy out a duplicate in Latin in case any lawyers got involved; and Mr. Smithers and Miss Saint-Jean signed them with Beauregard and Isabel as witnesses (I could not stand as a witness because of my operating under an alias). Mr. Smithers agreed to keep the sale secret until the hotel was full-on bursting with supplies.

Acquiring the saloon would be a trickier venture because it was owned by the Largo Trading Company—or really, directly by Seth Larsen—so we decided to defer that acquisition for the moment. We did not want to arouse premature suspicion—though of course the chickens could not be kept in the coop much longer.

I spent a couple of days at the Johnson farm making final preparations for the great chicken drive. The buckboard was loaded with coffee and flour and blueberries and asparagus and even (Isabel wanted it as a keepsake) old Sam Grant's picture, and anything else that might be of use to us and would fit.

The magician Fu Yu was astride a *mah* at the front, his multi-colored fan held close to his shoulder as a saber; behind him was the heavily loaded buckboard driven by Isabel, led by draft horses and with her cows on lead lines tied to the back; then came the pigs, with Beauregard, a deft man with a horse, keeping the porkers in line; and finally, bringing up the rear in dramatic fashion—for we had dozens upon dozens of squawking chickens—were Sergeant Bill Crow and I, riding on either side of the fryers, mindful not to trample them beneath our horses' hooves.

I had carefully instructed Fu Yu in the art of command. He raised a fan overhead and then lowered it slowly to the horizon and shouted, "Twoop, fowawd ho!" The chicken drive had commenced. It was a stirring moment.

Fu Yu shook his fan open, applied its gentle breeze, and rode ahead at a leisurely pace. Behind him, Isabel's two big draft horses did their best to pull their heavy load. Beauregard kept the squealers calm by serenading them in his low Southern drawl: "Swing looow, sweet bacon 'n' grits, comin' fo' to launch my morn'; swing looow, sweet bacon 'n' grits, comin' fo' to launch my morn'."

As for myself, the orders came naturally: "Yo there, Billy Jack, keep that fryer in line....Don't let that chick escape....Broilers to the rear!"

As absorbing as the trail work was, our journey would be relatively short, so the chance of having many chickens fall out or get rustled was slight. That allowed me to discuss a thought that troubled my conscience with Sergeant Bill Crow. I confessed how I had given my word to Chief Linewalker to kill Indians no more forever—and how I had obviously violated that word in defense of Isabel. I asked him, "What would your priest say about that?"

"He would say any vow made under compulsion—not valid; it must be an act of free will. And I say, any vow made to Boyanama Sioux is worth less than mud on a stick. Boyanama Sioux are my people's enemy; my people despise Boyanama Sioux; and I'm very sorry you're their blood brother—they're a tribe of scar-faced vermin; in French, *vermine cicatrisée*; in Spanish, *parásito con cara de cicatriz*."

"But surely a vow is a vow."

"Not under compulsion; not to Boyanama Sioux. You did the right thing protecting Miss Johnson. Every man has a right to self-defense and an obligation to defend others; my priest would say, 'Bless you, my son.'"

"I've always been a man of my word."

"You still are; you gave your word to Miss Johnson to protect her. That's more important. The Church teaches a hierarchy of duties. If your vow obliges you to do good, it is unbreakable. If it is compelled by scar-faced vermin, if it leads to evil actions going unpunished—then it must be broken. To do otherwise is selfishness and vanity."

"I've never broken a vow before."

"Name them."

"My vows?"

"Yes, the important ones."

"I took a vow to defend my country at West Point."

"That's a good vow."

"I kept it with honor."

"Any other?"

"I've taken a vow not to drink."

"That's a good vow."

"Also, not to gamble—at cards and the like."

"Fine vow."

"Most important, I took a vow of marriage to one Libbie Bacon—the finest woman in Michigan, if not the world."

"You vowed to marry bacon?"

"No, Sergeant, her last name was Bacon—look, it doesn't matter. I was married—to a woman—my wife."

"Just one?"

"Yes, of course, just one—you're a Christian, aren't you?"

"Catholic Christian, Hail Mary! But different tribes, different customs."

"Not the Custer tribe, I'll have you know."

"But you're also Boyanama Sioux."

And I'll be darned if Billy Jack didn't hint at a smile—the cheeky Indian.

"Get that rooster back in line!" I commanded.

෧෨

We rode on, the sun beat down, and sweat dripped from my brow. It wasn't just the heat but the awesome responsibility of chicken-herding, where any misstep could deprive us of eggs in the morning or fried chicken at night. To break the tension I sang, soft and quiet, a little song I'd made up: "*Whoopee ti yi yo, git along, little chickies. Whoopee ti yi yo, git along, little chickies. It's your misfortune and none of my own. Whoopee ti yi yo, git along, little chickies.*"

I was thinking up new verses when Billy Jack rode up alongside me and said, low but distinct over the squalling of the chickens, "Sioux following us."

I wasn't surprised. "How many?"

"War party—close to thirty."

"Thirty? To watch over four men and a woman?"

"They're Sioux; they fear chickens."

I could see why—the squawking, strutting, nervous, flapping rabble before me would unnerve anyone—but I knew the Sioux better than that. You don't send out thirty scouts. They were a raiding party—they meant to steal our asparagus, our chickens, our dumplings.

"Major Gillette," I called ahead, "we've got a Sioux raiding party following; I reckon they're after our ham and eggs."

"Careful, there, porky, careful," he said to a stumbling trotter. "Follow that buckboard, you Macon bacon," he encouraged another. Then, turning carefully from his charges, he came alongside. "Well, Yankee General, sir, all I can say is that if they're man enough to try it, I expect we'll give 'em the same treatment we gave 'em at Miss Isabel's place."

"Sergeant Bill Crow thinks there are thirty of them."

"Thirty? My, my, they did learn their lesson last time, didn't they?"

"What about a charge to disperse them?"

"Might make sense if it weren't for the lady."

I thought of Fu Yu defending Isabel with his fan and figured Beauregard was right. "And if they charge us instead?"

"A chicken stampede might confuse them a mite; they've probably never seen one."

"No, Major, I don't suppose they have. Have you?"

"No, but it could distract 'em: they chase the roosters, we get the buckboard to that group of trees—give us some cover, dismount, hold 'em off."

"And lose our chickens, Major? We've got a herd to drive; I'm not giving it to the Indians."

"Fair enough, Yankee General, sir. I defer to no man in my love of vittles. But your decision then, sir?"

"We're going hell-bent for leather into Bloody Gulch. My chickens will scramble as fast as their forked feet will carry them. Your pigs will fly..."

"...and Isabel's wagonload of blueberry biscuits will roll."

"Yes, Major; are you ready? It might mean leaner pork chops, but they'll be whole."

"General, sir, ready for your orders!"

"Ride up to Fu Yu; tell him, 'Forward ho, chop-chop,' and wiggle your arm in front of you. He'll get the idea, or he'll be eating our dust. Give the order to Isabel. As soon as her draft horses gain speed, we'll follow."

"Yes, sir!" and he bolted away.

I saw Isabel smack the reins; the wagon wheels picked up speed; Fu Yu screamed as he was almost run over; and I called to Billy Jack, "Yee-hah, drive those chickens, drive 'em!"

The straining horses pulled away; the cows, slow to comprehend, strained their lead lines in tardiness; the pigs' trotters moved like mad trying to keep up; but the hardest job by far belonged to Billy Jack and your devoted husband. The crazed chickens threatened to skitter off in sixteen different directions. But we cut them off at every turn, screaming, "Feed to the front; feed to the front! Cluck-cluck; cluck-cluck!" driving them forward.

Still it was impossible to keep pace. As overloaded as the buckboard was, the horses' hooves quickened, speed building on speed. The cows mooed their disapproval but ran to keep their lead lines slack. The squealing pigs under Beauregard's expert management were no match for the swiftness of the draft horses, but even they were pulling away from us, trotting as rapidly as their trotters would carry them. As we fell farther and farther behind, we struggled to keep order and direction among the cluckers. Isolated now from the main body of our force, we were an easy target. Billy Jack and I rode with rifles drawn, constantly looking to our rear, occasionally using a rifle barrel to slap a chicken back in line.

It was a harrowing few miles, as you can probably imagine: heat burning dust onto our faces like powder, rivulets of sweat cutting through it; crazed squawking chickens deafening our ears; our eyes straining at the simmering horizon. But there, finally, it was—Bloody Gulch, the trickling red moat, a narrow bridge with a few men standing by, and the buildings behind.

Across the bridge were Dern and his gang. They escorted us into town, halted us before the hotel, and surrounded our supply train. Fu Yu, still mounted, looked grim and held his fan like a dueling pistol. Isabel on her buckboard, biting her lip, looked in need of manly reassurance. Beauregard, tall in the saddle, watched his pigs as calmly and defiantly as an Irish wolfhound with its paw on a mewling kitten.

I rode to the front. "Fu Yu: guard those chickens—and don't make them disappear!"

Dern said, "Well, I do declare, Marshal, you are the most unpredictable lawman I done ever hear tell of. You arrive with a travelin' show and you return with a heap of pigs and chickens. You throwin' a barbecue or somethin'?"

"If it's any of your business, Dern, I can assure you a hot time is on the way."

"Would that be soon, Marshal?"

"Soon enough."

"With chickens, pigs, blueberry muffins, and coffee?"

"And a whole lot more."

"And a show?"

"Oh, a big show."

"I wouldn't want to miss that."

"No, you surely wouldn't. Right now, though, we're going to set up a pen and a smokehouse and whatever else we need behind the hotel."

"Behind the hotel? Where them spa waters are? I hear tell them dancing girls are there all the time."

I hadn't thought about that, but the need for a taller fence for the girls played into my other plans.

While I sat in the saddle thinking of the spa waters, the girls using them to rejuvenating effect, and the need to fence off our livestock, Dern said, "Marshal, just how big a corral you thinking about?"

"Dern, I make it a habit to think big. We're going to tear down buildings you don't need—like that telegraph office—and use it for lumber."

"Now hold on there, Marshal…"

"You told me yourself, Dern—no one here needs a telegraph, except for me. That office is a waste of good lumber. I'll rewire the telegraph through the hotel and contact Washington as necessary."

"But that office ain't your property."

"I'm commandeering it." I cupped my hands around my mouth and shouted: "Waka-waka Wolverines"—my war cry for our acrobats. They tumbled out of the hotel in their baggy, black, silk shirts and trousers, swords in their fists, purple scarves tied around their heads. I told Dern, "These men will disassemble the telegraph office and reassemble something more useful at the hotel. They have boxes of nails and hammers waiting for them—bought from your own general store—Larsen owns that too, doesn't he?—so everything is present and correct."

"Mr. Larsen approved all that?"

"He'll approve it *ex post facto*."

"That Indian talk?"

"Do me a favor, Dern. Tell Larsen I want to meet him—tomorrow. I've got a business proposition for him."

"A business proposition from a marshal?"

"I expect he'll want to see me—you go tell him."

"See you where, Marshal?"

"At the saloon—he's got an office there, doesn't he? That's as good as anywhere."

"Not the Trading Post?"

"He afraid to come into town?"

"You're pretty cocksure, ain't you, Marshal? I reckon men in your line of work don't live long."

"Not in yours either, Dern. And that's my line of work. You tell him I'll meet him at the saloon. Any time—I never sleep."

"All righty, Marshal. You take good care of those hogs and chickens, you hear—even those dairy cows—and yourself. We'll be seein' ya soon, I reckon."

He tipped his fingers to his hat, and he and his desperadoes rode away. I chalked that up as a victory. A few browbeaten shopkeepers emerged—curious what we'd delivered.

"Major, the acrobats are under your command—set them to work. Fu Yu, Hercules—keepee, keepee piggy-piggy, chickie-chickie together-together," I said, motioning with my hands, in case my Chinese was not clear enough. "Keepee-keepee shop-keepers away-away."

Hercules did as he was bidden: foot-stomping the ground whenever a pig or a chicken took a wayward step, and folding his arms and scowl-ing—like a sour-tempered genie protecting a seraglio—when a curious citizen got too close. Fu Yu for his part kept the animals together with deft stabs of his fan—much like a fencer with his épée—shooting it open when more emphasis was needed.

I dismounted and helped Isabel off the buckboard. Once again, as I lifted her, I was taken by how tall, lithe, and long-legged she was. I took her hand, grabbed my horse's reins, and led these two pretty fillies to the hotel, tying the horse to the hitching post and escorting Isabel to the parlor.

"Smithers!"—we had kept him on as a clerk and waiter—"Bring us two sarsaparillas." I regarded Isabel's bottomless blue eyes earnestly and said, "We took every bottle in the General Store. If you don't like sarsaparilla, we could squeeze your dairy cows—but, well, I figure they're probably a mite tired."

"Oh, sarsaparilla's fine, Marshal—it would be a treat."

And indeed, I must say that Isabel's undisguised joy at being under my protection and her girlish, giggling enjoyment at her first few sips of sarsaparilla were, in some avuncular way, deeply rewarding. We were just settling down to sharing reminiscences of the trail when Miss Saint-Jean came sashaying into the parlor wearing a yellow spangled corset, black stockings, black high heels, and a yellow tricorn hat—all of which made her look like a queen bee. Her theatrical training leant itself to such bold entrances. She was accompanied by Rachel, whose company—I felt a sudden pang of guilt—I had too long neglected because of duty.

"You must be Miss Isabel," Miss Saint-Jean announced, without waiting for me to do the honors. "I'd like to introduce you to Miss Rachel, who is Mr. Armstrong's ward; are you his ward too?"

"His ward? Why no, no, but I guess you could say I'm under his protection."

"Oh, aren't we all? Did he mention that you'll be in my employ?"

"He did say something about a cancan line—but I wasn't quite sure..."

"No, I expect you weren't. I believe it was a bit of a surprise for his ward as well, which is why I thought you might find her a useful companion in the days ahead. She's a regular member of our troupe now; she can help you find your way."

"Oh, well, thank you," she said, looking at Rachel, "that would be most kind."

All three women then looked at me as if expecting me to say something, so I stood up, sarsaparilla bottle in hand, and said, "Yes, that would be most kind indeed—and I expect you have much to talk about. I'll leave you ladies to discuss your business while I supervise the men." With that, I made a hasty retreat to the front porch.

There was a rocking chair out front, and I confess that after our long and dangerous ride I felt uncommonly weary; I wanted only a moment to sip my sarsaparilla; and the chair looked tempting as all get out. I plopped into it and rocked it gently back on its hind legs so that it leant against the hotel. I sighed, took a swig of sarsaparilla, and as always, my dear, thought of you.

CHAPTER FIVE

In Which We Set About Digging In

I needed only a brief interregnum of such peace to finish the sarsaparilla and creep warily back into the hotel to deposit the bottle behind the front desk. Then I was out on the street, striding down to where the acrobats, armed with claw hammers, were noisily ripping the boards from the telegraph office. Beauregard was handling the more challenging task of disconnecting the telegraph equipment.

"We'll have this done sooner than you can sing 'Dixie,'" he said.

That was an exaggeration, of course, but the men did work swiftly, and soon we were all gathered behind the hotel with stacks of boards, boxes of nails, and Beauregard instructing the acrobats using a combination of sign language and drawings he'd prepared. I had my sleeves rolled up and was pitching in—I'm not one for inactivity—standing on Hercules's back so that I could hammer down the roof of the chicken coop. Fu Yu was actually inside the coop, singing what I presume were Chinese lullabies to calm the birds, while Billy Jack secured the chicken wire. We had built a milking shed for the cows, and the pigs had a nice muddy area penned off with a sort of lean-to where they could hide from the sun. There was a small grove just within the farmyard fence, where we could occasionally shade ourselves during our labors. From a military point of view, this impromptu farmyard was virtually indefensible. We could erect a few barriers to slow an attacker and could perhaps, if necessary, keep a sentry on guard (as the chickens were the most easily affrighted, I considered Fu Yu for this duty, given his way with birds), but any attack in force would succeed. The sooner we had these animals converted into sustenance, the better.

It was hot and I was yearning for another sarsaparilla when I heard a woman's voice calling: "Oh, Marshal...*oh, Marshal!*" I finally recognized that it came from the bathing area, where one of Miss Saint-Jean's show-girls was standing wrapped in a massive towel, like a squaw wrapped in an Indian blanket. We had built a tall double-sided picket fence to protect the women's privacy, but from my perch on Hercules's back I could just make her out.

"Yes, my dear, what can I do for you?"

"Is it all right if we take the waters? It's so dreadfully hot—and the waters are so refreshing."

"Are they? Yes, well, all right then. Just a moment." I noticed that others from the troupe were lining up behind her, so I had to work quickly. I hammered in a few more nails and was nearly done when Hercules grunted theatrically in what sounded rather like an enormous belch, and I looked over my shoulder. Dern was ambling towards us.

"I took your message to Mr. Larsen. He'd like to see you tonight—and he don't approve of what you're doin'."

"Fortunately, we don't need his approval," I said, still standing on Hercules. "He doesn't own this hotel, he didn't own the telegraph office, he doesn't own this chicken coop or the farmyard we're building, and he certainly doesn't own this town—even if he thinks he does."

"It's a company town, Marshal. He'll see you at the saloon—his office; nine o'clock."

"And you'll be there?"

"If Mr. Larsen wants me." He motioned at Hercules. "What about him?"

Funny, I hadn't thought of that before; but a little extra muscle wouldn't hurt. I nodded. When I turned to resume my hammering, I was greeted by the laughter of showgirls splashing in the spa.

Unfortunately, Dern had not yet ambled out of earshot. "Well, howdy-do, Marshal. And will they be there? Looks like you got yourself a plum nice view."

"An educated man," I said, "is not afraid to see a lady in a perfectly respectable bathing costume. There is work to be done, and I am doing it; and part of my work here is to protect them from you."

"From me, Marshal? I wouldn't hurt a fly. I reckon they might like me."

"Well, you reckon wrong. We're a traveling troupe—no time for romance with cowhands."

"I ain't exactly a cowhand, Marshal—I got me a good job; one of the best around, in fact. I work direct for Mr. Larsen. Probably more future in that than bein' a marshal."

"If that's a threat, Dern, you should know that I've already survived the great war, a mess of Indian fighting, and much else besides. It will take more than you or a trumped-up Indian trader to put me in my grave." I pointed my hammer at him. "Let me give you a bit of advice—don't even try."

"Well, surely not, Marshal. I keep tellin' ya, I'm a peaceable sort of man. I'll let Mr. Larsen know you'll be seein' him."

6∂℃

Hercules and I were punctual. Larsen's office was up a flight of stairs on the side of the saloon away from the stage. Dern and another gunman were standing by the door, waiting for us.

"Howdy, Marshal. We could order you up a beer, if you like. Mr. Larsen won't care. He does some of his best negotiating over whiskey and beer."

"We'll go straight in, if you don't mind."

"This here is Wyeth," Dern said, and the other gunman—a stubby, dirty, loutish-looking sort—didn't offer his hand or nod but simply stared at me in a dull, bored, sneering way until Dern added, "he's here just to even up the numbers," at which point Wyeth still said nothing but pointed to the door, as if asking me to open it.

So, I did, and walked in followed by Hercules and Dern. Wyeth came in last, closed the door behind him, and leaned against it, which I suppose was meant to scare me—cutting off any escape route. But retreat was not on my agenda.

Larsen sat behind a very large desk of swirling pine, the swirls matching the contorted look of repressed anger on his face. He seemed to have drunk too much coffee and to need someone to shout at—and sure enough he did. He shot up from his chair, pointed at Hercules, and said, "Is that your negotiator? Marshal, I don't know what you're up to—but it sure as blazes isn't the law. You're a troublemaker, and I don't like troublemakers. And I don't want you in my town."

"Well, Mr. Larsen, I don't think this is *your* town. You don't own it, you're not the mayor, and as I recall, you're supposed to be running a trading post under a federal government contract. It seems to have grown quite a bit—like taking over that Delingfield place…"

"Delingpole!"

"…taking over this saloon; taking over the General Store; and I hear you've got other businesses."

"I don't own the General Store; I let Mathis keep it; I only supply it. And what's that to you? It's called enterprise; it's called working for a living."

"Well, for starters, I'm buying this saloon."

"You're what? It's not for sale," he bellowed and thrust himself back into his seat. "Get out of here—you're wasting my time."

"You're selling it to me for a dollar. I've got it right here." I pulled a dollar from my pocket and held it up.

"What's your game?"

"That's the wrong question, Larsen. The real question is what's yours? The federal government has had its eye on you for a long time. I could make them quite a report, the sort of report that could put you away for years, probably forever. So, I think you're going to want to sell me this saloon for a dollar."

"Get out of here! Dern, get him out of here!"

"He touches me," I said, "and your whole trading company comes down around your head like a wagonload of manure on a mouse. I don't have to do anything. The report is written—and unless I get this saloon for a dollar, and get it right now, I'm not going to be in any position to stop that report from reaching Washington."

"Report what? You've seen nothing criminal here—except what you've done yourself: gunning down Indians, knocking down the telegraph office."

"And the mine? I wonder what President Grant, let alone the governor of this territory, would think of your mining operations? And I wonder what your foundry does? I wonder where all the children are? I wonder where Indians get Winchester repeating rifles—you have any idea? I sure as heck do."

"Those guns are for hunting—I'm allowed to sell them."

"They're for intimidation."

"Marshal, you're a fool—and you're wasting my time."

"Am I? I figure you'd rather have me running a saloon than running a report out of here right now, wouldn't you? Answer me that."

"I don't have to answer anything. People in this town know me. No one here would ever testify against me. In fact, I could sue you, Marshal, for defaming my character."

"You could try that," I said, "but I think you'll come to a different conclusion. Your lawyer might too. You can have him look at this. This here is a bill of sale made out to Miss Sallie Saint-Jean. There are four drafts: one for me; one for you; one in Latin for your lawyers, should you wish to get them involved; and one for Miss Sallie Saint-Jean. You'll note I'm not a signatory to the contract. I'm merely acquiring the property acting as her agent. That doesn't violate my official role as a U.S. Marshal, but it does ensure that everything will be done according to the law. Tomorrow morning, I'll come back here to take possession on her behalf, and you'll have my copy and her copy signed and waiting for me on this desk. If it's not here, you're going to be in hotter water than a boiled rabbit in an Indian stew—and I mean one that's got a basket of cabbages dumped on its head. You got that? I mean every word of it. That's all, Larsen. Goodbye."

The dastardly bully sat there speechless, brooding, his lower lip jutted forward in a sort of fat boy's pout. I turned to Wyeth, and he looked past me at Larsen. Larsen merely scowled and waved us away. Wyeth grudgingly rolled his heels aside. I opened the door, turned to Larsen, and said, "I'll be back in the morning; have those papers ready."

I closed the door behind us, and Hercules and I walked slowly down the stairs. The saloon was doing a roaring business with the Largo men. No one looked our way; they were absorbed in gambling and drinking and telling tall tales. If Larsen signed those papers, the saloon would be deserted tomorrow. I looked to see if we were being followed. The door was still closed.

⁀⊇⁀

In the hotel parlor I found Beauregard, examining what looked like an account book. "Evening, Yankee General, sir. I've got Billy Jack training the Chinamen in night fighting behind the hotel. If he'd like to join them," he said, pointing a pen at Hercules, "he's welcome, though I reckon he can take care of himself."

"Every man can use extra training," I replied and nodded at Hercules, motioning to the rear of the hotel, saying, "Cluck-cluck, oink-oink, moo-moo helpy-helpy fighty-fighty chop-chop," which was the best I could manage in Chinese. It was apparently good enough, as Hercules turned his massive bulk and stepped out of the parlor

"From what I've seen," said Beauregard, "I'd take Hercules against those acrobats any time. Granted, if it's a kicking fight, they're high kickers, as high as Miss Sallie's dancers, or just about. Never seen fighting like that—and hope I never will either: prettier than effective, I'd reckon. Also, not sure about that card sharp Fu Yu. I tried to tell him a lady's fan has no chance against a gun, a tomahawk, or a knife."

"What'd he say?"

"Nothing—just flipped his fan open and stared at me like a basilisk."

"Don't be fooled by appearances; he's an impressive man. You saw his work on the chicken drive."

"Why, yes, Yankee General, sir, that was an impressive bit of work—best I've ever seen from a Chinese magician on a chicken drive."

I was glad to have my opinion confirmed. "So, what do you have there, Major?" I said, indicating the account book.

"Been toting up our supplies, and by my calculations we can hold this position longer than those Texas boys held the Alamo."

"But with a different outcome, I trust."

"Well, they had Travis and Crockett and Bowie..."

"Yes?

"...and we've got you, Yankee General, sir, and a critter company more irregular than Forrest's cavalry."

"We'll have the saloon, tomorrow."

"Well that's something—bourbon for the officers."

"Larsen'll be cautious until his hired guns arrive; that'll give us time. You can inventory the saloon in the morning; might be enough food there for another few days."

"Food, yes, but, Yankee General, sir, you've given me an idea: that saloon probably has more bourbon than a Kentucky colonel has horses."

"Well, yes, I suppose, Major. It *is* a saloon."

"What I mean, sir, is that we could use that to great effect."

"I doubt it, Major. You might be a drinking man, but an Oriental army led by a teetotaler and an Indian scout doesn't need much medicinal whiskey. None of us can hold our liquor."

"Actually, sir, I was thinking about our defensive position. Here we are at the hotel," he said, planting the salt shaker. "Here's the saloon next door," he said, moving the pepper into position, "and this is the boarded-up church," he said, repositioning the sugar bowl. "Now, Yankee General, sir, imagine the surrounding environs of Bloody Gulch, and what's our greatest vulnerability?"

"Well, our salt and pepper shakers are effectively surrounded," I said, plucking a couple of napkins from a neighboring table and placing them around the condiments, "we're badly outnumbered; we can't defend our chickens, let alone anything else; we lack artillery and most especially cavalry; and we can't even pray for a miracle unless we fix up that church. If I had my druthers, Major—and the livery stable had the horses..." I plucked a knife from a set of silverware and used it to flip aside one of the napkins. "We'd charge out of here, with every man, woman, and child of Bloody Gulch securely mounted; and I'd race Larsen's men to the safety of Fort Ellis—and beat them there as sure as Phil Sheridan. But besides being surrounded and outnumbered—and trapped—and our supplies limited to what we can requisition from the hotel, the saloon, and the General Store, I'd say we're fine."

"Well, sir, a man besieged can turn things to his own advantage, or so Marse Robert used to tell us. Think about a cornered wildcat. His one advantage is that no one can hit him from behind. His enemy— his tormentors—might be bigger, stronger, more numerous, but he knows exactly where they are: right in front of him. Turn that wildcat into a man, give him a rifle, put him behind some cover, and everything in front of him becomes a target."

"Your point, Major?"

"My point, Yankee General, sir, is that we can turn our position here into a defensible, tight, little island by digging a trench—a sort of moat, like the Bloody Gulch itself—around our two strongholds, the hotel and the saloon—and incorporating the church and the school, because we don't want them to fall to the vandals, do we? But more than that, sir, what if we lined the back half of the trench, behind the hotel and the saloon, with tin? I don't know if you've noticed, sir, but there are some tin roofs just cryin' to be put to better use. We block that section off, fill it with liquor, and set it alight: no enemy could cross that. Instead of attacking us from all sides, we'd force our enemy to the front; and we can reinforce our front with some homemade obstacles and wire entanglements and maybe breastworks."

"By Jove, Major, that's brilliant."

"Well, Yankee General, sir, we learned some hard lessons at Petersburg."

"On both sides, Major, on both sides."

"Sure enough, but I have something else in mind too. Have you ever seen a map of the Battle of New Orleans—not Beast Butler's, but Old Hickory's? His force was ragamuffin too—no Chinese acrobats to be sure, but pirates under Jean Lafitte, blacks and coloreds, free and slave, Indians I reckon, militia of course, and some good ole Southrons with squirrel guns facing off against the British army—and he forced the British to attack down a sort of funnel, as I recollect. Don't know why we can't do the same."

"No reason indeed."

"Now, of course, he did have field batteries, which we lack, and a real army and all, but..."

"But it's a plan," I said, warming to the idea.

"In my humble opinion, sir, Old Hickory was the best general this country ever had between Washington and Lee—and if that plan was good enough for him, I reckon we can get by with it too."

"We might not have artillery, Major, but Larsen's men aren't redcoats, either."

"No, sir, they aren't. More to the point, then, Yankee General, sir, I have your permission to take possession of all such liquor as I require and to rip this town to pieces for our common defense?"

"Not only do you have my permission, Major, I order you to do it."

"Thank, you, Yankee General, sir. We'll start tomorrow with hammers and shovels—form a regular work party."

"Well done."

"Also, Yankee General, sir, Sergeant Bill Crow has returned from scouting the enemy. His report: they're tightening the noose. Company men are posted at every farm. Indian war parties are riding patrols in between. We got Miss Isabel out in time, sir, but the others..."

I smacked my right fist into my left palm. "We'll rescue them, Major. We have to."

"Long and the short of it, sir, is that in Billy Jack's estimation they're pinning us in place—either for an Indian attack, like the one that roasted our English cousin, Delingpole, or for Larsen's hired outlaws."

"I left Larsen at the saloon. We could grab him now—make him a hostage."

"I reckon he's got a praetorian guard of pistoleros just waitin' for you to try that, sir. They'd gun you down—in self-defense, mind you—and then we're all at their mercy."

"You're right, Major, might not be prudent."

"If it were to be done, when 'tis done, then 'twere well it were done later, I reckon."

"What was that, Major?"

"If we're going to grab him, sir, I think we'd be well advised to grab him at a strategic time of our choosing. Billy Jack knows where the Company headquarters is, the Trading Post; he says there's always a passel of Sioux and Cheyenne lingering around it, but…"

"No, I mean, what you just said—*Hamlet*?"

"Up North they might call it that, sir. But my point is that instead of grabbing him at the saloon, which they might be expecting, and might end up with you getting killed—what if we, in due time, slipped out and surprised at him at the Trading Post."

"And run a gantlet of Indians?"

"At night—most'll be asleep."

I stuck my tongue in my cheek and was doubtful.

"I'm a gambling man by profession," continued Beauregard, "and if you want my professional opinion, I'd wait for the element of surprise. That's what Mosby would do. And I reckon the moral effect on Larsen's men—having him pulled from under their noses, at night, when they'll wake up confused—would be a heap more powerful, as Billy Jack might say, than a run-of-the-mill gunfight in a saloon. Think about old George Washington at Trenton, sir."

I gave a long commanding stare at Beauregard's exposed eye; it betrayed nothing. "All right," I said, "tomorrow morning we take possession of the saloon; then, in due course, at the Trading Post, we'll capture Larsen."

"In disguise," said Beauregard. "As Indians."

"As Indians?"

"Yes, Yankee General, sir: another element of surprise—sort of like those Boston boys at the Tea Party."

"Very well, then, as Indians," I agreed, without the slightest idea how we would do that.

⁖

Our roosters crowed us awake. Given our shortage of manpower, they acted as sentries and sounders of reveille. After accidentally sitting on Billy Jack (he was huddled under blankets and looking out the window, and my bleary eyes mistook him for a chair), I completed my morning ablutions and tripped down the stairs to the hotel parlor and breakfast.

Awaiting me was Rachel with plates of bacon and eggs and biscuits and cups of coffee for the two of us. "I knew you to be an early riser, General," she said, "so I tried to be ready for you."

"Thank you so much, Rachel."

"My pleasure, General. I was hoping we could talk."

"Of course, my dear—what about?"

"About this town, about the trouble we're in, about…you do—please tell me you do—have a plan to get us out of here, don't you, General? The girls—Miss Saint-Jean's girls and Isabel—seem to think we're in danger."

"We are—but there's no reason to fret; the challenge is not beyond my military powers. In fact, I see our position as somewhat similar to that confronted by Andrew Jackson at the Battle of New Orleans—and that, my dear, led to one of the greatest victories in American military history. I intend to smash the enemy here and then ride our wagons over his bones to our next theatrical engagement."

"You think we can?"

"I think it is a certainty. I expect we'll have theatrical engagements from here to San Francisco and back again—perhaps all the way to New York."

"No, I mean, you think we can escape?"

"The Largo Trading Company? This town? Of course! There's nothing standing in our way aside from an army of company gunmen—untrained, I reckon; a handful of hired assassins; and outlaws have no discipline—and an unknown number of Sioux and Cheyenne war parties; and I've dealt with them before."

"Yes, I saw one of those battles."

"That one was a fluke. You know my reputation. You trusted me to lead you to safety—and look at you now, tucked away here in Bloody Gulch, as safe as a treed possum with a lifetime's supply of fruit, crickets, and snails. It's only a question of strategy. The major and I spent most of the night developing a defensive plan, drilling our Chinamen in infantry tactics, and thinking up appropriate punishments if they miss roll call this morning, which I expect they will. Whether we break out—which I would love to do—or if we massacre the enemy on our front porch, our victory is a foregone conclusion. The key question is a business one: should we head east or west for our next theatrical engagement?"

"I'm so glad you're thinking of business," said the unmistakably businesslike tones of Miss Saint-Jean, waltzing into the parlor. "My balance sheet could certainly use some—in the column dedicated to income and profits. But I assume, as usual, Marshal, that you're planning on killing my customers rather than putting them in the stalls." She wore a purple hat that reminded me of Robin Hood and a corset of royal purple that did not, along with black stockings and shoes with heels so long that they could have been used for dowsing rods. "I assume you don't mind if I join you—I own this hotel now, don't I?"

"And the saloon, ma'am. I hope to take possession this morning. I concluded negotiations last night."

"You did, did you? For a good price, I hope."

"One federal dollar, ma'am, which I paid on your behalf, after all you've done for me."

"A grateful man is a rare find," she said to Rachel. "I guess I'm obliged to you, Marshal, even if that dollar was mine to begin with."

"I am not only grateful, ma'am, but dutiful and devoted. I intend to make your troop immortal in the memory of our countrymen. As men today venerate the memory of Andrew Jackson, so too will future generations remember with pride how Miss Sallie Saint-Jean's Showgirls and Follies, commanded by General Custer, won the Battle of the Bloody Gulch Hotel, Spa, Saloon, and Theatre."

"Uh, Marshal, I believe your name is not General Custer, but Marshal Armstrong," reminded Miss Saint-Jean.

"Oh, yes, so it is."

"I also believe I need some coffee."

"Oh, I'll get it for you," said Rachel, and she skipped away to the kitchen with a lightness of foot that I credited to her recent work on the stage.

"So, you bought me a saloon. Well, I suppose I should be bubbling with gratitude; but in sheer business terms that saloon is probably worth what you paid for it; it's lacking a certain something, don't you think?"

"Customers, you mean."

"Precisely—Boss Larsen won't want his men drinking there anymore, will he? And given the rate at which you eliminate customers, I'm not sure you're the best business partner I could have."

"Ma'am, if you mean to impugn my business acumen, feel free. I do not claim to be a businessman. I am what I am—a soldier, a writer, and perhaps in my retirement I could join you on the stage. For now, I am impersonating a marshal and leading an army of acrobats—and doing so, I will remind you, at your suggestion."

"My suggestion was that you put that badge of yours to good use. And I guess you are trying, Marshal. But good intentions, as I've told many a man, are not enough. A woman expects a man to be capable—to be handy—to do something, to be something."

"Well, I must say, madam, being the youngest general in the Union Army was certainly something; being a household name for military valor was certainly something; entertaining a wide readership with tales from my life on the plains was certainly something." Before I could add that marrying you, Libbie, was certainly something, Rachel returned with a coffee pot in one hand and a cup for Miss Saint-Jean in the other. Her appearance prevented me from responding further to Miss Saint-Jean's unwarranted remarks. Rachel set the pot on a trivet on the table, poured Miss Saint-Jean a cup, and said, "Would you like me to fry you some eggs, ma'am?"

"No, dearie, I've found that coffee is all I need—that and Marshal Armstrong's counsel; it's *so* helpful in navigating life's calamities, most of which *come* from Marshal Armstrong."

"If you want my advice," I said commandingly, "I would say to stay here while I go to the saloon."

"Whatever for?—I *have* been in a saloon before, Marshal."

"It's not that. It might not be safe."

"Is anything safe when you're involved?"

"I mean there is a chance that Larsen will have set a trap for me—or for us. He knows I'm coming to pick up the papers. He might have arranged an ambush."

"I'll take my chances, Marshal. There isn't a man who's ambushed me yet—except maybe you. Now finish up; I want to get to work. And where is that man Smithers? If he intends to stay in my employ, he needs to manage that kitchen."

"Oh, I don't mind doing it," said Rachel. "I like being helpful."

"Nonsense, no ward of Marshal Armstrong's should be a scullery maid." Then she inclined to Rachel and said, as if in confidence, "Never do something when a man can do it for you. They're the ones who need things to do—and they might as well do them for us. Our job, dearie, is to keep them busy, preoccupied, and entertained. Not a bad racket once you get the hang of it."

I felt I should excuse myself from this womanly conversation, but just as I was about to stand and take my leave, I saw Beauregard and

Billy Jack slouching on opposite sides of the doorway to the parlor; their opposing angles reminded me of the top half of a saltire.

"Good morning, ladies, and, Yankee General, sir. Thought I smelled coffee, and I reckoned you might need help drinking it."

"Why, take a seat, Mr. Gillette," said Miss Saint-Jean, "and you, Mr. Indian…"

"Sergeant Bill Crow," I reminded.

"Sergeant Crow, will you please go find Mr. Smithers and threaten to scalp him unless he gets cooking in the kitchen? I have a bevy of young ladies who will soon be joining us and expecting their morning coffee."

He saluted, which he needn't have done—Miss Saint-Jean held no official rank in our army—and said, "Yes, ma'am," and, as Indians do, seemingly evaporated.

Beauregard strutted in and I thought, not for the first time, how Southern gentlemen often seem to mistake themselves for high-stepping stallions.

Rachel said, "Let me get you a cup, Mr. Gillette."

"I do declare, Miss Rachel, you are the sweetest child in creation."

I eyed him with appropriate suspicion, but Miss Saint-Jean redirected the conversation.

"So, when does the Largo Trading Company lay siege to my hotel and my saloon?"

"I reckon we have at least a few days," I said. "Larsen will wait for his hired gunmen."

"And if they don't oblige you on that?"

"We'll be ready. But I think they will. Larsen's a boss; he's used to getting his way; he'll be overconfident; he'll think that because he's got us surrounded he can take his time and do things his way. But we'll have a few surprises for him."

❧

After our convivial breakfast, the four of us (Beauregard, Billy Jack, Miss Saint-Jean, and your devoted husband) strolled down to the saloon—at first with the careless happiness that follows a good meal and good company. But as we approached the saloon, I whispered for them to be quiet, and I put my hand on Miss Saint-Jean's shoulder to restrain her from moving ahead. As I did so, I marveled at its perfect roundness; how strong and supple it felt; how much like your own shoulder, dearest Libbie; and I wondered whether women gain strength from opening their arms to the elements; whether they gain power from exposing stockinged legs to bracing drafts; whether they gain balance from walking in perilous high heels. I am, as you know, Libbie, not much of a scientist, but even my mind can be inspired to scientific inquiry with the proper stimulus.

But for the moment I pushed such academic questions aside and whispered a command: "Wait here."

I waved Billy Jack to the opposite side of the saloon doors. He crept off the floor planks onto the dusty street and did a crouched run to where I wanted him. No bullets ensued. I motioned for Beauregard to stay low, and he and I waddled to the entrance like well-armed ducks. We paused and listened. No sound.

I whispered across to Billy Jack, "On the count of three, we all go in. Billy Jack, you cover the left. Beauregard, you cover the right. I'll run in and leap over the bar. One, two, three—now!" We burst in, each with revolver drawn, and I bolted for that bar fully prepared to having zinging bullets cutting the air fore and aft of me. I was so intent on my target that my mind and body registered nothing else. I expect I could have had my head shot off, and like a headless chicken continued forward. Up and over the bar went my boots, and I landed hard but stable and firm on the barkeep's side. I thought the bottles above me might start exploding, ignited by lead. But there was silence, except for the faint creek of leather and of Beauregard and Billy Jack's weight shifting on wood. I stood, my eyes swiveling for targets. But nothing moved. The saloon appeared deserted—its bottles and glasses, tables and chairs left just as they were after a usual night's closing.

"Cover me," I said, and I carefully crept around the bar and then to the stairway that led to Larsen's office. I knew, as I mounted the stairs, that I'd make a tempting target if any hidden gunman had me in his sights. But there was no click of a hammer, no glint of daylight slanted through a window onto a gun barrel, no footfall save my own. I made it to the landing. All was quiet. I knocked on the door. No response. I tried the handle: unlocked. I stepped inside. Larsen's chair was empty. On the giant desk were the documents, pinned there by a knife. I stepped to the desk, yanked out the knife, and a voice behind me said, "Morning, Marshal."

I consider myself a brave man, but I concede that the hairs on the nape of my neck stood up. I turned around slowly.

In the dawn shadows, sitting in the corner behind the open door, was Dern. His boots were propped up on a waste paper basket. "Mr. Larsen asked me to stay behind, just to make sure you were satisfied. We tried to do it right and proper. As I always say, Marshal, we don't want no trouble. I can verify his signatures; that's me signed on as his witness."

"Thank you, Dern; very efficient." I shuffled through the papers. "It appears everything is present and correct. Are you looking for a job?"

"I got me a job, Marshal."

"Telegraph's not around anymore—and you weren't much good at that job anyway."

"Have you tried that telegraph, Marshal? I reckon it won't be much use to you—Indians always knocking down the wires."

"I'm sure we can find you another job."

"Mr. Larsen takes good care of me. I reckon he might take good care of you too."

I wasn't quite sure what he meant by that. Surely he wasn't trying to bribe me. So, I said, "Thank you, Dern, that's all. You may go. You can tell Mr. Larsen you did your job."

Dern emerged into the daylight of the window. "There's more to my job than that, Marshal. Just a word to the wise, you might want to get out of town. Some folks are comin' you're not going to like. They're goin' to want a drink, and they're not goin' to want a marshal delivering it."

"I appreciate the warning, but I reckon I'll stay. Have to, anyway. As I'm sure you know, there's a cordon around the town."

"I could find you a way out. Not just you, Marshal, but all those girls. They don't deserve what could happen to 'em. Some of the men comin' here ain't too kind."

I gave him a long, assessing look and said finally, "Your Mr. Larsen wants me to stay; and as an investor in this saloon—a saloon that doesn't officially belong to me, but to Miss Saint-Jean—that suits me fine; I intend to protect my investment."

"Oh, he wants you to stay all right—let's just say for other reasons."

"To each his own. Goodbye, Dern. I trust you'll pay us a visit; first drink's on me."

"Goodbye, Marshal—and I hope I ain't toastin' your funeral."

I followed him out to the landing and watched as he descended slowly, his spurs jangling, his eyes on my colleagues.

"Goodbye, gamblin' man," he said to Beauregard. "Injun," he said, tipping his fingers to Billy Jack. Then Miss Saint-Jean sashayed through the swinging doors. Dern halted. He wavered for a moment, frankly appraising her, from Robin Hood cap to spiked heel, and tarrying in between. Finally, he said, "I surely do hope Mr. Larsen looks kindly on you ma'am; I surely do." He pushed through the saloon doors and was gone.

I needed to dispel the ensuing silence with action—and gave orders: "Beauregard, get your account book and make a tally of our alcohol, ranking it in order of inflammability. Miss Saint-Jean, these papers in my hand confirm the saloon is yours; let's make preparations to defend it. I'd be obliged, ma'am, if your ladies learned some new dance routines—they can practice here; the sight and sound of them will inspire the men..."

"What men?"

"Our men."

"You and Beauregard?"

"Well, it's a start—and I'd be obliged if you'd form a sewing circle. I need an Indian costume. So does Beauregard. Billy Jack and Rachel can advise." She looked exasperated. I turned with relief to Sergeant Bill Crow, a proper Indian scout and soldier, and gave some more orders:

"Sergeant, take Hercules and grab every shopkeeper you can find. Tell them we're obliged to destroy their businesses, but will give them work building a moat."

"Oh, they'll leap at that for sure," said Beauregard.

"Major, you have your orders."

"Yes, sir, and where might I find you, Yankee General, sir, if I need you—as if I didn't know."

"I don't know what you mean to imply, but I'm rousting our China-men out of bed. Billy Jack, come with me—let's find Hercules."

Thus began the fortification of the Bloody Gulch Hotel, Spa, Saloon, and Theatre.

At the hotel, Billy Jack and I marched into the kitchen. There amongst the pots and pans, the dozing Mr. Smithers, and an affectionate cat, prowl-ing for mice, we grabbed pot lids. Then through the deserted parlor, up the red-carpeted stairs, to the fourth floor where the Chinamen were boarded. Without pausing to knock, I flung open the door. "Get up, you lazy laundrymen!" I crashed pot lids together and nodded at Billy Jack to do the same. "What do you think this is? A Shanghai siesta? Sleepy-sleepy—naughty-naughty! Must wakey-wakey early-early in the morning-o, in the army-o! No rolly-cally, no breakfast! Now musty-musty doey-doey hardy-hardy labor-labor!" This I thought was a fairly good stab at the sort of Cantonese English that is the *lingua franca* of places like Hong Kong. I looked to Billy Jack, the linguist, for his approval. "Is that about right?"

"Right as rain, sir. In French, *droit comme la pluie*. In Spanish, *cor-recto como la lluvia*. In Latin, *rectum sicut pluviam*."

"Hercules, get these men organized into a labor detail, savvy? Acro-batty fronty-fronty." Hercules regarded me sullenly or perhaps uncom-prehendingly, but the acrobats tumbled over each other, forming a line for inspection, and saluted.

Fu Yu did not join them. He sat on his bed, his wide magician sleeves occupied by doves cooing and waltzing.

I put my face in front of his. "Who do you think you are—you Peking prestidigitator!"

The doves scattered, but he remained calm. He reached behind my ear and pulled out a joker card.

"Get in line!" I shouted, and he hopped over to stand by his fellows.

Dramatically, I paced before the short, black-silk line of acrobats. I dropped any semblance of Cantonese and spoke the most powerful English I could muster. "Tumblers, acrobats, I am assigning you to Major Gillette. Your mission will be the most important you have had thus far. Using hammers and other tools, you will be deployed to demolish every building in Bloody Gulch, save for the hotel, the saloon, the church, and the school. This destruction will not be the destruction of the Vandal or, perhaps more relevant to you, the Mongol. It will be the destruction we see in nature, of autumn making way for spring, of buildings coming down so that others might be go up, of dry brittle noodles, useless to you in that state, soaked in boiling water so that they might be sucked off chopsticks and provide you with nourishment.

"For to everything there is a season—a time to tumble, a time to make others tumble; a time to build up, a time to tear down; a time to bend steel bars with your bare hands," I winked at Hercules, "a time to dance the cancan," and I thought of Rachel and wished she were here to be inspired by this moment, "a time to deal cards; and a time to turn cards into doves," I looked to Fu Yu, who shot a fan out from his sleeve and waved it before his face, dramatically.

"Every board and building we take down will be material for Major Beauregard to build defenses—de fences and de breastworks," I said, smiling wryly at my little jest. "We will waste nothing. Everything that can be usefully requisitioned from the General Store will be put to good use. We are not termites, eating away this town's foundations, we are Trojans defending Troy. *For Troy—and for Bloody Gulch!*" I waited for a rousing Chinese cheer. But they only stared in amazement, and I figured that was good enough. "Sergeant Bill Crow, lead them away!"

In short order, Major Gillette had them working like the Trojans I had told them they were, and the air was bursting with the sounds of harmonious hammers, rasping saws, and the lovely thunk of boards fitted on boards. We built a small and nicely arched bifurcated passageway with one corridor connecting the saloon to the hotel and the other connecting the saloon to the barnyard (I envisioned the saloon as our supply depot, to which we could evacuate the pigs and chickens and dairy cows if necessary). Beauregard erected such impediments to an aggressor's attack that he deemed feasible, and since the telegraph was useless, we raised telegraph-wire fences to keep the enemy out just as ranchers erect barbed-wire fences to keep cattle in.

I assigned Hercules, Fu Yu, Billy Jack, and myself to digging the trench. This, I pointed out, would allow me work in the open air without a shirt, illustrating for the men, in my own muscular development, the benefits to be gained from vigorous outdoor activity. I also hoped to inspire the remaining civilians to join us after we tore down their establishments.

In that job—the job of destruction before the reconstruction—Hercules was a great help, stifling each proprietor's protests by clasping one giant hand over his mouth and placing the other on top of the proprietor's head, threatening to twist it off and break his neck—at least that worked with Mathis, who ran the General Store, and Llewellyn, who ran the livery stable.

With Ives, the blacksmith, it was a different matter. Big and burly, bearded and bearlike, Ives was not a man to be trifled with. Hercules couldn't even get close to him. As the Chinese strongman approached, Ives sensed a challenge. He grabbed what looked like a sledgehammer, ready to do battle. Billy Jack fetched me to defuse the situation.

"Ives," I said, marshal's badge glittering on my chest, "my friends and I have come to take possession of your property. I regret this extreme measure, but as you undoubtedly are aware, Seth Larsen and the Largo Trading Company plan to turn Bloody Gulch into cinders. They want to show you and everyone else here that unless you're willing to be slaves to the Company, they're going to destroy you. They've been destroying everyone's self-respect in this town already. We're about to bring that to a halt.

"We intend to make a stand at the saloon and the hotel. We need to tear down your business for its lumber—so we can build more defenses.

Larsen's going to destroy it anyway. And we can put you to work—we have plenty of work for strong men—fighting men too, if you're up to that, and by the look of it, you are."

"This is my business, Marshal, my livelihood; I built it with my bare hands."

"It can't be much of a livelihood with only one customer, the Largo Trading Company. And at what cost in honor do you buy that scant livelihood? I'm a man of the law, and I've heard what's happened here: your women held hostage, your children stolen from you and put to work, your comrades, your fellow men, slaves to Larsen.

"You built this business with your bare hands—so take it down the same way, plank by plank. With every plank you take down, with every sacrifice you make, you'll be losing little but gaining much; your prof-its—whatever they are—will be suspended, temporarily, but your honor will be restored forever.

"Take it down, Ives, and join us. Mathis and Llewellyn already have. They're practical men of business—the only ones left in this town—and they know there's no future going on like this. This large Chinaman you see before you, Hercules, helped convince them of that.

"I challenge you, Ives, from all that is manly in your heart, to join us, so that from this day until the end of the world you will not hold your manhood cheap but take pride in standing with us at the siege of the Bloody Gulch Hotel, Spa, Saloon, and Theatre."

He looked at me under black eyebrows. He lowered the sledgehammer, spat on his hands, and rubbed them together to stimulate thought, as working men do. Then he cocked an eye at me and said, slowly, in a deep low voice, "Well, Marshal, if you put it that way, I don't have no woman and don't have no kids, so I guess it was easy enough for me to look the other way, or just to mind my own business—which is all I've done. But I suppose, now that I figure it, that was kind of short-sighted, wasn't it? I expect I should be comin' along; I expect I should let your boys help me take this place down. I'm a handy man with a hammer and a shovel—and a rifle, if it comes to that. You can count me in."

"Well done," I said. I grasped the blacksmith by the hand and shoulder and welcomed him to our merry band. And so we set to work, each in his own style: Ives silent and dedicated; Llewellyn, who ran the livery stable, grumbling and spitting tobacco juice, staining the grey beard that sat on him like a bib; Mathis, the proprietor of the General Store, whose eagle-eyed gaze seemed to assess the worth of every board and every nail that we ripped up or hammered down; the Chinamen singing their highly annoying, discordant songs (oh, for a regimental band to trumpet out "Garry Owen") or yelping like jackals when a steel hammer hit a yellow thumb; Beauregard, suave and efficient; Billy Jack, stealthy and mysterious; and I, your devoted husband, manly and strong.

Everyone did his part, though I occasionally suspected Mathis and Llewellyn of malingering, and wanted them horsewhipped. Major Beauregard persuaded me, however, that, as civilians, they could not be held to military discipline. He suggested a midday glass of beer to help them deal with the heat, which I allowed, and which Rachel and Isabel delivered from the saloon. Ives declined the beer dispensation, working diligently and soberly, and patiently instructing the Chinamen.

Beauregard, I noticed, kept a flask of bourbon handy, but never showed ill effects. For me, the beverage of choice was fresh milk, of course, my beloved "Alderney"; and I was most grateful for it. The Chinamen waved off Alderney as if it were poison. I allowed them no alcohol, so they and Billy Jack subsisted on branch water.

All in all, I have to confess, Libbie, I was having a wonderful time, working outside in the glow of the day; the cancan girls watching me appreciatively from the balcony of the hotel; evenings spent, soothing glass of Alderney in hand, watching the ladies in turn, as they perfected new aspects of their dramatic art.

Days passed in such fruitful labor and nights in such theatrical rehearsal; and every day Billy Jack scouted the enemy cordon and reported that he saw nothing—or at least nothing new: Larsen's men occupied the outlying farms; Indian patrols kept a watchful eye on our destruction and reconstruction of the town. Behind the hotel, protecting the farmyard, we erected a five-foot-high palisade with a ten-foot-high watchtower. The trench was dug, lined in the back with tin and filled, in that section, with the most inflammable spirits we could find (so not beer but whiskey). I had reckoned on a splashy pond of alcohol, but Beauregard, after experimenting with a tiny trickling rivulet (which we kept from evaporating by covering that portion of trench with wooden planks), concluded that such a pond would far exceed our supply of spirits. Better, he figured, was placing the bottles strategically in the tin-lined rivulet, like torpedoes, and stacking a supply of rocks nearby so that that the bottles could be broken and the whiskey set alight in an emergency (he and I and Fu Yu, as officers, each carried a box of matches). This, Beauregard pointed out, would also allow us to withhold a small store of whiskey for medical emergencies. What could I say but, "Well done."

The Confederate Major devised other clever defenses as well. About sixty yards in front of the hotel and saloon we strung a telegraph-wire fence and dug a trench behind it. The fence would impede an attack—giving us more time to shoot—and the trench was a trap in which our acrobatic swordsmen could, with luck, dispatch the enemy.

I was happy with our defenses, the improved marching of our acrobats, and the fact that, after endless drilling, Fu Yu could evacuate all our livestock from the farmyard down our newly constructed corridor to the saloon in about thirty seconds, according to Beauregard's pocket watch. Fu Yu's driving of the animals was, as you might imagine, thrilling to witness: the dairy cows, the chickens, the porkers, all stampeding, but in good order and in near perfect safety, down the corridor. The odd chicken casualty was added to our dinner buffet.

Amidst all this activity, my mind was constantly at work on an audacious military stratagem, and one night, after Miss Saint-Jean's rehearsal, I stayed behind in the saloon, stein of Alderney in hand, and asked Beauregard to abide with me.

"Major, you've done a tremendous job fortifying the town; now we go on the offensive."

"Abducting Larsen?"

"Think bigger and bolder, Major—more Moses than Mosby."

"Well, Yankee General, sir, I count myself a religious man—but what the Sam Hill are you talking about?"

"We can capture Larsen later. We have a more urgent, pressing need. We need to increase our manpower, Major. That's our biggest weakness. It's not so much that we're surrounded, it's that we have so few men."

"So, you want me to go recruiting?"

"No, Major, I intend to dismantle Larsen's empire through a series of lightning raids. We're going to liberate the men, women, and children of greater Bloody Gulch and bring them here. The women and children we'll keep safe. The men we'll enlist."

"Well, Yankee General, sir, it would be daring to infiltrate the enemy and seize Larsen. But liberating the farms, mine, and foundry, and bringing those people here—that's a different order of magnitude."

"It's important to think big, Major."

"Each of those positions is guarded, sir... "

"No more so than the Trading Post."

"...and even if we achieved this miracle, our supply situation would be untenable."

"Major, never let logistics deter audacity. The men we liberate will give us an army equal to Larsen. We won't have to endure a siege. We'll break out."

"Begging, your pardon, Yankee General, sir, but assuming we take one objective at a time, how do we keep our sole advantage?"

"You mean me?"

"I was thinking of surprise, sir."

"And so was I. We will operate incognito, Major, just as you suggested. Indians patrol between the farms, don't they?"

"Such was my reconnaissance, sir."

"Then we will be a small detachment of Indians going from one farm to the next. We'll take our objectives in stages—starting with the women."

"I believe you said, sir, that our chief need was *manpower.*"

"Indeed, Major, but never forget—duty before necessity."

"I'll remember that, sir."

I pulled the plans I had sketched from my pocket. The most important document was a map I had drawn—not to scale and not including terrain, but it neatly depicted the general idea. In an arc above the town I had written, "Farms with Women." I had our position marked by two adjacent rectangles labeled "Saloon" and "Hotel" and two small adjacent squares labeled "Church (defunct)" and "School (defunct)." From the rear of the rectangle labeled "Hotel" I neatly marked a path with dashes to the farms and back to the hotel front. At the first dash I had sketched my own profile with the inscription "Rescuer Hero Starts Here." At the last dash, my profile crowned the words "Rescuer Hero Finishes Here."

I watched Beauregard closely as he examined the plan. He was so taken by it that he flipped up his eyepatch, revealing the steely blue eye beneath, absorbed in the details before it.

"Are you all right, Major?" I said, pointing to his eyepatch.

He flipped it down and said, "Yes, sir—just ensuring I hadn't missed anything."

"The plan's central components are all there."

"Your plan, sir, is truly redolent of the North's strategic genius."

"Well, Major, I *was*, at one point, the army's youngest general."

"You don't say, sir? Remarkable, sir, truly remarkable."

"You, Major, will accompany me on the rescue mission, as will Sergeant Bill Crow, and Miss Johnson."

"Miss Isabel, sir?"

"We'll need her to guide us to the farms. We'll start on foot—easier to sneak out that way. At the first farm, I hope to find a wagon and horses. Then it's just a matter of making one call after another, picking up our passengers at each stop—sort of like a stagecoach."

"Genius, sir, genius."

"Thank you, Major. If the plan works, we will share the glory."

"And our disguises, sir? Will we share those?"

"Miss Saint-Jean's dancers have already sewn our Indian costumes. Their work is never far from my thoughts."

"I've never had any doubt of that, sir."

"Mathis, Llewellyn, Ives, and Smithers will stay here under the command of Miss Saint-Jean."

"Under her *command*, sir?"

"She would accept nothing less. The Chinamen will be sentries; she will prepare the saloon for those we rescue."

He looked around. "Yes, sir, just the place for a bevy of farm women."

"Frontier farm women, Major. And given the situation, I expect they will not faint at the thought of residing in a saloon."

Beauregard stood, saluted, and said, "It is an honor, Yankee General, sir, to serve under your command. Will you join me in a toast, sir?"

I raised my stein of Alderney as he pulled his flask from his hip pocket. "To you, sir, and to our sacred, chivalric mission: saving the women of Bloody Gulch! May God have mercy on us all!"

"Hear, hear!" I said. And I hoped He did.

CHAPTER SIX

In Which Things Go Kaboom!

Less than twenty-four hours later, I stood in the parlor of the hotel. Miss Saint-Jean and Rachel were there to see me off. Isabel was at my side. Miss Saint-Jean wore a black felt fez with a red tassel, a sparkling black corset with red pinstripes, black silk stockings, and of course her black high-heeled shoes that could drive both nails and a hard bargain.

"When Isabel and I return," I said to Miss Saint-Jean, "we'll have a wagonload of new talent for you. Isabel assures me that the women on these farms are not hard and plain and best-suited to stand behind a plow, but handsome migrants from the better areas of Sweden and Norway and thereabouts. They have plenty of potential as cancan dancers."

"Thank you, Marshal, that was my foremost thought."

"I assumed so. As for the younger girls at the Blake homestead, they can be put to work mending, sewing, cooking, whatever you see fit. I leave them to you."

"I had no doubt you would."

"We'll be back before dawn with every woman from every farm in greater Bloody Gulch, and with every girl held hostage at the Blake homestead. Goodbye, Rachel, my ward." I gripped her shoulders and kissed her on the check. "If I don't return, I will die gratified that I at least gave you a profession of which you can always be proud." She looked baffled, so I added, "The theatre, dear girl, the theatre."

"Oh, yes, thank you, General."

I would have extended my remarks, but Rachel and Miss Saint-Jean seemed distracted, which was understandable, I suppose, given that I wore nothing but a breech clout, a yellow bandana (once a cavalryman, always a cavalryman), and my Indian medicine pouch tied with a leather thong around my neck. A black wig hid my blond locks, and mud caked my skin so that I would look and smell more like an Indian.

Isabel's disguise was more modest. She wore a tight-fitting, knee-length, deer-skin tunic with matching moccasins, which Rachel assured us was the height of fashion with the Boyanama Sioux. She too had her blonde hair tucked up into a wig, but we refrained from covering her natural, radiant, sun-kissed skin with mud; it would have seemed, somehow, sacrilegious.

Waiting for us in the farmyard were Beauregard and Billy Jack. Beauregard had declined the breech clout option and instead disguised himself as one of the Indian bounty hunters we had met at Isabel's farm. He wore a flat-brimmed, large-domed, black hat, black pants, and a black vest over a red and white check shirt. He had removed his eyepatch and kept it in his pocket as a good luck charm. Billy Jack, meanwhile, had ditched his bowler hat and shirt, tied his hair in two long braids, and wore a vest, dark pants, and went barefoot. Isabel was unarmed, but Beauregard, Billy Jack, and I each carried a Winchester rifle.

Our first challenge was to leave our fortified position without being spotted. By Billy Jack's calculations, the enemy scouts had a blind spot, extending at a 45 degree angle west from the farmyard's northwestern corner. That invisible line would be our path. We had taken the trouble to dig a tunnel beneath the farmyard's enclosing wall so that we could creep beneath it under cover of darkness and emerge, we hoped, without being seen.

We slipped quietly down the tunnel and crawled out the other side, leaving the safety of the fortification behind us. We slithered along, avoiding moonlit strips, and inched across the planks covering the whiskey-filled trench. My main concern, of course, apart from not succumbing to the alcoholic fumes, was protecting Isabel's knees from splinters and scrapes. About my own skin—tough and leathery as an old cavalryman's should be—I cared not a whit. I checked on her continually as we crept along, ensuring that her tunic was stretched as far over her knees as possible to give them maximum protection. But she was a self-reliant trooper, boldly slapping away my hand at one point when I tried to provide assistance. That little scuffle caused Billy Jack to turn around and say, "Shh! In Spanish: *Silencio*! In French. . ." I crawled forward, and the translations ceased.

After that little diversion, we moved as stealthily as teetotal lizards until we reached a wedge of tall grass next to a line of fir trees. Here we paused and caught our breaths. Billy Jack stood up slowly, like a crane rising from shallow water. Satisfied that we were unobserved, he motioned for us all to stand. Now we moved more swiftly, darting from fir to pine, deft feet stirring the underbrush as little as possible.

We made good time to the outskirts of the first farmhouse—"the Foster place," Isabel called it—with Billy Jack guiding us into another semi-concealed position behind rocks and scrub where we could observe our target without much exposure. The guards, if they were there, were not visible. Billy Jack assumed they were inside and asleep. We trotted—slowly and crouched—to the farmyard. There was a wagon, perfectly suited to our purposes, just inside the front gate. We left Isabel there and advanced on the farmhouse. I took the point; Beauregard and Billy Jack covered my flanks.

I approached the front stoop with catlike tread and ascended the steps to the front door. Fortune favors the bold, so I tested the handle and found it turning in my hand, unlocked and inviting me in. I accepted fortune's invitation, easing the door open. Directly in front of me, asleep in a chair, was a big bearded galoot, a shotgun resting on his lap, a candle burning on the table beside him. I gambled that he was alone and entered the room. No one shouted or shot at me, so I tiptoed over, slipped the shotgun from his loose-fingered grasp, and crept to what I assumed must be the bedroom door. I opened it without hesitation, and there, lying on a bed, was a young woman—in her twenties, I reckoned—asleep, her golden tresses splashed over her pillow like sunbeams across the clouds, her beauty like that of a goddess from ancient Greece. Instinctively, I knelt, reached for my Indian medicine pouch, withdrew the toothbrush and a pinch of salt, cleaned my teeth, then returned the brush to the pouch and stood—ready now for anything that might happen. I came over and touched her gently by the shoulder. She stirred, vaguely, and I gripped her shoulder with more force. Her eyes revealed themselves, a bright—panicked, in fact—blue; and I clapped a hand over her mouth before she could scream. I lowered my lips to her ear and whispered, "Fear not, I am not an Indian. I have come in disguise to rescue you. I am Marshal Armstrong from town. You may have heard of me." She nodded; I suspected I had been the subject of gossip. I gently helped her rise. She was dressed in a beautiful white sleeping garment, almost like a wedding dress in its stylish cut. She slipped her feet into white deerskin moccasins at the foot of the bed.

"The guard is sleeping. I need to gag him and tie him up. Can you help me?"

She nodded and soon returned from the kitchen with a rag to stuff into his mouth, and some twine stout enough to bind his hands and feet. I asked for one more item: work gloves. These she procured from a drawer in her bedroom, and while they were tight on my hands, they would offer my knuckles some protection if I had to bust the villain's nose.

He lay snoring in his chair until I rammed the gag home. His eyes shot open and the rag stifled his tongue. I put my fingers over my lips, jabbed the barrel of the shotgun into his gut—and he got the idea. The young golden-haired lady tied him up and did a right good job of it; she had hog-tied beeves before. For good, if superfluous, measure we blindfolded him and I growled in his ear: "Sioux hate you fat white man." I hoped those words and my mud-covered body would throw him off our scent.

I took the young woman by the hand and we dashed to the wagon like eloping young lovers. Seeing Isabel there, however, reminded me that this was no romantic dream but a martial reality of search and rescue. Beauregard and Billy Jack stood by with horses from the barn—a team of two for the wagon, and mounts for each of us cavalrymen.

Isabel was all nursely comfort, saying, "Judith, are you all right?"

"Isabel, oh, Isabel, thank goodness it's you—yes, I'm fine. What's going on?"

"You are delivered, madam," I said. "Think of me as Moses and you as my people. But we must make haste, there are many more to rescue."

For the sake of our imposture, Billy Jack had not saddled our horses, only draping them with a blanket; and though I managed, grabbing two fistfuls of mane, to leap aboard, I confess that landing on the horse's bare back wearing only a breech clout was a very different feeling from what I was used to—and a not altogether comfortable one.

I will not bore you with all the details of our mission of mercy, save to say that I was struck by how each femme du farmhouse seemed more beautiful than the last, though perhaps it was the moonlight, and none of course could compare, dearest one, to the image of you engraved on my arm, let alone the reality of you!

At each farmhouse, with the help of the farm-lady-fair, we tied, gagged, and blindfolded Larsen's blackguards, and I soon became quite proficient at it. As expected, we passed several Indian patrols during our midnight ride of liberation, but Sergeant Bill Crow did an excellent job of spinning the Indians a yarn.

The interrogation went something like this:

"What are you doing?"

"Taking the white women to one farm; Larsen is worried about raids from the mighty warriors at the hotel."

"Mighty warriors?"

"Have you not seen them?"

"We have seen the marshal"—you can bet they had!—"and the little yellow men. They are not mighty warriors."

"Did you not hear about the Battle of Johnson Farm?"

"Yes, there is a dangerous Crow. That man is beyond mighty."

Or so Billy Jack told me. I never actually heard any of these conversations, because he would ride ahead to meet the Indian patrols, guarding us from curious eyes. Whatever yarn he spun them, we had no trouble with the Indians.

The Blake homestead, however, was a different challenge; it was the toughest nut to crack because it had three guards over eleven young children. There we approached openly, parking our wagon next to another on the property. Isabel and her fellow femmes du farm waited while Beauregard, Billy Jack, and I dismounted and walked straight to the house. The three guards eyed us skeptically from their rocking chairs on the porch.

"A patrol said you were coming; never heard that from Mr. Larsen."

"He decided at supper," said Billy Jack. "He tell us, 'Move quickly.' He fear men at hotel and saloon. Great warriors, he say. He fear they come for women and children. Must move."

"Well, we got the little varmints ready. They're all dressed and holdin' their dollies and whatnot. Haven't hitched the horses to the wagon; reckon you can do that. Didn't have time. Horses are in the barn."

Billy Jack turned to Beauregard. "Sightless Southern Eagle, get horses."

"Yes'm, big chief."

The guard added, "Them girls are your responsibility now. And you're welcome to it. I'd rather be working in the mine than minding these little, lazy, no-good layabouts; all they do is whine and complain even though we feed 'em and treat 'em proper."

A troop of nervous little girls were led onto the porch.

"No need worry," I said, in my best Indian uncle voice—but my manly appearance, so consoling to grown women, affrightened these little ones.

"Naked Warrior Who Talks, take children to wagon."

I led them—like a breech-clouted, Winchester-toting, mud-spattered, tattooed, Boyanama Sioux Pied Piper. At the wagon, Isabel smiled, encouraged them with pleasantries, and got them settled, while Beauregard brought up the horses.

Billy Jack mounted up, and I, more carefully this time, did the same. Isabel took the reins of the children's wagon, Judith Foster acted as wagon master for the femmes du farm (or Miss Saint-Jean's future cancan dancers, as I preferred to think of them), Beauregard leapt aboard his horse, and we were off. There was a moment of extreme risk when we circled back to the hotel, of course. We halted at the ditch, hurried the women and children across the planks, stowed the wagons by the abutting line of firs, and unhitched the horses and brought them across. We were vulnerable to attack at any moment, but apparently our Indian watchers were too baffled to act.

All was now hustle and bustle. With the horses stabled in the farmyard, I took it upon myself to introduce the femmes du farm to the cancan dancers who were eager to help, bless their hearts, get them situated at the hotel. I entrusted the children to Miss Saint-Jean in the saloon. They were noisy and harder to herd than chickens, but she soon had them boarded in Larsen's office and adjacent rooms on the second floor.

It was dawn before I took a breather and treated myself to a bottle of sarsaparilla in the hotel parlor and pulled from my breech clout a folded sheet of paper. It was the map I had drawn outlining our rescue plan. I glanced at it fondly and, I confess, shook my head in genuine admiration for the simple genius it represented—the genius of your very own Autie. With that thought in my mind, I finished the sarsaparilla and feel asleep in the chair.

⌒⌖⌒

I awoke in, of all places, a soapy bathtub with Hercules standing next to me holding out a large sponge, which I accepted. Billy Jack, who was sitting in a chair facing me, explained: "Miss Saint-Jean wanted you cleaned up and dressed. She didn't like the look of you in the parlor. Said it was bad for business."

I didn't know what to say to that, so I said nothing—I was still half asleep—and set about scrubbing myself clean with the sponge.

"All's well, Sergeant?"

"All's well, sir. Miss Saint-Jean is preparing dancing costumes for the women. The children are asleep at the saloon. They stayed up all night talking in high-pitched voices. They reminded me of the Chinamen."

"Hmm—well, Sergeant, I doubt they're related linguistically—Western girl-talk and Cantonese—but I could be wrong. Are they under guard?"

"The Chinamen?"

"No, the children."

"Yes—Mathis and Llewellyn. I assumed it was civilian duty."

"Well done. And the cordon around us? Any movement?"

He shook his head. "No movement. All is quiet. I think they are stunned—like the Romans were when Hannibal brought elephants over the Alps."

"I reckon I'd be stunned too—but I'd do something about it; right away. Where's Beauregard?"

"He's drilling the acrobats. The women are watching."

"By his invitation, I'm sure. I should have figured as much—that Dixie Don Juan."

Clean, dressed, and with a cup of coffee inside me, I decided to show our new arrivals who was really in charge. I stepped onto the veranda of the hotel, Billy Jack and Hercules beside me. Beauregard was on our improvised parade ground, standing with a gentleman's cane (part of the booty we had acquired from the General Store). The acrobats had formed a human pyramid. Fu Yu stood at the top. Doves emerged from his sleeves, and he released the birds skyward. The women—those we had rescued and Miss Saint-Jean's veterans—watched from the balcony, gasping, cheering, and applauding.

"Billy Jack, saddle me a horse, and bring him here on the double!"

I nudged Hercules in the ribs and motioned for him to step into the street. I placed my booted foot in his stirrup-shaped hands, clambered onto his shoulders, and his hands clamped over my feet like shackles. We walked onto the parade ground, the strongman acting as my stilts, and I balanced as adeptly as any acrobat.

"Good morning, ladies," I declared. "I am General, and U.S. Marshal, Armstrong Armstrong. My subordinate Major Gillette and I are pleased to welcome you as our guests. Last night, we rescued some of you. I was the half-naked Indian of savage mien and startling physique—but do not be afraid: I am a gentleman, not a savage, and a gracious respecter of the fairer sex." This was greeted with appropriate polite applause.

Billy Jack ran onto the far side of the field, leading the horse I'd named Marshal Ney. I waved for him to keep running towards me and shouted: "How do you say 'one, two, three,' in Chinese?"

"*Unos, dos, tres,*" he shouted back, which didn't sound right to me, but I tried it on Hercules, and bang on the count of *tres* he threw me into the air and I spun myself so that I landed perfectly astride the saddle as Marshal Ney came trotting by. The feminine gasps and cheers were easily the match of anything Beauregard had elicited. Billy Jack tossed me the reins, and I raced the horse down the dirt track, turned dramatically, *volte face*, and charged the human pyramid. Fu Yu screamed and jumped off the pyramid, doves shooting from his sleeves like fireworks, but the acrobats held steady, and Marshal Ney and I leapt over them to more cheers. I pulled the good marshal up so that he reared, jabbing his front hooves like a prizefighter showing off for the ladies, and whinnied his victory roar. I trotted him beneath the balcony and bowed in the saddle. Marshal Ney pawed the turf.

"What a marvelous performance! What style! What grace! What courage! What dash!" These words, I guessed, were forming in their minds—their children's too, for the little ones were gathered at the front of the saloon, cheering and clapping, with Isabel as their shepherd.

I dismounted and said, "Ladies, I am at your service. Meet me in the parlor and I will brief you on my plans." Marshal Ney whinnied his assent, and I gave him a well-deserved pat on the neck and draped his reins over the hitching post.

I took a commanding position in the center of the parlor and was soon surrounded by admiring glances and the susurrus of cotton and silk. "Ladies," I said, "we are gathered here today in an epic struggle against the Largo Trading Company. We are engaged in a war to decide whether women, such as yourselves, and children, such as those next door, and your boys and menfolk can live as happy families undisturbed by Seth Larsen's greed. Soon we will take the next step toward victory. We will raid the mine and the foundry and bring your men and boys back here." Cheers erupted, but I bid them cease. "In the meantime, meals are at seven, noon, and seven. The children will dine at the saloon; you may take your meals with them or here at the hotel. I, most often, will be here, contemplating matters of tactics and strategy.

"Though you are our guests, we count on your assistance. Miss Saint-Jean will carefully arrange your schedules so that you may help with the children at the saloon, oblige as needed in the farmyard or the kitchen, and still be fresh for cancan rehearsals in the evening. Your rehearsal nights could be long, ending at the discretion of Miss Saint-Jean, who," I chuckled, "is a stern taskmistress. That is all for now, ladies. Dismissed."

But instead of dismissing they fluttered around me, bombarding me with questions, which, for the most part, I dodged for the sake of military secrecy. I pressed my way through the throng and outside to the safety of Marshal Ney's back. Before an avalanche of fluttering feminine fear could come pouring out the hotel door, I applied my spurs to the good marshal and we sped away. I needed to think. Billy Jack was soon riding beside me.

"General, I thought you might want a council of war."

"Decent of you to come along."

"Do you have a plan?"

"For the mine and the foundry? Nothing as detailed as the plan for rescuing the women; just an idea. I do know we can't repeat the Indian trick."

"Indians have many tricks. I have another, adapted from a book I read, given to me by the priest. Ives and I have been working to build what we might need: a giant cannon."

My face, I'm sure, betrayed my amazement, because he continued: "It is in sections, but can be assembled quickly. We made it from the scrap of the torn down buildings. It cannot fire, but it can fool the enemy. We load it with the Chinamen and drag it to Larsen. We offer to exchange it—our cannon for the imprisoned men and boys. It is the Quaker Gun as Trojan Horse."

"My goodness, that's a clever idea. But could it really work; could it fool Larsen?"

"We make the exchange at night. In the dark, he will not look in the horse's mouth, the mouth of the cannon. He is greedy. He will take the gift. He'll think it's a weapon he can turn against us. That's how we surprise him."

"Is the cannon ready?"

"Nearly. We've worked hard into the night while others sleep, using muffled hammers and working by lamplight. The parts are hidden in the grove by the farmyard fence. It can be ready in two days. You, or Major Gillette, can offer Larsen the exchange."

"Beauregard knows?"

"No. No one. We kept it secret. May I show you?"

"Of course!"

We rode to the grove. Hidden there, beneath bushes and branches, were the materials of the giant cannon; sections of barrel that could be fitted together; wagon wheels; and limber. I tapped the barrel and asked: "Wood wrapped in tin?"

"And disguised with paint."

I thought of the acrobats squeezing themselves down the tube—they were flexible little fellows and could probably manage.

"Two days, you say."

"Yes. Give me two days. Then write Larsen a message and I will deliver it."

"He'll want shells; you can make dummy ones?"

"Yes, certainly."

"Then, by Jove, let's do it! I'll draft the note to Larsen—and I'll do it now, while I'm inspired; no need to dawdle. Orders, battle plans, books, notes, I can write them all. Have you read *My Life on the Plains*? Brilliant literary work, if I say so myself. I can write quickly and with popular appeal, but this, this is a different challenge, an invitation to a gunfighter—or to a villain who hires them. To the hotel, Sergeant—to the hotel!"

The women, thank goodness, had abandoned the parlor. I sent Billy Jack to find the major, and I grabbed a sheaf of paper from behind the reception desk, as well as pen and ink, and set to work.

"Dear Mr. Larsen. . ." No, that wouldn't do. I wouldn't call him "dear." "Larsen." That was better. "Larsen, we rescued the ladies and the girls. Now we will trade for the men and the boys. In our possession is a giant cannon, once belonging to the Chinese Emperor Hu Dat Mhan. We will trade this priceless—and deadly—weapon for the boys imprisoned at the mine and the men enslaved at the foundry. You could not build a weapon like this if you had a thousand years. We deal from a position of strength. We can raid your positions and liberate captives at will—we've proven that. But our next raid could result in casualties—needless casualties among your men. As a professional soldier, and marshal, I would rather avoid this. We will give you an incredible weapon, but first you must hand over your remaining hostages—all the men and all the boys. Once they're reunited with their families, and once you give us your word that we have free passage out of town, we will provide you with the shells that feed this monstrous cannon. We will have our freedom, and you will have a weapon beyond compare. You have forty-eight hours to decide. If you agree to these terms, we will deliver the cannon at midnight. If you do not, you will feel its wrath—and perhaps be its first victim. RSVP. Sincerely, U.S. Marshal Armstrong Armstrong (Brevet Major General, U.S. Army, 1865)."

Beauregard appeared in the doorway. "Yankee General, sir, Sergeant Bill Crow said it was urgent."

"Everything we do is urgent, Major. Hours and days are precious—we should use them wisely."

"Thank you, sir, I appreciate that. Was there something in particular?"

I handed him my note. He read it and looked at me with an arched eyebrow. "Emperor Hu Dat Mhan?"

"An embellishment; acceptable given the circumstances."

"And this cannon?"

"The handiwork of Ives and Billy Jack, assembled at night in the grove behind the farmyard. I'm surprised you don't know about it. You're responsible for assigning the sentries."

"I am—and my nightly sentries are Ives and Sergeant Bill Crow."

"So, they outsmarted you."

"Well, I didn't expect them to be Yankees pulling shenanigans behind my back."

"Thank goodness they were; thank goodness I can rely on someone around here to go above and beyond the call of duty, instead of showing off for the ladies."

"Yankee General, sir, is that why you called me here, to dress me down because the ladies of Bloody Gulch seek my company? Well, sir, I can say I was only behaving as an officer and a gentleman."

"Major, I want your thoughts on that note. If you were Larsen, how would you respond? We plan to load the cannon with Chinamen."

"And fire it? That would be as messy as a woodpecker trapped in a tub of molasses."

"No, you Confederate Casanova—have you never heard of the Trojan Horse? We wheel the cannon into Larson's Trading Post and bang, Chinese acrobats leap from the barrel with blood-curdling screams."

"Well, sir, I can confirm that would certainly frighten me."

"Do you think it would work?"

"After last night's performance, sir, I reckon you have Bonaparte's gift."

"Genius?"

"Luck, sir, something even greater than genius."

"So, you're in favor?"

"Well, sir, if we have the cannon, we might as well use it—and that's as good a way as any."

"Indeed. In two days, we'll have Billy Jack deliver that note. In the meantime, we must prepare for battle. The acrobats need to be trained. We'll need a mock cannon for them to practice loading themselves in and firing themselves out."

"Well, sir, I reckon we could knock the bottom out of three wooden barrels, lash them together, and then prop them on a water trough for elevation."

"See to it."

And he did. I watched the men train, and my confidence rose with every drill. The Chinese order for "fire," as advised by Billy Jack, was: *Sechuselvesonfire*. This he said was not classical Chinese but a dialect version that most Chinamen understood, and ours seemed to, as they leapt out screaming and waving their curved swords. It was, in its own way, an impressive demonstration.

When not supervising such drills, I watched over Ives and Billy Jack. They worked hour after relentless hour until, on the afternoon of the second day, the snout of an enormous cannon poked into the sky from behind the grove.

Billy Jack stood beside me, wiping the sweat from his brow.

"Good gun, you think, sir?"

"A fine gun, indeed, Sergeant. I think it's time you got the message to Larsen."

"Yes, sir," he said

"Seize the day, Sergeant."

"Yes, sir, *carpe diem*."

"Indeed, Sergeant, *carpe diem*—which reminds me: how do you say 'seize the cannon' in Chinese?"

"In Chinese, sir, it would be, '*Carpe Dayboom*.'"

"Very good—on you go now."

I set Ives and Hercules as guards over our Quaker Gun. In the hotel parlor, I ordered a stout glass of Alderney and sat down with a sheaf of battle plans—each sheet of paper outlining a scenario we might face. Beauregard ambled in. I eyed him cynically.

"Afternoon, Major, no ladies' tea to attend?"

"I saw Billy Jack riding out to Larsen, and I thought, Yankee General, sir, we might want to discuss our plans again."

"Major, take a look at this." I pulled out a chair and handed Beauregard my latest sketch. "That," I said, pointing to a long barrel, "is the cannon, wheeled before Larsen. The balls bouncing out of it are the acrobats. You note that the balls, in figure two, form a circle around the letter L. The L is for Larsen."

"So, I take it then, sir, that the bouncing balls have taken Larsen captive?"

"Yes. We hold him until the men and boys are released into our custody."

"And then the bouncing balls go bouncing back to Bloody Gulch?"

"Yes—if possible. If we have to fight it out then and there, I'll be ready. But I'd rather bring the civilians to safety first."

"Brilliant, sir. Sherman or Sheridan could not have done better."

"Thank you, Major. I had the pleasure to know both."

"Pleasure's all yours, sir." He handed me the paper and tilted his hat over his eyes. Leaning back in his chair, he said, "For now, sir, with your permission, I reckon a siesta's called for. It could be a long night."

⤜⤛

It certainly was. When Billy Jack returned I was still in the parlor committing my plan to memory while Beauregard slept in the adjacent chair. Billy Jack looked at him, then at me.

"You saw Larsen, Sergeant?"

"Yes, sir, he agreed to see me. He read your note and then stared at me for a long time. Finally he told me to go away."

"That's all?"

"That's all. I believe he wants to verify we have the cannon."

"Well, Sergeant, his scouts aren't worth much if they can't verify that."

"No, sir."

"So, we wait to see whether he accepts our offer."

"Yes, sir."

"Any reason why he wouldn't?"

"He might try to steal the cannon."

"Not worth it—too risky. In his mind, by our terms, he gets the cannon for nothing."

"What about his hostages?"

"He'll regard their surrender as temporary; he'll reckon he can recover them in a trice. He'll deal with us."

Beauregard tilted his hat back from his face. "When a man's bluffing, you can always force his hand."

"Meaning?"

"What if we gave Larsen a taste of Old Blunderbuss?"

"And just how do we do that, Major?"

"We've got plenty of gunpowder. An explosion's an explosion. He won't know where it's from."

I sat tall in my chair, my scalp tingling with excitement. "That, Major, is a splendid idea. Explosions motivateth the man. How close do we set it off?"

"Well, the closer, the more effective—the riskier too. I reckon if we're careful we can get a barrel of gunpowder out the same way we left for the farms. Only need two of us, if we roll it along. Get the barrel as close to the enemy as time and prudence allow. They'll hear it, wherever it goes off."

"Right, let's do it. Beauregard, find your barrel, and get a fuse and make sure you have your matches. The three of us will go—in disguise."

"Not Indians again."

"We have no choice. There's no time to make new costumes—and without a black wig my hair shines like a morning star, beckoning all to follow."

"You reckon, so, Yankee General, sir?"

"Yes, I reckon so—and I reckon we should get moving."

"Poor Mother Gillette—she did not raise her son to be an Indian."

"Or a gambler?"

"Well, Yankee General, sir, a gentleman *can* gamble; he will risk *all* for honor."

"And a Crow—if not a Sioux—can be a gentleman," said Billy Jack. "In Spanish, *hidalgo*. In French, *gentilhomme*."

Beauregard nodded. "Better an Indian than a Yankee—beggin' the Yankee General's pardon."

"Gentleman," I said, "let us forget the last war and prepare for this one."

⚬⚬⚬

Sans clothes, sans mud (there wasn't time for that), sans everything save breech clout, black wig, yellow bandana, and Indian medicine pouch with salt and foldable toothbrush, I was soon ready, as were my colleagues. We gathered in the farmyard, our whispers covered by the baritone mooing of the cows, the scattered cluck-clucks of the chickens, the truffle-hunting snort-snorts of the pigs, and the sighed breathing of the horses.

Beauregard and I rolled out the barrel. Billy Jack followed carrying an armload of branches. We rolled the barrel down the tunnel that ran beneath the wall and pushed it up and out the other side. The next obstacle was the trench. We had to risk the danger—of both sight and sound—of rolling the barrel across the wooden slats that covered it. We moved painfully slowly, thinking sound was our greatest enemy. It was quite dark, and the Indians would not be looking for a barrel rolling across a makeshift bridge unless they were alerted to it by the creaking of wood rolling on wood. To forestall this possibility, Beauregard had brought a dark blue towel, loaned to us by Miss Saint-Jean, in which we swathed the rolling barrel to muffle its passage across the boards. Once over the bridge, we moved in intervals, rolling the barrel forward, then stopping and hiding behind it, then rolling it forward again. Every time we stopped, Billy Jack leaned over the barrel with his branches, disguising it, so that we were like Birnham Wood marching on Dunsinane.

I need hardly belabor the point that this was arduous work, mentally and physically exhausting; and it tapped every resource I had as an actor. Each time we stopped, my mind told me, "Be a bush of Birnham Wood," and I struck the pose, held it, and controlled my breathing so that it mimicked the gentle swaying of branches in a breeze. The role was not, I must say, terribly satisfying—because I had to remain invisible to the audience and could win no applause—but it was successful; we were not spotted.

We spent hours advancing the barrel. Finally, we saw the outline of the Indian Trading Post in the distance. Lamps lit its windows, as if Larsen was engaged in some nefarious nocturnal activity of his own. When we reckoned we were close enough, we planted the barrel against a berm of dirt. Beauregard ran the fuse and a trail of powder. He lighted the powder; it puffed; and the flame went fizzing down the fuse. We took cover.

To a trained military ear, the explosion was not that of an artillery shell, but surprise, especially in the dark of night, can fool anyone. We covered our heads, earth went flying, as did shards of wood from the now disintegrated barrel, and when I looked up again the lamps at the Trading Post had gone out—as if Larsen's gang feared they were under attack. Perfect.

We hightailed it for the safety of the trench, but it was a long run, and as we ran our eyes and ears were alert for the sight or sound of pounding hooves, of an Indian patrol hunting for us. But apparently the patrols had collapsed upon the Trading Post, rallying against what they feared might be a coordinated assault. Still, it was a good three miles back to town, and it was a nerve-jangling half hour until we made it over the trench and back to the safety of our lines.

You might think that sleep would have been impossible after such an adventure, especially for someone like me, who needs little rest and upon whom action is like a tonic. But truth be told, when I staggered up the red-carpeted stairs past the red, velvet, flocked wallpaper to my room, I stopped only to wash my face in the basin before collapsing on my bed. I slept as soundly as any Indian ever had. I guess your Autie is getting old!

CHAPTER SEVEN

In Which I Make More Battle Plans

When I woke, I thought momentarily that I must have collapsed onstage, for my eyes opened to see Miss Saint-Jean's face directly in front of mine. She looked repelled. My black wig was in her hand.

"Armstrong, will you get out of that ridiculous costume and get downstairs? Larsen's men are waiting for you."

"Men? How many?"

"Only two. I think you can handle that. Get a grip on yourself. It's that weaselly one Dern, and the other one who looks like a killer."

I sprang upright and splashed water from the basin on my face.

"Get some clothes on, for goodness' sake. I don't want my girls seeing you like this."

There was a mirror in the room, so I took a look. "Why not? What's wrong? I'm still fit. I need to comb my hair, I confess, and I should let my moustache grow out, but Indians don't have moustaches..."

"Will you get your clothes on? I don't like Larsen's men lounging around; they're trouble."

"Well, if you'll give me a moment of privacy, madam."

Washed and dressed, I trotted down the stairs and there was Dern, sitting in a cocky slouch, and next to him the one named Wyeth. His eyes locked on mine and never wavered. He wanted me to reach for a gun I wasn't wearing.

"Well, howdy, Marshal. Sorry to have gotten you outta bed. I guess you really do live the life here now, dontchya? Sleepin' late, livin' in the hotel and all; havin' the saloon all to yourself—but I guess you don't, do you? You got all those kids…"

"What do you want, Dern?"

"Mr. Larsen is none too happy about you. He was tryin' to entertain a few friends last night, professionals he invited out here to do a job."

"That has nothing to do with me."

"Sure it does, Marshal. You hear that big explosion last night—kinda like when they blow out a mineshaft?"

"You know there's no mineshaft. And your boss knows what that was—it was a warning. Next time it won't miss."

"That so? Well, he told me you were interested in a deal. I'm to tell you, he'll take you up on it. And he's got a warning for you too. He's hired some new men. Friends of Wyeth's, in fact; they can make some noise of their own, if you catch my drift."

"Tell Larsen, we'll deliver our part of the bargain at midnight at the Trading Post. His part of the bargain has to be there too. You know what that is?"

"No, tell me, Marshal."

"The boys and men he keeps as forced labor at the mine and the foundry. We're setting them free."

"Are you now?"

"We bring them back here, do a head count, and if everyone is present and correct, we'll turn over the shells for his new toy, a cannon, and he can make his own mineshafts. You got that?"

"Oh yeah, I got it," Dern said, rising, and Wyeth rose after him. "You best watch yourself, Marshal. This is about the most dangerous deal you've ever made."

"I appreciate your concern."

"Mama always said, good manners don't cost nothin'. See you tonight, Marshal. I'll be there."

"I hope he is too," I said, nodding at Wyeth.

"Oh, he surely will be—and his friends."

Billy Jack and Beauregard framed the doorway to the parlor.

"Major, Sergeant, escort these two men out."

"Don't need no escort, Marshal. We can find our way."

"You tell Larsen what you've seen—tell him about the fortifications."

"That we will, Marshal. Quite a setup you got here. You expectin' trouble?"

"Anyone who comes looking for it will find it."

"I keep tellin' you, Marshal, this has always been a real peaceable town—least it was 'til you got here."

"Goodbye, Dern."

"Goodbye, Marshal. You take good care."

When Billy Jack and Beauregard returned, we sat down to a breakfast of strategy, biscuits, and coffee.

"Well, gentlemen, it appears our plan is unfolding as it should."

"Yes, sir, Yankee General, sir, what could go wrong now, walking into the enemy's camp with a fake cannon and who knows how many hostages to rescue—what do you reckon, a couple dozen at least?"

"Major, I thought we were agreed on our plan?"

"Yes, sir—but it's a bit like a shotgun wedding; I see no alternative."

"And you, Sergeant?"

"I trust your judgement, sir. I see it as Crow versus Sioux; Chinamen versus Cheyenne; and you and Major Beauregard versus hired gunmen."

"Well, that settles it—we can't lose. Make sure that cannon is ready, Sergeant. Major, write out wills for the Chinamen, leaving everything to Miss Saint-Jean, and have them sign them. I will make sure the ladies are aware of our plans. They'll need to make arrangements of their own."

⚬⚬⚬

The saloon was as packed as a chapel on Sunday and as noisy as a schoolyard playground. The ladies were having a matinee rehearsal, and the children were watching delightedly and squealing their approval. For many, no doubt, it was the first time they had seen their mothers in tights, kicking up their heels, and performing the *ballet du cancan*, as the French call it. For me, on the other hand, it was a happy confirmation of the talent we had stocked up here in Bloody Gulch. I had no doubt that most of these women, if not all of them, would return to their farms after Larsen's tyranny was broken. But it gave me a feeling of accomplishment to know that I had done my small part to bring culture and the arts, the theatre, to this frontier town, to have lifted not just the legs of these women in dance but their hearts in spirit; forevermore they would have stained-glass memories of the hours when they had perfected, to the best of their ability, the terpsichorean art and found within themselves a new and perhaps unexpected form of expression. I paused for a moment, overcome with a wave of emotion, and gripped the back of a saloon chair. An enterprising young girl approached me.

"Hiya, Marshal. Can I get you something?"

"Alderney, dear one, Alderney."

"What?"

"Milk, a glass of milk, if you please."

"Sure."

She skipped off to do her good deed, and I made my way to the stage.

Miss Saint-Jean, leading the rehearsals, looked askance at me, but my natural air of command compelled silence and I proceeded to address the women, who stood attentively, as I suppose one must when wearing such high heels. They were, naturally, dressed in the corset attire that was their costume *d'art*.

"Ladies, pardon the intrusion—the interruption—but I come bearing good news. Tonight at midnight, I hope to effect the recovery of your menfolk—fathers, sons, uncles, whoever they may be. I hope to restore them to you in the wee hours of the morning. I come to you, however, with a frank, full warning. The task we embark upon is dangerous, there is risk involved, the risk of armed combat, but we have measured the danger, trained for the mission, and expect success. I can tell you no more for now, but in the meantime I ask that you prepare to receive your boys and men, that you set up a medical station as a precaution, that you have meals ready to feed them and rooms where they can bunk. Most of all, ladies, I ask that you prepare yourselves to be the ministering angels, the loving mothers and wives, that I know you to be." I was about to say, "Dismiss," but instead concluded with, "That is all." And then I ran as fast as my boots would carry me to the relative peace of the farmyard and the ever-gracious company of Marshal Ney.

I saddled him and rode out along our trench line. That made me an easy target for any passing sniper, I knew, but I trusted that fate and my destiny held bigger things for me than to be gunned down before we effected the liberation of this town from its slave master. I trusted my star. Someday, I thought, the midnight ride of Marshal Armstrong—the ride that freed the people of Bloody Gulch—would be as memorable to Montana's citizens as the midnight ride of Paul Revere is to the people of New England. Heroism does not dim with age. Heroes do not fade from memory. They are immortalized in song and story, in statuary and stone, and no society—certainly not the United States of America!—that seeks to perpetuate itself can neglect its ancient, or not so ancient, heroes: its George Washingtons, its Andrew Jacksons, its Davy Crocketts, its Winfield Scotts, its McClellans, its Custers! (I can hear Beauregard interjecting, "Its Lees, its Stonewall Jacksons, its A. P. Hills!" and I will grant him that.)

Perhaps I, as Custer, had gained enough glory—by the measure of most mortal men I surely had—from the war. If it be, then, Marshal Armstrong who gets the glory now in this battle against evil, I thought, so be it. My only regret, darling Libbie, is that my alias precludes you from publicly sharing in the glory. For you are the one whose memory, and Indian-engraved tattoo, is ever in my thoughts and on my arm whenever I take the field of honor.

Our preparations moved swiftly. As twilight deepened into night, we were ready: the wagon horses were harnessed, the cannon and limber were hitched, and the cannon was loaded with acrobats. They tumbled in willingly. Hercules drove Fu Yu in at the end of a ramrod.

I patted Marshal Ney's neck and whispered in his ear, "This is your night of immortality, noble beast."

Sergeant Billy Jack doubled as our cavalry bugler for this mission, wearing a bugle suspended from a baldric. He took the reins of the wagon and slapped the horses. Hercules, looking like an emissary guard from the court of the Emperor Hu Dat Mhan, walked alongside the cannon, bearing his ramrod like a staff.

The creak of the limber's wheels, the horses straining (but not too much) under the harness, the thrill of riding into the dark, the expectation of danger awaiting us, my marshal's badge shining in the moonlight like a heraldic badge worn by a knight errant—it was, perhaps needless to say, a dramatic moment. I looked back at the hotel and the saloon and saw the women, arrayed like ladies fair, waving their handkerchiefs at me—each one a portrait of feminine devotion, hope, and, no doubt, prayer.

Our first obstacle was immediate. Beauregard and Ives had spent much of the day supervising the construction of a bridge that would allow us to transport the cannon across the trench. The span of the trench was only about four yards, but the weight of the cannon, loaded as it was with Chinamen, was considerable, and neither Beauregard nor Ives seemed as confident about their handiwork as I reckoned they should be.

Beauregard rode ahead and pulled up at the bridge. Ives was still inspecting it, squeezing the boards with his hands, tapping them with his fist. The major gave the bridge a good, long look and said to Ives, "You reckon it's safe?"

"It'll see the cannon across—maybe not back."

"One way's good enough."

Beauregard's horse showed trepidation, but he trotted over the boards and they held steady.

The horses pulling the wagon were far more skittish. They pawed the turf and whinnied their disapproval until Billy Jack shouted, "*Giddy-up!*" and whacked the reins. They bolted across, but the boards creaked and started to splinter under the weight of the loaded cannon, and Hercules, rather than crossing the bridge himself, jumped into the trench and scrambled his way up to the other side.

Now it was my turn. Marshal Ney looked at me skeptically and, as so often happened, I knew that my horse and I were of the same mind. We would put on a show for the ladies. I wheeled him around and then, with twenty yards between us and the bridge, we faced the span and charged. Trooper that he is, he leapt the trench, touching nary a splintered board, and pranced for the next twenty yards until he figured, no doubt, that darkness was closing in between us and our audience of ladies fair.

After that we ambled our way through the darkened yellow scrubland that separated us from the Indian Trading Post. Now and again, we heard Indians using owl or dovelike hoots to pass word of our progress.

Eventually, in the distance, we saw the lamp-lit windows of the Trading Company, guiding us like a lighthouse—but to the shoals of danger rather than away from them. As we drew closer, black, shadowy figures appeared—a silhouetted army of brigands.

"Armstrong!" It was Larsen.

I rode to the front. "*Marshal* Armstrong."

"You're as much a marshal as I am an Arapaho. How many marshals sell cannons?"

"How many Indian agents use slave labor—white slave labor?"

"That's what *you* call it. I'm a government contractor."

"And I'm a U.S. Marshal."

"I don't know what your game is—but you're no marshal. I think you're a thief; a cocky, no account criminal; a gunman who will finally meet his match."

"I haven't met it yet."

"Well, we'll see about that. No one takes what's rightfully mine."

"And what's rightfully yours—your slaves?"

"They're not slaves. They're gainfully employed. But you wouldn't know about that, would you? Not you, nor your Carolina cavalier friend."

Beauregard puffed out his chest. "Virginia, sir. I have nothing against the Old North State nor against the old swampy Palmetto State, but I am a Virginian, sir."

"You're a traitor—you and all your other *Ivanhoe*-reading, slave-driving, secessionist rebels. If you want to talk about slavery, look at him…"

"At me, sir?" said Beauregard. "You speak of slavery, sir. What of the wage-slavery of Northern factories—or your heinous doings here…"

I held up my hand. "That's enough. I fought in that war once—we're not fighting it again."

"It looks like some still haven't learned their lesson," said Larsen.

"I reckon some carpetbaggers think they can still take advantage," replied Beauregard.

"Major, that's enough. And as for you, Larsen, I should tell you that I was a highly decorated Union General in the war."

"Is that so? A marshal and a general. Were you selling cannons then too—to secesh like him?"

I instinctively felt for my holster. "I should blow your head off."

"Beggin' the Yankee General's pardon, but shouldn't we trade him the cannon before we blow his head off?"

I took Beauregard's point. "As you wish, Major." To Larsen I said, "Are you prepared for the trade?"

"Yes. Wyeth, bring up the men; Dern, the kids."

We heard the clanking of chains, the shuffling of feet in the dust, and then the bent men and the humbled children emerging from the shadows. My rising gorge forced the words from my mouth: "You villain! You've bound them like prisoners."

"Only way to keep track of 'em; might miss their meals otherwise, mightn't they? They've had everything provided: work, food…"

"Chains."

"Yeah, chains—no charge for that. Now about that cannon…"

My mind quickly placed Larsen in tactical perspective. He stood at the summit of a triangle, captives flanking him on either side to the base of the Trading Post. On a parallel line with Larsen, extending to his right and left, was a ragamuffin force, rifle-toting Indians intermixed with gunmen like Wyeth. I reckoned he had about a dozen men or more on either side; that made the odds at least three to one in his favor. Our hidden sword-wielding Chinamen had no rifles or revolvers, but their capacious silken sleeves held their own surprise.

"We'll unlimber the cannon when you unchain your captives."

"You know, I could take that cannon from you right now."

"You could try; you'd also be dead. I'd drop you before your men knew what happened."

"And you'd be dead too, Armstrong."

"In some ways, I'm dead already. Now you unchain those boys, or you'll learn what happens when a soul goes to hell."

That seemed to unnerve him a little. "Wyeth, Dern, see to it."

I don't think a word was said, but you could sense the inward rejoicing of the boys as they were freed from the grip of those chafing, biting, iron shackles. As the chains came off, some boys rubbed their ankles; others, more boisterous, swung their legs, rediscovering their freedom. The men were more subdued, not daring to move much, and quite obviously bracing themselves for whatever might happen next. They watched curiously as Hercules pushed the unlimbered cannon to the front.

"Now then, Larsen," I said, "send over the boys and the men. The cannon is yours; the limber too. We'll keep the wagon. If any of those men and boys can't walk, they can ride. For your sake, Larsen, I hope they're not many."

The men, though emancipated, were still unsure of their freedom, and shuffled forward with cautious backward glances at their former prison guards. The boys, on the other hand, were willing to take a chance. They sprinted to us. Billy Jack jumped down to shepherd the boys and hoisted two of the bigger ones up to take the reins and drive the wagon. Larsen scowled and grimaced like Simon Legree, and his teeth glimmered in the darkness.

"All right, Armstrong, you've got your ungrateful, worthless rabble. Now clear off and leave me that cannon."

Whispered instructions, initiated by Billy Jack, passed through the boys and men like a cool summer breeze.

"What's all that jabbering about?"

"It's the sound of freedom, Larsen. We're organizing our men for the march out."

"Well get on with it!"

I pulled gently on the reins so that Marshal Ney eased out of there like a gunman backing out of a saloon. Behind us erupted a chorus: "For he's a jolly good fellow, for Marshal Armstrong's a jolly good fellow, for he's a jolly good fellow, which nobody can deny!"

A spark shot up from the barrel of the cannon; Larsen's men drew back; and then crawling from the barrel, like a worm from an apple, came Fu Yu. He dropped, feet first, to the ground and his hands popped from his sleeves, holding two glittering sticks; he waved them, sending off pea-sized sparks in all directions.

"What the devil is this?" said Larsen.

"Giddy-up!" shouted the boy teamster, and the freed slaves trotted or quick marched after him

On cue, the magician tossed aside the sticks, and in their place appeared two small bombs—fireworks really, a Chinese specialty— which had rolled down from his sleeves. He bowled them at the enemy and they exploded in spectacular fashion, a rainbow of colors shooting into the sky, with a symphonic frenzy of whizz-bangery soon joined by the blood-curdling "AAAAiiiiiiiieeeee!" of the acrobats, who came tumbling out, hurling fireworks bombs of their own, before drawing and swirling their swords. My Winchester and Beauregard's and Billy Jack's joined the explosive chorus, and while Larsen's blackguards returned fire, they were running away, some of them with their hair smoking or their pants smoldering from the fireworks. I could hear the horses in

Larsen's corral, about thirty yards to the west, whinnying and colliding against the wood railings in their panic.

I was tempted to press the attack, but Beauregard said, "General, sir, we got what we came for," and I had to agree.

"Billy Jack, sound recall for the Chinamen."

Billy Jack bugled our signal for retreat, and the Chinamen responded instantly, their discipline as sound as that of Napoleon's Old Guard. We backed away in good order—cautiously, but with due regard for speed—and when it became apparent that Larsen's men were too shocked to pursue us we turned our focus to hurrying along the former slaves to the safety of fortified Bloody Gulch. Beauregard and I jumped our horses over the trench, the boys and men slid down one side and climbed up the other, and we got the unloaded wagon over the bridge before it collapsed. Ives, who was waiting for us, handed the acrobats axes. Together they demolished the remains of the bridge and turned the resulting woodpile into spikes to slow an invader and affright his horses.

The reunion of the long-separated families was touching in the extreme; the tears shed could have flooded the trench around the town. Beauregard, with that deep concern for others that is one of his abiding characteristics, seemed on the lookout for any young woman not being reunited with a husband; he was dedicated to the proposition that no woman should be left without a dancing partner. I, with higher thoughts, sought out Isabel. I wanted to ensure she found her father—and to protect her from unwanted attentions. Beauregard, however, was already at her side.

"Well, hello, Yankee General, sir, isn't this a happy event? You know Miss Isabel, of course, and this is her father, Mr. Cyrus Johnson."

"I'm much obliged to you, Marshal," said Mr. Johnson, who was dressed in a torn pink undershirt and grey trousers. He was white-haired, red-faced—from the sun or the foundry work or the exertion of running I don't know—and had inquisitive blue eyes that reminded me of an owl's. "It sounds like you had quite a battle on your hands, quite a battle—but quick, though, wasn't it?"

"A triumph of strategy, Mr. Johnson, and really only an opening engagement in a greater war—the war of liberating this town from the greed of Seth Larsen."

"Greed—yes, yes, that is exactly the issue. Larsen is consumed by greed—and we have all suffered for it, but now reunited with my daughter, well…"

"Yes, I know how you feel, sir," interrupted Beauregard. "It has been my pleasure—or I should say, honor, sir—to be your daughter's guardian. I have come to deeply appreciate her character—she is a fine, fine, young woman."

"Yes, she is, isn't she? Her guardian, did you say?"

"Not in any legal sense, sir, not in the sense that Marshal Armstrong is connected to so many of the young ladies of the chorus who perform at his saloon, but in the sense of shielding her from Larsen's Indians and ruffians."

"Oh, I see."

"I do not mean to alarm you, sir, but we have had a few dangerous moments."

"Really? How dangerous?"

"Oh, daddy, you mustn't trouble yourself," said Isabel.

"She's quite right, sir; the tales of how I saved your daughter's life are quite harrowing, and now is not the time; now is a time for celebrating."

"Saved her life?"

"You, as her father, sir, would surely have done no less. I acted only *in loco parentis*."

"In what?"

"In your stead, sir."

I could take no more. I politely but firmly shoved Beauregard aside. "What he means to say, Mr. Johnson, is that he and I have done everything possible to guarantee the safety of your daughter—and as you can see, she is quite well."

"Quite well, yes, quite well, quite well indeed. I must tell you, Marshal, this ranks as one of the happiest days of my life. Reunited with my Isabel, seeing all this happiness around me. Why, why, I'm nearly overcome."

I was distracted for but an instant, patting my pockets for a hand-kerchief, when Beauregard squeezed past me and took both Johnsons by the elbow. "Come, sir, let us—you and I and Isabel—step into the saloon. I assure you, sir, that this is no ordinary saloon; it is a perfectly decent place for women and children. The marshal, in fact, boards them there. We can celebrate with a glass of sarsaparilla—or something stronger, if you prefer."

"Oh, I have no objection to something stronger—especially after what we've all been through."

"You are a gentleman, sir, after my own heart."

I sighed as he escorted them away. Isabel offered me a long, tender, over-the-shoulder glance; it was so full of sincere admiration that I could but return her look with the hope that my eyes expressed my deepest appreciation and understanding of her feelings. And then I stood, alone, the lonely hero, for what must have been a full five seconds, before a pair of small, thin, feminine hands embraced my arm, the one with your picture on it. It was Rachel.

"Oh, General; oh, Golden Hair," she teased, rubbing her knuckles into my side. "You have done it again, haven't you?"

"Rachel, you might be my ward, but don't take liberties."

"General, you and I have been through a lot together."

"Yes, my dear, we have."

"You are a one-man army…"

"Well, I had a bit of help."

"You are a liberator—like Abraham Lincoln!"

"No, Rachel, not like Lincoln. He was a Republican. What this coun-try needs is a good Democrat in favor of lower taxes, a return to sound money, free trade, a smaller, reformed government that spends more on the army, and honest administration—especially after two terms of that baboon Grant. Don't you agree?"

"Oh, I do so agree, General; I do so agree."

"Well, had things gone differently in June, I might have been tapped—who knows?—by the Democratic Party to carry their standard. As it is, I can only toil in anonymity, liberating men, women, and children held captive by a corrupt Indian trader, a government monopolist, a western carpetbagger—he does have a carpet bag, doesn't he?"

"Oh, I'm sure he does."

"Yes, it fits, doesn't it? The swine. I bet he voted for Grant."

"I don't doubt it."

"No, I don't doubt it either. Our country was not meant to be run by government traders, it was meant to be run by we the people, working on our own, building farms, like Delingplane or whatever that Englishman's name was, or Isabel and her father."

"I think I should like to live on a farm—as long as it was safe from Indians."

"And that's the one place," I said, warming to my subject, "where our corrupt government should be doing more—protecting our people from savages. If you saw what I had to deal with to get adequate supplies in the Army, you'd be shocked. They take every economy they can and then go and waste it all on giving weapons to monsters like Larsen and the Indians."

"General, perhaps we should go to the saloon. I didn't mean to upset you."

"It is righteous anger, my dear, righteous anger. But yes, let us go, there is nothing like a soothing glass of Alderney to quench the fires of anger."

"Alderney?"

"Milk, dearest one, milk."

So, it was that Rachel and I sidled up to the bar next to Beauregard, Isabel, and her father.

"Why, Yankee General, sir, I thought we had left you to your myriad duties. But then what duty is greater than acting as a guardian to your ward?"

I said nothing, which only emboldened him. "Mr. Johnson, sir, might I introduce you to Miss Rachel Armstrong, one of the marshal's wards?"

"Charmed," he said. Then to Beauregard, "You say, she's *one* of his wards?"

"Oh, yes, I'm not quite sure how many there are. Quite a few among Miss Saint-Jean's showgirls, I believe."

"Is that so?" he said, giving me a peculiar look.

"Have you ever bothered to count them?" asked Beauregard, grabbing a handful of peanuts from a bowl on the bar.

"I take it as my duty, Mr. Johnson—as a lawman—to protect the innocent, to serve the weak, to apprehend wrongdoers."

"And to guide rehearsals—he's quite good at that."

"Mr. Johnson, you know as well as I do that the West is a dangerous place for women. The fair sex needs protection. I take that duty very seriously."

"I can attest to that, sir. Never, in all my years have I seen a Yankee more considerate of women—and more blessed I might say in the numbers under his care—than Marshal Armstrong. Were he not an upright Christian man, he might be a sultan with a harem."

"You will take that back, you scandal-mongering secessionist."

"What, sir, that you are an upright Christian man?"

"No, that I am a sultan with a harem."

"But you misunderstand me, sir. I meant to pay you a compliment."

"You can pay for our drinks instead, you bourbon-soaked rebel. I should warn you, Mr. Johnson, that Mr. Gillette is a professional gambler and an inveterate drinker."

"You don't say? Why, I like a little game of cards myself. And my father always held that a drink, in moderation mind you, was good for the heart."

"So, true, sir, so true. If a man cannot enjoy a simple game of cards— why, the mind staggers at the thought. And as for drink, sir, yes moderation is the key."

I'd had enough of this and led Rachel away to a table, to which Smithers—the hotelier acting as a waiter—delivered my glass of Alderney and Rachel's glass of champagne.

"Would you like a sip?"

I shook my head.

"It's delicious—and the color of your hair. Can I still call you Golden Hair?" Her eyes glowed, as if a match were burning behind them—a match lit by a previous glass of bubbly, I guessed.

"I'd rather you didn't."

"All right, then, *General*."

"Marshal."

"Such an adventurous time we've had together. To think it started out just you and me."

I looked her full in the face, and I would be lying if I didn't confess— and it was not just the Alderney speaking—that she was an astonishingly handsome woman. It put me in a philosophical mood.

"Yes," I said, "it did start like that, didn't it? And to think here we are, godparents to a soon-to-be liberated town."

"Godparents?"

"In a manner of speaking—charged with this town's physical, moral, and spiritual safety."

"That's your job, General, not mine."

I drained my glass of Alderney. "So it is—and a new challenge awaits: the siege of Bloody Gulch. I must prepare."

She gripped my forearm. "So soon? You just freed all these people. Shouldn't you celebrate?"

"I would like to, ma'am, and I begrudge no man his share of joy, but a commander is burdened with duty."

"It must be terribly taxing."

"Yes, indeed it is. Some think that a soldier's life is mere fighting or brutality; and there is that, of course. But for the officer, the commanding officer, especially above the rank of major, it requires courage, yes; muscle, of course—feel that arm, girl—and steely nerves, without a doubt; but most of all high intellect."

"Oh, I can see that."

"I know some people think I'm impulsive, but they're wrong; I'm trained, and by my own lights well read, in the art—the *art*, mind you— of war. Yes, an officer needs daring and dash. He wants his men eager and straining at the leash, but as a commander, everything I've ever done on a battlefield has been the result of study. I study every military situa-tion that might arise; I imagine it. And when I become engaged in a campaign or a battle and a great emergency arises, my mind focuses on everything that I have ever read or studied or imagined. That's why my decisions are instantaneous—because my mind instantly sorts through all my hours of study, every scenario I've imagined, every counter to every move of the enemy that I had considered. The result: victory. That, dear, is why I was the Boy General; that is how I became a Cavalier in Buck-skin...But, Rachel, I apologize, I must be boring you."

"No, General, you're not. I've been away from educated people for a long time. You're a great man, General, a fascinating, brilliant, and courageous man, and I love listening to you talk, just being in your presence."

Truer words from the heart, I expect, were never spoken, so I said gently, "Yes, I can see that. I quite understand, my dear, and if it is a comfort to you, I will sit with you and drink Alderney until the cows come home." Of course, as the cows were already home, in our impro-vised farmyard, I stayed up all night, during the course of which I received a seemingly endless parade of grateful men, women, and children who came by to pay their respects, offer me their thanks, and tell my ward Rachel how lucky she was to have me as her protector.

True enough. But the larger truth, of course, is that the mistress I truly serve, the one who gives strength to my stern right arm, is you, darling Libbie. But that is a secret shared only between us, a crazy old Indian tattooist, and those who see me shirtless or with my sleeves rolled up—and I try to save that for the truly deserving.

I did in fact roll up my sleeves in the parlor of the hotel where I waited on coffee that morning while everyone else slept off the evening's fes-tivities. I was drawing up battle plans—contingencies for various siege scenarios I could envision, and while I remained confident in our defenses, many of the scenarios would have struck most men as night-mares.

We were massively outgunned. By what exact numbers it was impos-sible to know. Our enemy knew we were pinned down, if not by him then by the civilians we were pledged to guard. He had his own private army, now supplemented by professional gunmen who likely knew neither shame nor honor. Still, save for one charge—foolhardy, my critics will say; betrayed, I will aver—into the maw of an Indian army larger than anyone had ever seen, I had never lost a battle, and I would not lose this one. There was too much at stake.

I looked down at you on my arm, and it seemed as though your portrait came alive and spoke to me these words: "Take courage, Autie. Ask Miss Saint-Jean to put on a show to calm everyone's fears. Your genius will win through again." And I thought, "Yes, darling Libbie, as always, you are exactly right."

As I was thinking this, Beauregard stepped into the parlor. I was glad to see him, because an officer should always be an early riser, and he looked none the worse for wear.

"I trust you had a pleasant evening with the Johnsons, Major?"

"Yes, quite pleasant, sir. And you with your ward, and your well-deserved adulation?"

Smithers, whom I'd earlier rousted out of bed, stumbled in with my cup of coffee. I sent him away to fetch another for Beauregard.

"The time for bunting and confetti, for champagne and celebration is over, Major. We need to think about the looming siege."

"You're right about that, Yankee General, sir. I assume you have a plan."

"Yes. First, we'll stage a show for the families of Bloody Gulch."

"A show? You mean a military show? Raid Larsen?"

"I mean nothing of the sort, Major. I mean a proper show. I mean singing and dancing and magic—and card tricks too, if you like. Morale is vital to any defensive strategy, and we need civilian morale high for the challenges ahead. You understand?"

Smithers handed Beauregard a cup of coffee, and then wandered away, as if sleepwalking.

"Well, sir, we had no shows at Petersburg—and never heard tell that Vicksburg did either."

"Precisely my point, Major."

"Your point, sir, is that the Southern Confederacy was defeated by a lack of proper entertainment?"

"Indeed, it wasn't just Sherman who crushed the South. Your people lost hope. But imagine if Miss Saint-Jean's dancers had toured Dixie. Imagine their high-kicking to 'The Bonnie Blue Flag.' Would that not have strengthened Southern resistance?"

"Well, Yankee General, sir, I can't honestly say..."

"Your man Jefferson Davis, though a Democrat, had too narrow a view."

"Well, I didn't know him, sir, but he was a soldier, a Secretary of War, a United States Senator..."

"That's all very well, Major, but that's exactly what I mean. He had the *curriculum vitae* of a leader, the knowledge, the substance one would want, but that is only half of the equation. One must understand the human heart; one must know how to inspire—it is in that half of the equation that art displaces science."

"And you believe, sir, that the art of the cancan is crucial to our defense of Bloody Gulch?"

"It seems obvious when you say it, doesn't it? But that too is part of leadership—seeing the obvious point that everyone else, in their convention-bound thinking, misses. I'm glad you saw it, Major."

"Yes, sir, well, I assume the responsibility for the show can be delegated to Miss Saint-Jean, and that you and I can apply ourselves to the more traditional, tactical aspects of defending a position such as we have here."

"It is, of course, a question of a hierarchy of priorities."

"Yes, sir."

"And in that light, I'm sure you will agree that my focus should be on the show."

"I see—and what should my focus be, sir?"

"Naturally, you will want to perfect your card trick act."

"Naturally."

"As you have not performed on stage before, I assume it will require a great deal of practice and rehearsals."

"I assume so."

"But, Major, you and I are men of action who require little sleep. Any spare time we have from rehearsals and planning for the show we can devote to military planning, narrowly speaking."

"I'm gratified to hear that, sir. I reckon I'm better suited to that than the stage."

"'Know thyself,' Major; that is a worthy admission."

"Thank you, sir. I see you're already sketching out some plans. Might I see them?"

And so I spent the rest of the morning ignoring the pressing responsibility of organizing the show in order to discuss lesser tactical matters with Beauregard. But one must take advantage of circumstances, and as Beauregard was awake and at the breakfast table and everyone else remained slumbering, it seemed an acceptable diversion of my time from matters theatrical.

That afternoon, however, my focus inevitably shifted to Miss Saint-Jean. She again reminded me of Robin Hood, with her interesting feathered cap, but this time her theme was green—green hat, green corset, green stockings, even green high-heeled shoes. We sat at a table before the saloon stage. Most of the children were outside running and shouting, though a few girls were sitting at tables playing quietly with dolls.

"I remember when I was their age," she said. "You know, the great thing about being a kid is believing everything's possible."

"Everything is possible," I said, "if you're willing to work for it."

"Yeah, well, what's on your mind, Marshal? You get full credit for the rescue—now how do we feed these people, and keep from getting shot or scalped?"

I dismissed these elementary questions with a brush of the hand and turned the conversation to what really mattered: rehearsals, new acts versus the standard show (which of course none of the captives had yet seen), and whether the farm women of Bloody Gulch should be performers or members of the audience.

It took Miss Saint-Jean a surprisingly long while to understand the importance of these questions. She wanted to talk about the siege—and I suspect it offended her, as a keen woman of business, to discuss theatrical matters in which there would be no immediate profit (because I intended the show to be performed free of charge). In the end, though, I got the answers I wanted. We came up with a rehearsal schedule that would allow for a full-scale performance in three days' time; and we decided to stick with the standard show, because even it needed some brushing up and she wanted to stick with the true professionals (and Rachel) and not involve the farm women.

I came away from our meeting thoroughly satisfied and confident in our future. I walked the streets of Bloody Gulch with a jaunty air, whistling "Garry Owen." The freed boys saw me, fell in behind me, and were soon marching in step. I sang so that they could learn the words:

Let Bacchus' sons be not dismayed
But join with me, each jovial blade
Come, drink and sing and lend your aid
To help me with the chorus:

Instead of spa, we'll drink brown ale
And pay the reckoning on the nail;
No man for debt shall go to jail
From Garryowen in glory.

We'll beat the bailiffs out of fun,
We'll make the mayor and sheriffs run
We are the boys no man dares dun
If he regards a whole skin.

Instead of spa, we'll drink brown ale
And pay the reckoning on the nail;
No man for debt shall go to jail
From Garryowen in glory.

Our hearts so stout have got us fame
For soon 'tis known from whence we came

Where'er we go they fear the name
Of Garryowen in glory.

Instead of spa, we'll drink brown ale
And pay the reckoning on the nail;
No man for debt shall go to jail
From Garryowen in glory.

The boys were quick learners, admired the tune (as well they should), and I soon had the makings of a regimental band. I set them to making drums and whittling whistles. With the boys thus occupied, I wondered what I could do with their fathers. They were civilians, of course, but even civilians have their uses. Beauregard and Ives were standing by the trench, discussing additional fortifications, when I accosted them.

"Well, Yankee General, sir, I'd say two things. One, as farmers, they can slop the hogs and take care of the farmyard. We could also use a labor detail to help us build lunettes in front of the hotel and the saloon."

"Well then, Major, you shall have them."

So—in short order, Libbie—I had my drummer boys working on their instruments, their fathers working on entrenchments, Miss Saint-Jean's company (including the farm women, though they would not be part of the actual performance) working on their act (with the younger girls as an audience); and all seemed right with the world. All I needed now was a scout like Billy Jack to keep an eye on the enemy. That was obvious enough. What was less obvious was where my own path of duty lay: Should I scout with Sergeant Bill Crow or should I join Miss Saint-Jean in supervising the rehearsals? Though I normally take only my own counsel on such matters, I found myself so torn about this decision that I saddled Marshal Ney, road across the trench into the dangerous near wilderness, and consulted the good marshal, for I have always trusted the instincts of dogs and horses. Yet Marshal Ney gave me little guidance—dutifully cocking his head and listening patiently, but offering no assent—via a flicked tail, a rotated ear, or an exultant whinny—to one option or another.

I was sighing and nearing despair and drifting too close to enemy lines when Sergeant Bill Crow rode to my side. I revealed my dilemma to him, and in his sacerdotal way he said, "The show is women's work; scouting is a warrior's work; you are a warrior. Billy Jack and you should scout the enemy."

In saying this, the sergeant revealed his savage heritage, because the theatre is, of course, manifestly not—exclusively or even primarily—the realm of women. Still, I had to concede that your Autie was put on this Earth to be a soldier, and few things are more exciting for a soldier than scouting enemy positions. I had the perfect opportunity, even responsibility, to do that now, or not quite now, as I looked up and realized that if I rode any farther from our lines, I might soon lack a scalp, a head, and other important parts, so we rode back to the farmyard.

Unsaddling Marshal Ney, I asked, "All right, Sergeant. When do we go again?"

"Tonight. Scouts never wait for anything but darkness."

This time we did not disguise ourselves as Indians. Billy Jack, of course, needed no Indian disguise anyway; and he sourly dismissed my former Indian costume as pointless. He told me instead to dress in dark clothes and wear a black hat, and truth be told, I was ready for a new reconnaissance role.

We moved out on foot. The moon was obscured by clouds, which made our progress a mite easier, as we scrambled like wary lizards from our trench into the underbrush. The yellow fields of tall grass ahead of us were cut by narrow channels, natural trails, and through these we advanced. We were a hundred yards from the trench when I heard the first, eerie, Indian, night-owl calls. Already flat on the ground, I pressed myself flatter. I caught Billy Jack's eye, which betrayed nothing. He didn't move and neither did I. I had a knife tucked in a sheath inside my boot. I pulled it out, even though the blade might reflect the moonlight. I reckoned I might not have time to reach for it if an Indian sprang from the tall grass.

Ears are more useful than eyes in the darkness, and my ears tingled to catch any audible hint of movement. I kept my eyes on Billy Jack, and

I'm glad I did because he cupped his hands around his face and hooted—
it would have scared the devil out of me if I hadn't known it was him.
Even so I had to wonder what he was up to. He motioned for me to crawl
ahead, and I did, boldly, assuming that whatever he had said in owl talk
provided us with some sort of protection. There were hooted replies, and
Billy Jack hooted again. I paused and looked over my shoulder, trying to
find Billy Jack in the tall grass. Then I nearly leapt off the ground, stifling
a curse, as something smashed down my hand. My head shot round and
I half expected to see a bear towering over me. Instead, I saw a moc-
casined foot and a tree-stump leg. A rifle barrel jabbed my face; behind
the rifle stood a war-painted Indian. Though I daren't look back, I felt
a hand clasp my boot, then my belt, and finally my shoulder. I heard Billy
Jack at my ear: "Crow."

"What do you mean? Like a rooster?"

"No, we're all Crow—except for you, Boyanama Sioux."

The rifle tilted away from me.

"Sergeant, what the blue blazes is going on?"

"You need cavalry. No cavalry available, so I bring Crow. These are
all Crow."

"Well, thank goodness for that. How many are there?"

"Fifteen—they left their horses behind; necessary to sneak through
Larsen's patrols. Tonight we take mounts from Larsen. He has horses—
a barn with saddles too. We can outfit cavalry."

"Sergeant, you are one exceptional Indian."

"The cannon was one plan; Crow reinforcements another; did not
want to reveal either until I knew they were real, not just ideas."

"Well," I said, and nodded at the Crow who had flattened my hand,
"he seems real enough."

"His name is Sonny Sioux-Killer."

"Well, then, our sort of man."

"Yes, let us go. They have already swept the area ahead. The Sioux
have no sentries. They are all at the Trading Post with Larsen: big confer-
ence. While they are distracted with talk, we'll take the horses."

"Well done, Sergeant. Let's go."

With the Crow scouts leading the way, we advanced through the scrubland like panthers on the prowl. Soon we saw the lamps glowing through the Trading Post windows, the outline of the corral fence off to the west, the horses moseying around its confines—lonely, I thought, and in need of riders—and a large barn limned behind.

"Horses enough for all," said Billy Jack.

"Let's go get 'em."

I was astonished that Larsen had no guards posted. I suppose having the town under his thumb had made him careless, and he discounted our ability to take the offensive. That proved he didn't know with whom he was dealing.

Several Crows sprinted up to the corral. We could hear voices in the Trading Post—it sounded like an argument—but no footfall of pacing sentries, no creaking leather of tired guards stretching and yawning in the darkness. The Crows began cutting out our mounts, stroking the horses' noses to keep them calm.

"Pick me out a good one," I said to Billy Jack. "I'll cover you."

Winchester ready, I kept a bead on the Trading Post. I strained to make out the loud, rough, raucous voices, but they talked over each other and there were too many of them. The one definite sound, like a bell in the night, was the clinking of whiskey bottles, heating the conversation. Larsen's gunmen were blowing off steam, he probably wasn't there, and the Indians had abandoned their patrols for firewater. There would be hell to pay when Larsen found out what had happened.

Reins were placed in my hand. "General, we go." Taking an Indian pony for himself, Billy Jack gave me a sleek black gelding. I looked at the fine, black, leather saddle. Stamped on it in gold were the initials "SL." Poetic justice, I thought. I shoved my boot in the stirrup and swung aboard. Seeing my Indian platoon all mounted, I raised my arm and drew it level with the horizon, pointing our way to Bloody Gulch. It won't surprise you, Libbie, that I got more pleasure from this raid on Larsen's corral than I did from rescuing the hostages. I was thrilled to have Larsen's horse—or at least of one of his saddles—and elated at the addition of Crow Cavalry. I guess when it comes down to it, I prefer horses to people—except for you, dearest one. And I guess when it comes down to it, I'd rather be a cavalryman, or a Crow scout, than an emancipator.

I decided to name my new horse Edward, after the Black Prince. He leapt over our trench, wound expertly through Beauregard's defensive line of stakes and strung wire, and I patted his neck in congratulation. He seemed a fine beast. "Well done, good and faithful servant," I told him. I expected he would get on well with Marshal Ney.

CHAPTER EIGHT

In Which Siege Warfare Begins—and Ends

The next day the siege of Bloody Gulch began in earnest.

The weather was warm, and the children were hoop-rolling outside the saloon and playing on the parade ground in front of the hotel. I was with Beauregard in the parlor, rehashing the previous night's adventure— when I heard a mother's scream.

Outside, arrows smacked into the parade ground like hail; children fled (with less panic than you might expect); and mothers grabbed little hands and ran to the saloon and safety. Flaming arrows targeted the hotel. One thudded into the post next to me. I yanked it out, stamped on it, and pounded the few stray embers in the post with my buckskinned elbow.

"Beauregard!" I shouted, though he was standing just a few paces away. "Get the acrobats on the roof with towels, rugs, buckets of water, anything to beat down the flames. Get Hercules to help."

Billy Jack appeared just as I needed him. "Sergeant, have your men mount up; let's teach these Sioux a lesson."

"Yes, sir!"

Beauregard lingered. "Begging the Yankee General's pardon, but if there's cavalry work to be done…"

"Major, I gave you an order—the hotel's on fire."

"I'm better with a horse and a gun than I am with a fire brigade."

"All right, but get the Chinamen moving; put Ives in charge; then saddle a horse and join me—there's not a moment to lose."

His drawl might be slow, but in action Beauregard is like a tiger. Five minutes after I gave the order, I was astride Marshal Ney, Beauregard was mounted beside me, and a line of Crow cavalrymen was formed behind us. We were armed with Winchester repeating rifles.

"All right, boys! You don't need a speech from me, just an order! Let's go get 'em! Crows—*charge!*" Our horses leapt to the fray, hooves pounding for the trench, the flaming arrows arcing over us like misaimed artillery shells. The Crows whooped and hooted as our horses cleared the ditch and we saw the enemy arrayed in the tall grass a few dozen yards ahead of us.

"*Come on, boys!*"

Our horses burst upon them—and the Sioux, confronted with these unexpected monsters, fled, many with arrows half-cocked but not daring a Parthian shot. I had a command decision: we could either pull up and form a firing line or plunge into the fleeing Sioux, making their panic febrile. I figured the Crows wouldn't hear my shouted orders anyway, so we plowed ahead and were soon amidst the enemy. Some Crows fired their Winchesters, others swung them as clubs, and above all the screaming and howling I heard the gruesome pops and smacks of wooden stocks and metal barrels cracking into skulls. Personally, I rode down and shot the enemy at point-blank range.

Libbie, you are a soldier's wife, and you know what this sort of combat means—blood and brains, jaws and eyes splattered onto our horses, the fallen pummeled beneath our horses' hooves. The Sioux did not ask for, and the Crow did not offer, mercy. We shot and hammered and beat the enemy until we left the yellow grass littered with red, broken, bloody corpses. Crows dropped from their horses to take scalps, noses, whatever else they wanted, and I spurred Marshal Ney ahead. My blood was still up. I wasn't done.

"Let's give Larsen a personal message," I shouted to Beauregard, and he followed me as I raced for the Trading Post. We pulled up in sight of it. A cordon of gunman was forming, some still strapping on their gun-belts. They'd heard our shooting. Larsen was no doubt inside, hiding behind them.

I held my Winchester aloft as a sign that I was there to talk, not shoot. "You men listen to me. If you know what's good for you, you'll clear out. I just left a trail of scalped Sioux behind me. My advice to you is let Larsen fight his own battles—and you tell him, next time he sees me, he better have a white flag of surrender."

Beauregard and I turned our horses. No bullets pursued us, no shouted threats or insults, no counstercharge of Sioux cavalry held in reserve. I reckoned the enemy was in shock. We trotted back to our men.

Billy Jack's Crows were remounted and ready for action.

I asked, "Any casualties?"

"None."

"The enemy?"

"Dead."

"Bows, arrows?"

"Taken; knives too."

"Good work, Sergeant. We'll leave the Trading Post for another day. We're done here. Let's move out. They might need us at Bloody Gulch."

We galloped back—and the civilians knew immediately that we were victorious. The Crows were ecstatic, yip-yip-yipping and holding out their prizes, like dogs bringing back shot ducks. The civilians, meanwhile, had things well in hand. A line of men and boys had formed an—unneeded, as it turned out—bucket brigade for the saloon. The Chinamen were standing on the hotel roof smiling and waving at us. There were thin trails of smoke, and charcoaled splotches here and there, but the hotel and saloon were safe and secure; the acrobats had performed well.

We rode up to the hotel. I dismounted and handed the reins to Billy Jack. Waiting for me on the hotel porch was Miss Saint-Jean—a mirage-like vision in a corset, Robin Hood hat, tights, and heels—this time all in pink. It took me a while to adjust to this peculiar and unsettling picture, so familiar and yet so exotic, like something out of the tales of Scheherazade. Her face had that sardonic expression I knew so well and found so provocative.

"Well, Marshal, is this our future—fire and arrows?"

"Not from them. They're dead. Children safe?"

"Yes—and their mothers aren't much rattled; comes from being farmers' wives I expect."

"Hotel and saloon?"

"Safe for now, Marshal; only minor damage. I appreciate your concern for my property."

"Protecting your property—and you, madam—and all who live in Bloody Gulch honestly and uprightly is my duty."

"Yes, yes, I appreciate your 'honestly and uprightly, and duty,'" she said, trying to imitate the commanding tenor of my voice, before giving it up. "But my duty is to get my girls safely out of here. We will not stand as targets for flaming arrows that might destroy our costumes or set our hair on fire."

"Do not fear, Miss Saint-Jean: Larsen is right where we want him."

"Really? Surrounding us here, igniting the hotel, chasing the children off the streets with arrows? I expected better from you, Armstrong. I want Larsen gone. We can't stay here forever. We need to book engagements; we need to get moving; we're a traveling troupe—and we're not traveling now; and we're not making money."

"You're rehearsing a show!"

"For charity! That doesn't count, Marshal. All you've done is gain me property that might become my grave."

"Miss Saint-Jean, you'll soon be traveling again—and the profits will roll in like your acrobats."

"My profits, Marshal, are a lost cause—at least for now; and you've taken my acrobats for soldiers; and my girls are getting restless."

"Restless? We're under siege, for goodness sake; we're fighting the enemy; we've liberated captives; you're putting on a show; these are exciting times!"

"I'll take my excitement at the cashier's till."

"Liberating an entire town from a villainous, evil carpetbagger surely gives your life more purpose than that, madam."

"If I need any purpose, I'll get it from a Sunday sermon, thank you very much. If you want to do something really useful, why don't you repair that boarded-up church and school? If you keep us trapped here— if you keep rescuing people—we'll need more room. But whatever you do, Marshal, just get on with it."

"Miss Saint-Jean, we just came back from scalping Indians—isn't that *getting on with it*? Bloody scalps are dripping on the parade ground, my pants are flecked with Indian blood, my horse's hooves are coated with gore. I take your point about restoring the church and the school—and I'll set work parties on it as soon as possible, but in the meantime, madam, do you mind if I scrape the Indian brains off my boots?"

"You don't have to be dramatic, Marshal. That's my business."

"Yes—and don't you have a rehearsal?"

"Yes, I do: another one of my many charitable efforts on *your* behalf; but I'd rather have performances I can take to the bank."

And with that she spun on a high heel and ambled down to the saloon with a walk that, if I may be blunt, would have brought some men to their knees.

But not your dear Autie—and not Beauregard; he and I are made of stronger stuff. He came up beside me and said, "That, Yankee General, sir, is an extraordinary woman."

"Yes, she is, Major—a constant reminder of duty."

"Duty, sir?"

"We need to prepare for a counterattack."

"No white flag yet from Larsen?"

"No, not yet, Major. But having tried bows and arrows, he'll turn to bullets now. Pass the order to keep the women and children inside. Have you enough men for the lunettes and our perimeter defense?"

"Untrained men—and we don't have arms and ammunition for all of them, either. I suppose those Indian bows might help for a short spell, if the Chinamen can use them, along with their swords, but we're not equipped for a long siege."

"Larsen will want his revenge—sooner than later. And we'll make him pay for it. I need to draw up more plans, and I need to think things through. But for now let's arm the farmers and put them at the lunettes guarding our front. The Chinamen will guard our rear flank, basing themselves at the farmyard. We'll keep the Crows mobile, as cavalry."

"Yes, sir."

"Put Ives in command of the farmers and Fu Yu in command of the Chinamen."

"Yes, sir."

"Once you have our approaches guarded, come see me in the hotel parlor. I need to mull over scenarios and battle plans. We'll have a council of war."

"Yes, sir."

At the hotel, I immediately set to work with paper and pen. When Beauregard joined me, I was able to illustrate, with diagrams, my new basic strategy: "I expect the main attack at our front," I said. I illustrated the point with arrows pointed at adjoining rectangles labeled "Hotel" and "Saloon." "There will likely be a diversionary attack against our rear," I added and illustrated this with a rectangle in which I wrote, "Moo-Moo," and, "Oink-Oink," representing the farmyard.

"We should encourage the attack on our front," I continued, "by only lightly defending our lunettes." I drew our front trench and three crescent shapes behind it. "The men at the lunettes should be prepared for a fighting withdrawal to the saloon and the hotel." I sketched stick men running away.

"The goal is to draw Larsen's men in so that Billy Jack's cavalry can sweep behind and cut them down from the rear. We can't, however, let

Larsen's men advance too far or we might imperil the women and children; and I want to keep their husbands and fathers safe too."

"Well, Yankee General, sir, if we're going to keep husbands and fathers safe, the only dispensable men we have are you, me, Ives, Billy Jack, and the Chinamen—and I suppose the Crows, if it comes to that."

"Precisely. The Chinamen must guard the farmyard. Billy Jack commands the Crows. That leaves you and me and Ives with a lunette for each."

"Well, sir, that's about the lightest defense I can imagine—in numbers, if not in quality."

"With Winchesters, we can hold our own—long enough for Billy Jack to mount a charge anyway."

"So, it's death or glory, then."

"Glory, major. We can't afford to die; these civilians need us."

"My sentiments exactly, sir."

"So then, Major, I'll defend the lunette nearest the hotel."

"Of course, sir. Miss Saint-Jean's showgirls will be there, won't they?"

"Yes—and they, Major, as you can appreciate, are my special responsibility; I got them into this; I need to get them out."

"A noble sentiment, sir; I would expect no less."

"Also, my horses: Marshal Ney and Edward. That lunette is closest to the stables and the farmyard."

"Exactly. And for me, sir?"

"Next one over. There's an argument to be made, of course, to put Ives in the middle and have professional soldiers on either side, but that advantage is outweighed by you and I likely being unable to communicate across that distance once the bullets start flying. I'd rather have you nearby so that I can give you orders; you can pass orders to Ives. Ives can fall back onto the saloon, where the male civilians can support him as necessary and protect their womenfolk and children."

"Brilliantly conceived, sir."

"Thank you, Major. All right, then. Let's get to work."

So we did. Before taking up my own position at the lunette, I inspected the men, beginning with the Chinamen in the farmyard. Fu Yu was in position at the watchtower; Hercules stood ready—rock in one hand, torch in the other—to smash the whiskey bottles and fire the bridge over alcoholic waters, if necessary; and the acrobats amused themselves by reflecting the sun's rays off their swords and into the eyes of any spying Sioux. Crow cavalrymen marched their horses like sentries along the rear perimeter of our position, ready to form up for a charge on Billy Jack's orders.

I entered the hotel, which had a holding force of only three men, and unlikely ones at that: Smithers, Llewellyn, and Mathis, each of whom, rifle in hand, kept watch from a front-facing window. In case of emergency, they could call on reinforcements from the Chinamen or, sprinting down the corridor connecting the hotel to the saloon, from the husbands and fathers.

The saloon was the next stop on my inspection tour. If the mood in the hotel was one of expectant, somber, nervous near-silence, the saloon was boisterous with the revels of happy warriors. Of course, it didn't hurt that, onstage, Miss Saint-Jean's showgirls were dancing and high-stepping like manic marionettes, Miss Saint-Jean was pounding out a rousing tune on the piano, and the children were making a happy ruckus. Their mothers, meanwhile, kept redirecting their husbands' eyes from the rehearsal to the saloon windows.

From the rowdy good humor of the saloon, I stepped out onto the dusty streets of Bloody Gulch and inspected the lunettes. Ives was in his, counting up the ammunition in his cartridge boxes. Beauregard was absent, attending to other duties; and when I looked at my own empty lunette, I had a sudden, inspired idea. It would take time to execute, but Larsen gave me that time, because, to my surprise, he did not attack—not that day; not that night.

A good dog, surprised by a snake, will fight to the death. A weak dog, once bit, will shy away, yelping, tail between its legs. That, I reckoned, was Larsen. I took him for a coward.

I decided to take advantage of Larsen's cowardice, and tapped Billy Jack to help me execute the sudden and inspired idea that had struck me at the lunettes. Using his woodcraft skills, his talent with ax and blade, and stripping out of my clothes, we made a dummy Custer and slipped it into my lunette in the dark of night.

I reckoned I needed a disguise and, despite Billy Jack's protests that it was unnecessary, I returned to my Indian costume of black wig, medicine pouch, and breech clout, with the added panache, of course, of my yellow cavalry bandana.

I took my stand with the Crows. If Larsen would not attack us, then our Indian cavalry would attack him. I waited impatiently through the night and early morning. By 7:30 a.m., I had waited long enough.

"Sergeant, have Sonny Sioux-Killer take command. You and I will scout the enemy—or provoke him. We'll ride straight across the bridge to those fir trees, then we'll arc south, riding parallel to our own perimeter. If they've got scouts, or a picket line, they'll be there. If not, we're going after them."

We rode out. We were easy targets, but that was by intent. I wanted our enemy to show himself. Yet no sniper opened fire. Nowhere did we espy any Sioux.

If this was a shocking turn of events, it was nothing compared to what we found next. Billy Jack and I turned our mounts to the Trading Post. We rode through the tall grass and the corridor of trees that led to Larsen's headquarters. To our astonishment, it appeared entirely abandoned. The corral was empty. There was neither horse nor man to be seen anywhere. I dropped Edward's reins over the hitching rail.

"Sergeant, stay mounted, keep your eyes peeled, and look for tracks. I'm going to investigate."

The Trading Post was a large, long, two-story, A-framed cabin, with two, big, front-facing windows. The curtains were drawn. Given the air of abandonment about the place, I saw no need for caution. I walked up to one of the windows, bold as you please, and took a gander: tables, chairs, a counter, but no a sign of life—no dogs looking for scraps, or cats looking for mice, or people looking for supplies. I stepped over to the front door, confident I wasn't walking into a trap.

I opened the door, like any other customer would, and stepped inside. There was no seated gunman waiting to threaten me—nothing but wooden barrels on the ground, a few burlap sacks of salt or grain behind the counter, and shelves so sparsely stocked that I assumed Larsen's hired army had stripped them of every provision that would fit into a saddlebag.

There were stairs in the center of the room, and I followed these up to a sort of loft that was the Trading Post's second floor. It was partitioned into offices and, at the far end, a bedroom, but again neither mouse nor man was in attendance.

I descended to the main floor and followed it back to where it ended in a storeroom. There was a door behind the storeroom. I opened it and stepped outside. Billy Jack was waiting for me there. He looked down from his horse and said, "It looks like the Sioux have gone. I am not surprised: siege warfare is not Indian warfare. If I am right, they have abandoned Larsen, because they think your magic is stronger."

"Apparently, the white men do too."

"They went a different direction." He pointed to the northwest.

"What's there, I wonder?"

"I do not know, General. But I would say the siege is over."

"And the war?"

"The war never ends for Crow and Sioux, but these Sioux, at least, are gone. I believe they are gone forever, and will not fight for Larsen. The white men, I'm not sure. For them, it could be a strategic withdrawal: in French, *retrait stratégique*; in German, *Strategische Rückzug*; in Beauregard's tongue, *Joseph E. Johnston*."

"Very wry, Sergeant, very wry."

"I'm a student of the great war. I have studied the generals of both sides, including the Confederate Cherokee General Stand Watie."

"Yes, well, let's get back to town. I reckon the farmers—and their brides and children—can return to their homesteads."

"Yes, I reckon so too, General. I'll fetch your horse."

I had a moment to wonder, again, how much this wily Indian knew about me, but as sleek black Edward appeared, all introspective thoughts fled, and I stepped into the saddle and we galloped away through the tall grass, Edward leaping the trench and delivering me back to Bloody Gulch.

Beauregard exclaimed, "By Jiminy, look what the cat brought in! Hallo, Billy Jack! Hallo, Yankee General, Big Chief, sir!"

I reined Edward in at Beauregard's lunette. "They've gone. All of them: Larsen, the Indians, Larsen's gunmen; the whole bunch."

"Gone where, sir—or should I say, chief?"

"Don't be impertinent, Major. We don't know where, but the Indians are out of the way—maybe even at their reservation. According to Billy Jack, they've abandoned Larsen—our magic is too great. The gunmen—that might be a different story; Billy Jack saw their tracks heading to the northwest; looks like they stripped the Trading Post; so, they'll be well-supplied."

"Northwest? Up past the farms?"

"I assume so; we didn't follow the tracks."

"Yankee General, sir, I think I know where they are."

"Well, in the meantime, Major, these people can return to their homesteads. The siege of Bloody Gulch is lifted. The rebuilding of Bloody Gulch can begin."

"Huzza for that, sir, and congratulations."

"Thank you, Major."

"But, beggin' the general's pardon, I'm going after Larsen."

"Now?"

"With your permission, sir."

"Surely it can wait a moment, Major. Larsen's lost half his army, he's in retreat, he stripped his headquarters of supplies—which implies he's not coming back—I wouldn't calculate him an immediate threat."

"He's just biding his time 'til you're gone, sir, then he'll swoop down again like the vulture that he is and prey on these poor innocent people."

"All right, Major, very well. We'll pursue him and chop him down. There's nothing I'd like better than being the sword of justice. But in the meantime, let's deliver some good news to these poor people—and give them a thrill."

I nudged Edward forward and together, man and beast, we passed through the swinging doors of the saloon. The children shouted and laughed in astonishment and joy; their fathers eyed me with slack-jawed consternation; and their mothers sighed in appreciation for my return.

I raised my hand Indian-style and said, "Greetings, people of Bloody Gulch. Do not be alarmed, it is I, Marshal Armstrong Armstrong; I'm only disguised as an Indian. I bring you good news. You are all free to go home!"

I had to pause for all the cheers and rejoicing.

"The siege of Bloody Gulch is lifted. Your farms are returned to you. You can rebuild your town. And we will restore your church and your school."

I waited for the inevitable question, but in the pandemonium of celebration it never came, so I put it forward myself: "Now you may ask, 'But what of you, Marshal Armstrong—where will you go, what will you do?' To which I say, 'Your battle, dear people, is won; but my battle against Larsen continues, and Major Beauregard and I will carry the battle to Larsen wherever he might hide, whatever he might do, so that you need never again live in fear.'"

The thunderous applause set Edward's ears back. I backed him from the saloon and doffed my black wig, acknowledging the appreciative ovation of the people.

As Edward trotted to the hotel, a window sash went up, and a be-robed and perfectly coiffed Miss Saint-Jean stuck out her head. "Marshal, what are you doing? Get some clothes on!"

"Miss Saint-Jean," I shouted, saluting her with my wig, "your show can go on—here or any place you please; the siege is lifted; your showgirls are free."

"Are you serious—or should I say, as serious as a half-naked white man disguised as an Indian can be?"

"Quite so."

"Well, then, Marshal, hallelujah. I'll buy you a drink."

"Your company, madam, at dinner is all I require, with a refreshing glass of Alderney, and perhaps the addition of my ward and Miss Johnson."

"You old tomcat—but why wait for dinner?"

"I have business to attend to, Miss Saint-Jean. Until then..." I bowed in the saddle, sweeping my wig before me.

Billy Jack was still mounted, and waiting for me at the farmyard. "You want to continue the fight?" he said.

"You read my mind, Sergeant."

"Not hard for a Crow to understand Boyanama Sioux."

I gave him a sour look. "Major Beauregard is certain our fight isn't over. You agree?"

He nodded. "Man like Larsen has only one good end—and that is six feet under, as you white men say."

"And your Crows—will they fight with us?"

"No; they came to fight Sioux. They're not interested in this war."

"But you are?"

"I serve with you and Major Beauregard as pony soldier and scout."

"Well done. So then, Sergeant, how about we follow those tracks?"

"After you change clothes—I do not like riding with Boyanama Sioux."

I laughed and said, "As you wish."

⁊

I was at my washbasin, patting my face dry, when I heard a knock at the door. I was half-dressed—pants and boots on, but shirtless—and said, "Just a minute."

A woman's voice said, "Marshal—General—it's urgent!"

Knowing that my torso often has a calming effect on women, I answered the door immediately, shirtless. Rachel stood at the doorway.

"Why, Rachel, come in; what's wrong?" I closed the door behind her.

"Billy Jack's waiting for you on a horse outside. Where are you going? Are you leaving me?"

"Leaving you? Why, Rachel, no I'm not leaving you, if you mean abandoning you. If anything, I am further guaranteeing your safety. Billy Jack and I are going on a reconnaissance mission to see if we can track down Larsen."

"And if you do?"

"Well, that's valuable intelligence."

"You're going to fight him, aren't you?"

"Well, yes, I assume eventually."

"And what if you get killed?"

"Well, there's always that risk, but..."

"You do realize I'd be left entirely alone then."

"Well, not entirely—you have your whole career in front of you with Miss Saint-Jean. Never underestimate, my dear, the worthiness of the professional cancan dancer. You are, in your own high-kicking way, advancing the cause of civilization is these parts."

She turned her head, and was, I sensed, about to weep, as women do. So, I took her by the shoulders and said, "Look at me, Rachel, and listen carefully. You are my ward and I will do everything I can to protect you, but you must also realize that I am Custer of the West. Where I go, you cannot always follow; what I do you cannot do with me; my immediate future is one of being a knight errant. I will defend you always, but you must accept that I might be gone for long periods of time; that my battles for truth and justice are ones that you cannot always share. Right now, I have a mission to track down Larsen. That's my duty. Yours is to be the best cancan dancer you can be, and to repay Miss Saint-Jean for all the kindness she has extended to you—not in money, but in service, the service of the theatre, which is a very great service to the human heart. Do you understand?"

She grabbed my arms and tried to compose herself. "Yes, yes, Golden Hair," she said, looking up at me. "I...I understand." I thought she'd want to step back and take at least one good look at me before she left, but instead she cast her eyes down, caught her breath, and then fled. Don't ask me to explain it. That's just how it was. So, I shrugged my shoulders, put on a shirt, and trotted down to Billy Jack who held the reins to Marshal Ney.

"I reckoned you'd like a fresh horse."

"You reckoned right," I said, stepping up into the saddle.

Beauregard come trotting up on a horse as well. "You boys goin' somewhere?"

"Why, Major? Would you like to keep us company?"

"I surely would—like to keep you boys from getting lost too."

I chuckled and we led our horses over the trench.

"I can tell you where they are," Beauregard continued as we ambled in the direction of the Trading Post. "They're almost certainly holed up at old cousin Delingpole's place. It's at the end of a big box canyon to the northwest of here. It's a perfect hideout. Hidden from the outside by the canyon walls; a river runs through it, so there's no worry about water; plenty of game too."

"You know it?"

"Scouted near it—certainly heard about it."

"And you, Billy Jack?"

"I know it. The Sioux killed an Englishman there."

"Under Larsen's orders," said Beauregard. "Larsen took it over; it's his hunting lodge now. That's why I'm pretty sure he's there."

Billy Jack nodded. "Makes sense; strategic withdrawal."

"All right," I said, "but let's start at the Trading Post. We can test your theory, Major, by following the tracks."

"Yes, sir," said Beauregard, saluting, and we picked up our pace.

Billy Jack found the tracks easily at the back of the Trading Post, but Beauregard bid us wait. He dismounted and said, "I'd like to look around, if you don't mind."

"As you wish, Major. I'll go with you."

Billy Jack held the reins of our horses. Beauregard told him: "If you hear a gunshot or two don't come running; wait 'til you're sure it's a gunfight." Then he moved like a hound dog on the scent of a coon through the storeroom and into the main part of the store. He surveyed the counters, shelves, and barrels, then jogged up the stairs to the loft above, and headed straight for the offices, starting with the one on the far right. He threw open desk drawers, rifled through papers, then charged into the next office and did the same. At the third office, closest to the bedroom, a locked file drawer stymied him, so he blew the lock clean off with his revolver. He plunged his fingers into the files, pulling one after another, giving each a quick examination, and then pushing on. Finally he raised a document in his hand, like an Indian lifting a prized scalp.

"Take a look at this," he said.

It was a land grant. The paper was smudged and dirty, maybe even bloodstained, given some of the rusty-colored marks on it, but legible enough, most especially the name of the property owner, Jack Delingpole.

"Major, what's the point of this?"

"The point, Yankee General, sir, is that 'Cousin Delingpole' is more than a figurative expression. He actually was my cousin—my English cousin. His pappy exiled him and didn't want him back, Jack being a younger son and all, and he being English and all—that's the way things work over there. He served with me in the First Virginia Cavalry. That paper you're holding says he owns Bloody Gulch—the town, the Trading Post, *and* his homestead."

"I see. But he's also dead, Major."

"Yes, sir, I reckon that's so. But I also reckon that Cousin Delingpole's legal right to that land can be proved, which gives us another reason to put a bullet hole in Larsen."

"We had reason enough already."

"Well, sir, let's just say I'm glad to have it."

"But if this paper proves Larsen stole Delingplane's land, why didn't Larsen burn it?"

"Look at the scrawled addendum on the back. Cousin Jack deeds everything to Larsen as an agent for the Sioux. That's a fraud, I reckon. County clerk's office probably has a copy. Larsen had to make it look legal to prove his case. But I reckon with proper encouragement, Larsen'll confess that addendum came under duress."

"Meaning Indian torture?"

"Unto death, sir."

"Which would mark Larsen a murderer, or an accomplice anyway—not something he'll likely want to confess."

"All a matter of alternatives, Yankee General, sir; I intend to provide him with the right ones."

I handed him the deed, and he folded it and put it into his pocket and said, "I'll hang onto this for now. Just thought you should know. And there's something else, Yankee General, sir; there's not just a murder to set right, there's cousin Delingpole's treasure. I know about that too. I know where it came from and I reckon I know where it is."

"Not at the mine or the foundry?"

"No, but with your permission, sir, I'd rather leave that discussion for another time. The first objective is Larsen. Shall we go?"

I nodded.

We said no more, and I followed him as he trotted down the stairs and quick marched out the storeroom. To Billy Jack, he explained, "Just went over Larsen's books."

"With a gun?"

"Sometimes, Sergeant, that's the best way to reconcile accounts."

"Sergeant Bill Crow, take the point," I said, "and let's go get Larsen."

CHAPTER NINE

In Which I Seek Delingpole's Treasure

"Englishman's place is about ten miles," said Billy Jack as we rode through the tall grass. "Mouth of the canyon is about eight miles. We can expect sentries there."

"How many men?"

Billy Jack nodded at Beauregard, who said, "Brace yourself, Yankee General, sir, but I wouldn't be surprised if it's upwards of fifty, if you add up the farm guards, the mine and the foundry guards, his personal guards at the Trading Post, and the men who lounged around the town and the saloon. If you're looking for a war, sir, you still have one."

"And glad for it, Major. Glory is a corporate thing. Oh, I know out here in the West, men like Wild Bill Hickok, with whom I've ridden by the way, have fame that's unique, individual; but for me, it's all about leading men into battle—the duty and the cause. That's why I wear a badge, that's why I wore the uniform."

"An army of three, sir, is an army in reduced circumstances."

"It'll do, Major—first, we scout the enemy; tonight, at the hotel, we have a council of war. By tomorrow morning, I'll have a plan. We'll strap on bandoliers with our coffee."

Billy Jack visibly tensed, alert as a jackrabbit in mating season. That had me worried.

"What is it, Sergeant?"

"Pursuit."

"How many?"

He held up one finger. "Been tracking us, but coming rapidly now—too noisy for Sioux."

I heard nothing but trusted him. "How far away?"

He struck out five fingers. "Five minutes. From those trees," he pointed to a line of cottonwoods on our southern flank.

"Well, then, Sergeant. Let's form a welcoming committee."

We turned our horses to the trees and pulled our Winchesters from their scabbards. As sure as biscuits need gravy, a horse and rider came bursting out of the trees and rode straight toward us, the rider unfazed by three men holding rifles; and then I saw why.

"Rachel—what the heck are you doing here?"

"I told you, Marshal, General, you can't abandon me."

I sighed and glanced at my comrades.

"Yankee General, sir; you don't expect all your, uh, wards, to come ridin' after us, do you?"

"I am alone, Major Gillette," said Rachel.

Beauregard tipped his hat brim in reply. "Ma'am." Then he turned to me, "Well now, sir, I reckon this calls for a change in plan."

"It does nothing of the sort. Miss Rachel, you have made your decision. You have joined us on a dangerous and desperate reconnaissance. You must stay beside me at all times and do exactly as I say."

"I will follow you, General, wherever you lead."

"I reckon there's no doubt of that," said Beauregard, turning his horse onto the trail.

Billy Jack said, "I will ride ahead to see where sentries are posted."

"Very well, Sergeant," I replied. "Carry on."

Rachel fell in beside me, as ordered. "I was useful last time we rode together, General. Maybe I can be useful again."

"Maybe so, but for your safety, I wish you had stayed behind."

"Where could I be safer than with..." she leaned over and whispered, "*General Custer*?"

I had to confess, there was logic to that.

We must have ridden five miles or more when Billy Jack reappeared.

"Mouth of the canyon is two miles distant. We can skirt the sentries if we cut north. There is rocky country, big boulders, up there—good cover and perhaps a good view of the canyon. The only easy descent is where the sentries are, where a tongue of land slopes down into the mouth. But if we don't need to descend, if we only need to observe, the northern approach is better."

"Very well, Sergeant, take the point and lead the way."

Sergeant Bill Crow led us off the flatlands, up a slope, and into a grove of pines that opened onto a new landscape of rock, spurs of forest, and tree-flanked natural terraces in the hillside, along which we rode with scrubland and scree beneath us. We rode higher and higher up a winding hillside until we came out on a boulder-strewn bluff. We left our horses at a stand of pines and moved stealthily among the rocks until we had a good vantage point on the canyon. It was a spectacular view. The Delinquent-pool property—what was now Larsen's hunting lodge—was set still farther back, though we could see it well enough and note that it was constructed in a "Tudor" style, but with turrets on its four corners. In contrast to our stony bluff, the land below was verdant and the area leading up to the house was one vast, green lawn, but lined and broken up with hedges, which—always thinking tactically—could give us cover.

It was not a sleepy place. Larsen's men moved hither and yon like so many rifle-toting miniature cowboys. Those who didn't have rifles were digging trenches—where the green grass yielded to hard, dry soil closer to the house—and others were stuffing the dug dirt into burlap bags for parapets.

"Picturesque, Yankee General, sir, but we can't see all their traps and surprises from here."

"No, we can't. Let's take a three-pronged approach. Sergeant, go as far north as practicable and scout the enemy's rear. Major, I'll leave the enemy's left flank to you. I'll descend right here."

"Beggin' your pardon, sir, but, your, uh, ward?"

"Rachel," I said, "you must give me your word that you will follow my orders. You cannot come with me. The descent is too steep. The risks are too great. But I will entrust you with a grave responsibility. Stand guard over Marshal Ney. If anything goes wrong, you must lead him to safety. Do you understand?"

"Yes, General, I understand."

"All right—stay out of sight. Sergeant Crow, Major Gillette—off you go."

I'm about as sure-footed as a goat, but even I had to be supremely careful. It wasn't just a matter of finding footholds, but of finding cover, scampering across the canyon wall from one shrub to another, and doing so with the brisk, light feet of a dancer, so as not to send sprays of pebbles and dirt raining down the rock face. My recent period of training with Miss Saint-Jean's troupe proved invaluable in this regard.

Danger and daring have always been my friends, but with the sun beating down and the difficulty of the descent, I was dripping sweat. I was perched behind a bush, trying to look as inconspicuous as a fly on a horse's tail when I heard a commotion up above. Billy Jack peered down the canyon rim; he saw me—and he shouted.

"Patrol coming! We must leave!"

"I'll never get up there in time. Save Rachel. Save Marshal Ney. You have Beauregard?"

"Yes—will come back for you."

Then he was gone and I was in a fix. Somewhere up there was a Larsen patrol, and beneath, I could see cowboy hats tilted up. No one had spotted me yet, but if they sent a search party, I had no place to go—with the canyon wall behind me and a bush between me and a drop to the bottom. And then things got worse. Some bright jasper got the idea of shooting at the bushes along the canyon wall. Soon, inevitably, bullets would come crashing towards me. I had three choices. I could stand up, wave my arms, and surrender; I could charge; or I could try to make a fighting retreat with enemies fore and aft. A charge would be suicidal. And a fighting retreat on level ground was one thing, pinned to a canyon wall was quite another. There was nothing for it but to stand and shout: "Hallo down there! It's Marshal Armstrong! I've come to see Larsen!"

"Well howdy-do, Marshal. Watchya doin' up there? Front door's around t'other side. You're welcome to come on down. Been wonderin' when I'd see you again."

"Good to hear your voice, Dern. I was hoping to stumble across someone I knew."

"Well, you stumble on down here, Marshal, and we'll make you feel right at home; we'll be right hospitable."

I stepped carefully at first, but, like a rolling snowball, I gained momentum and finally half-ran, half-slid down the embankment. When I stood at the canyon bottom, dust swirled around me.

"Well, Marshal, you surely do know how to make an entrance."

I brushed off my sleeves. "You fellas don't make it easy."

"Easy way's up that way—a nice, gentle slope. There's a welcome committee up there too."

"Well, Dern, no need for anything special. I just came to see Larsen. We have some unfinished business."

"Oh, yes, you surely do. Those scalped Indians, Marshal—you didn't bury 'em. That was mighty impolite. They were Mr. Larsen's clients and he's none too happy—especially since the others ran away."

"You know who is happy, Dern? Every honest man, woman, and child of Bloody Gulch—that's who's happy."

"For now, Marshal. That'll change. Mr. Larsen has plans."

"I do too," I said, marching toward the house. "What's he got in mind?" Dern fell into step beside me. A gang of gunmen followed us.

"You won't like it, Marshal."

"If it's illegal, I'll stop it."

"By your lonesome?"

"If necessary."

"You got no friends here, Marshal."

"I've got you, Dern."

He snorted in amusement, and we finished the walk to the house in silence.

The house was surrounded by a picket fence. Two guards stood at the gate, two more stood on the porch, and when Dern led me through the front door we were greeted by two gunmen sitting at a table in the entryway—Larsen wasn't taking any chances.

"Whatchya got there, Dern? Is that the marshal?"

"Sure as shootin'. I reckon Mr. Larsen might like a word with him."

"Ain't you gonna disarm him?"

Dern pulled my revolvers and put them on the table. "Sorry, Marshal, house rules."

One of the gunmen at the table got up and ambled back to another room. He returned a moment later saying, "Okay, Dern, bring him back."

The room was a study, stuffed with books and bric-a-brac to which I paid little attention. My eyes were on Larsen. He sat behind a large table wedged into corner. He wiped his sweaty brow with a handkerchief.

"What's your name again?" he said. "I refuse to call you Marshal because I know you're a fraud."

"Armstrong—*Marshal* Armstrong Armstrong."

"Armstrong Armstrong, eh? You're not a very creative impostor, are you? I know why you're here—the same reason that I'm here; the only reason that would draw anyone but a cretin to this place. You heard about the Delingpole Treasure, didn't you?"

"I know nothing about Delingstone—never met him; never heard of him—at least not until I came here. Then all I heard was that you killed him and stole his land."

"You'll meet him sooner than you think. He's buried outside here. There's room for two. If you think I killed him, what makes you think I'll spare you?"

"I represent the law."

"You represent nothing but your own greed. Delingpole wasn't just an Englishman, he was a rebel against this country. He deserved what he got. Now you tell me, Mr. Armstrong, just exactly what you know about the treasure. Your life depends on your helping me find it; so, you better be forthright."

"What if I know nothing?"

"Then you're of no use to me—or to anyone else. Talk, Mr. Armstrong. Talk for your life."

Well, as you can imagine, Libbie, I was momentarily lost for words because I knew nothing about the treasure besides what Beauregard had told me—and I am opposed to lying on principle. But I am also opposed to dying when it interferes with my duty, and I was ever mindful of my duty to save Miss Saint-Jean, her showgirls, and the people of Bloody Gulch. Unwilling to let them down, unwilling to lie, I had but one alternative—to inhabit a role, to be an actor, to play a part, to be a *dramatis persona*, to be the character Larsen assumed I was. And so I proceeded.

"All right, Larsen. I'll tell you what I know—but it comes at a price. We split the treasure fifty-fifty."

"You are in no position to negotiate, Mr. Armstrong. If you cooperate, you save me time, but you're hardly necessary. I'll find the treasure with or without you."

"You won't find it, Larsen. I didn't come all this way on a rumor. I know exactly where it is—and I know why you haven't found it. I know where it is, because I met Delingfoot's partner. He had one, you know. They were together in the First Virginia Cavalry. I met him dying in the wilderness, scalped by an Indian, maybe one of yours. He told me where the treasure was."

"Why would he tell you?"

"Because he was dying, and he knew Delingpile was dead. He didn't want the treasure to fall into the wrong hands. He judged me for a good man; he gave me the secret; and apparently the treasure is enormous."

"Well, out with it; where is it?"

"Like I said, Larsen—we need to make a bargain."

"We'll make a bargain all right. You'll tell me so I don't torture you to death. There's a basement in this house. I made a dungeon, a prison out of it; and if you won't talk willingly, then we'll use force."

"Unlike your minions, Larsen, I'm not easily bullied."

"Dern, take him away. I'm done wasting time with this idiot."

The barrel of Dern's revolver nudged my backbone. "Let's go, Marshal." We left the room and proceeded to the entryway corridor. Behind the entryway guards were three staircases, two going up and one going down. We went down the flight of stone steps to a doorway that opened up into a dark, dank room. I couldn't easily make out its dimensions. All I saw was another of Larsen's henchmen sitting on a chair behind a square table on which were arranged a candle, a spittoon, and a game of solitaire. A big black dog—short hair, long teeth—snapped to attention beside him and snarled at me. The dog wore a studded collar and was chained to one of the several, stout, wooden pillars that ran floor to ceiling. The henchman's face was squashed between a beard and a low forehead; his hat was tilted back (he was scratching his head), and he spoke around a chaw the size of a baseball. "Who you brung me this time—don't look like one of ours."

"Look at that tin star, Buford. This here's Marshal Armstrong."

"The marshal?"

"No worries on that account. Mr. Larsen reckons he's not a marshal at all, just a common chancer, no better than the rest of us—maybe no use at all, if he's not willing to tell us what we want to know. But Buford, here," he said to me, "knows how to make people talk. He gets lonely down here. He knows all sorts of tricks to make the shyest man the most conversational man you'd ever want to meet, and you ain't the shyest of men, Marshal. You'll be talkin' soon enough. Buford'll see to it. His helper there is Bad Boy—and it don't seem like he's taken a shine to you."

Buford said, "He don't take a shine to no marshals—I taught him that—and no Injuns—that come natural. You mind your manners, Marshal, or I'll sic him on you."

Buford pulled a pair of handcuffs from a drawer. Dern jabbed his revolver and I stepped deeper into the darkness. Buford ambled alongside. He was short and stocky and stank of cheap, old tobacco.

"Now hold steady there, Marshal. I reckon you've clamped these on plenty another man."

My hands were behind my back. The handcuffs clicked shut.

Buford said to Dern, "You can just set him by that beam for now and help me with the rope."

I was shoved to a dirty stone floor, littered with hay, and then pushed against a wide wooden beam. They secured me against it with a thick rope.

Buford said, "I'll attend to you later, Marshal. I reckon I got time to finish my game—might even play me another; let you get used to things down here. We got us plenty of rats; they can get mighty familiar. You'll feel 'em before you see 'em. You let me know if they bother you. I could turn Bad Boy loose on 'em. He hates rats—but, as I say, he don't like marshals either; might rip you up by mistake."

Dern nodded to me. "Be seein' you, Marshal. Sooner than later, I hope. Buford's an old miner. He doesn't mind it down here. I reckon you will, though. It ain't just the rats you gotta worry about, or Bad Boy getting unchained. Buford can get plumb angry when people don't talk, can't you Buford? Likes to hit 'em with a shovel."

"That's a fact, Dern, that is surely a fact. Always keep my shovel handy for hittin' folks with—mind you, only if they deserve it."

"You know, Marshal, when stubborn folks won't talk, Buford gets pretty ornery. When he's done with 'em, they sometimes don't talk forever. Now, that would be a shame in your case, Marshal, because you're such an educated man with a lot to say. So, you play nice with Buford, and he'll play nice with you." To Buford he said, "Marshal here's going to tell us where the treasure is."

"Well, that is surely nice of him. Save you boys up top a lot of digging. I'll let you know."

Dern closed the basement door and the darkness, outside the pale glow of Buford's candle, grew inkier. But, Libbie, you know I fear nothing—least of all dogs or rats or any other furry creature; I've always had a way with animals, and if a rat came nibbling up to my ear, I believe we'd get along quite handsomely, just like I did with my pet field mouse (you remember him); and I've never met a dog that didn't love me.

As it was, I didn't hear the scurry of little rat feet but only Buford's sighs and grunts, the ping of liquefied tobacco hitting the spittoon, the creaking of his chair, and the shuffling of cards. I had the distinct impression that he had already forgotten me, so absorbed was he in his game, but staring in my direction, visible through the darkness, were the glowing canine eyes of Bad Boy. He was no longer snarling; he just sat prone, his long, dark face resting on his big, dark paws, regarding me attentively, as Rachel often did—and that gave me an idea: As I had helped effect Rachel's escape from the Boyanama Sioux, I wondered whether Bad Boy could help me escape from the tobacco-dribbling Buford and his torturer's shovel.

Beauregard, when I first met him at the saloon, had attempted to blink at me in Morse code. I doubted that at this distance, and under these circumstances, Bad Boy, even if he knew Morse code (which I had to concede he probably didn't), could have deciphered my blink-blinks. But I have long held the belief that horses secretly speak French (which is why it is on the curriculum at West Point) and dogs speak German. In the Army I have learned to speak fluent Irish, but my German remains scant. Still, if I could cobble together a few German phrases, I could plead my case. Buford would hear me, of course, but I decided I had to try.

"*Achtung!*" I said.

"Whatchya say?"

"Nothing, pardon me. Just a cough."

"Damp down here sometimes affects people like that. You want a chaw? I don't mind sharin'."

"No thanks. *Ich bin trappenzied. Ruff, ruff—needinzie your helpen.*"

"What's that?

"Sorry, just clearing my throat. *Gnawinzie das ropen, bitte, to freeinzie me? Ich bin ein nicen master, ich leben das hunden.*"

"Listen here, mister. You keep clearin' your throat like that, and I'll turn Bad Boy loose to tear it wide open for ya."

"*Ich bin ein hunden freunden. Helpenzie me, bitte.*"

"What the heck you doin' over there?"

I coughed dramatically. "Sorry—like you say, it must be this damp air. *Ich leben hunden. Mucho leben. Feedin generous. Helpenzie me.*"

"I'm warning you, Marshal. My patience has its limits. And I ain't finished my game yet. And Bad Boy ain't been fed yet. You wanna be his chow?"

"I fear no dog, Buford, just as I fear no man. *Das Master ist meanen, ja? Ich bin molto kinder. No strikenzie mit das shovelen; only petenzie.*"

"That so? Well then, how about I set Bad Boy loose? I'll keep my shovel handy to beat him off when you start screamin'."

"Do your worst, Buford. *Ven du bist freeen, ven die chain ist offen, helpenzie me.*"

I heard the chain clank. "*Get him!*"

The dog sprang. His fangs shone across the room; an instant later they were at my face, tearing the air as he barked; his breath hot; his eyes fierce; his growling like that of a bear tearing into an elk—yet it was all a tactical feint; his jaws clamped not on my flesh but on the rope that bound me. He put on a ferocious show for Buford—teeth gnashing, neck shaking violently—but it was my freedom at which he labored. "Bad Boy!" I shouted. "Bad Boy!"

"Heh, heh, they're usually screamin' about now," said Buford, rising from his chair. I heard the clang of a shovel blade on the cold stone floor.

Bad Boy's frenzied attack on the rope had shredded enough of it that I reckoned I could at least wiggle my way up to a standing position even if my hands were still cuffed. With my feet planted firmly under me, I pushed hard and shot up to my full height.

"What the devil?"

"No devil, Buford, but an avenging angel."

He swung the shovel at my head, but I ducked down, and threw myself at him. My legs were tripped by the still-binding rope, but I smashed my head into his chest. We both fell—he directly onto his back, I onto my side, rolling onto my back so that I could defend myself with kicks if need be. Before Buford could rise, Bad Boy was upon him. With a brutality I can scarcely describe, he took Buford's neck between those fearsome teeth and shook the life right out of him. I believe I actually heard his neck snap, and after a gargled yelp, Buford lay still and limp, like a giant smelly dishrag. Bad Boy trotted over to the table, pulled open the drawer with his teeth, clamped them onto Buford's ring of keys, trotted over, and dropped them in my palms. "Bad Boy!" I said, *"Bad Boy!"* He licked my face and waited patiently while I struggled to find the right key and remove the lock from my wrists. When I had done that, I took his paw with one hand and stroked his head with the other. "Well done, noble Bad Boy!"

Directly above me were Larsen and his army of gunmen. I needed a strategy—and for this I had to rely on my own wits. Bad Boy might be a great trooper, but he required leadership.

I stripped Buford of his gun belt. At least now I had a weapon—or two, counting Bad Boy. I bade him follow me and I opened the basement door. Slowly and carefully we tiptoed up the winding stairs. I knew that at the top we'd have Larsen's office on our right and two gunmen seated at a table in the hallway with their backs to us. With each cautious step we took, different courses of action raced through my mind.

I saw the gunmen's backs; I saw Larsen's closed door; and Bad Boy and I made our leap, bursting into Larsen's study, shouting (or I shouted; Bad Boy remained silent), "Aha!" Before us was an empty room. Quick as lightning, I slammed the door and jumped, Bad Boy beside me, behind the desk. We curled beneath it and I put my finger to my lips. *"No barkenzie,"* I whispered. The two gunmen charged in.

"What in blue blazes is goin' on? Was they comin' or goin'?"

Boots pounded across the wooden floor; the gunmen inspected the big windows at the opposite end of the study.

"He didn't leave this way—and only a ghost coulda got by us."

"Don't make no sense nohow."

"But you heard it and I heard it."

"Maybe best forget it. Folks'll think we're crazy from sittin' out there so long."

"They might be right at that."

"Mr. Larsen ain't here, so it don't matter to no one but us."

Boots creaked on the boards, and the door closed.

"Well done, brave and noble Bad Boy," I whispered to him, and he licked my face. "Now we must find a way out." The two of us crawled on all fours, edging around the desk and into the main part of the study. I dared not stand lest one of Larsen's innumerable gunmen should see me through the window. We dared not smash through the window, because we would fall into the enemy's clutches. And we dared not just sit and wait, because I am not one for sitting and waiting. Instead, I decided to pull a practical joke—one of my greatest strengths, as you know. If those two clodhoppers outside thought we were ghosts, we might as well act the part. I crawled to the door and, as eerily as I could, moaned, "Whaaaa! Boooo! Whaaaa! Boooo!" and Bad Boy joined my chorus, howling like a coyote.

Boots came running down the corridor, and Bad Boy and I hid behind the door. It came swinging at our faces.

"I don't like the look of this, Elmer," one of them said.

"Look of what? There ain't nothin' here."

"You heard it and I heard it."

I waited for them to inch their way into the room before kicking the door shut and shouting, "Aha!" again, this time with better reason. They turned on us, but we were ready—and they weren't. I grabbed my opponent's wrist, twisted it until he dropped his gun, and slammed my other hand, a fist of vengeance, into his jaw repeatedly. Bad Boy adopted my techniques to his own talents, sinking his fangs into Elmer's wrist, sending Elmer's gun clattering harmlessly to the ground, and then jumping onto him and pinning him to the floorboards, snarling at his face.

"Call him off! Call him off!"

My opponent was unconscious, so I consented. "*Achtung*, Bad Boy! *Haltenzie!*" and I took over, planting my boot on Elmer's chest. "All right, Elmer, my friend, you're going to help us out of here."

"There's no way outta here. You might have me now, Marshal, but I'll have you soon enough."

"Brave words for a man on his back."

"You're gonna get yours—oh, are you gonna get yours."

"Your friend downstairs got his—he got his throat ripped out. If you don't want the same, you'd better think fast, Elmer, because you've got one chance to save your miserable life, assuming you want to."

"Sure enough, Marshal, I want to live, but there *is* no way outta here—'ceptin' through all Boss Larsen's men. And they're not gonna let you through no matter what."

"We'll see about that." I lifted my boot from his chest. "Get on your feet." We were close enough to the door and far enough from the window that I doubted we could be seen from outside, but I didn't want to take chances. I bent down, picked up his partner's revolver, and directed Elmer with its barrel. "Draw those curtains. And if you so much as smile or wink or twitch your head, I'll put a bullet through your spine."

He stumbled over to the curtains, drew them quickly with a satisfying whoosh and then, slowly, with all due propriety, turned to face me.

"Now then," I said, "does this canyon have an outlet to the rear, less well-guarded?"

"No, Marshal, the only easy way out is up yonder. And that's chock-full of men. Otherwise, you gotta climb—and on that canyon wall you'll be a big target."

"Less of one without you and your partner. You drag your friend here downstairs. We'll try our luck out back. If you know what's good for you, you'll stay in that basement with him."

Elmer grabbed his compadre's boots and, maneuvering him like a wheelbarrow, dragged him out to the edge of the descending stairwell. There he bent down and hoisted him over his shoulders. He leaned against the wall for support as he descended.

"Heavy load," I said.

"He ain't heavy, he's my brother," he replied, making his awkward way down the stairs. Bad Boy and I followed them down. I retrieved the keys that I'd left on the stone floor, hoping one of them fit the door's lock.

Elmer dropped his brother to the ground with less care than you might think, and I said, "Sorry to leave you in this house of horrors, Elmer, but duty calls." I closed the door, found the right key, and locked him in.

Bad Boy and I then bounded back up the stairs. I had no intention of rushing from Larsen's lodge and attempting an ascent up the canyon walls—at least not yet. That suggestion was merely to throw Elmer and his gang off our scent. What we needed was a more thorough scouting of our enemy's position, and for that we ascended a narrow winding staircase—the left of two on either side of the front door. We stepped up and up and up until we were confronted by another door, which was unlocked—and none of the keys would lock it behind me. Next came a short flight of stone steps that opened onto a medieval turret with a wide view of the estate. Keeping low and hiding behind the crenellations, Bad Boy and I surveyed the enemy's dispositions. His main force was directly in front of us, the men digging trenches and building parapets. To the left, right, and rear (as best as we could see) there were scattered sentries, but it was apparent that Larsen assumed any attack had to come down the tongue of the valley. I scanned the canyon ridge and was nearly blinded by blinking, reflected sunlight on my right. It took me a moment to realize that it wasn't just the sun, it was a heliograph. I waved my hat—quickly, intermittently, and with care—hoping to attract no one's attention but the heliographer's, and hoping he was one of ours. I was rewarded with this message in Morse code: "C-R-O-W-G-E-T-C-A-V."

"Crowgetcav: what does that mean?" I whispered to Bad Boy—and then it struck me. It was Sergeant Bill Crow. He was going to fetch the cavalry, possibly from Fort Ellis. I was simultaneously elated and perturbed that the U.S. Cavalry might rescue me—and reveal my identity. But there was no way and no time to protest—the sunlight had stopped flashing, and Billy Jack had bolted. Either I could wait, or Bad Boy and I could take on Larsen and his army of fifty or more men ourselves. Naturally I opted for the latter course, calculating that our best chance to evade the enemy was to march right through him out the entrance to the canyon. I looked into Bad Boy's big brown eyes and said to him in English, because my thoughts were too complicated to capture in my sparse knowledge of German, "Bad Boy, if you wish to stay here and wait to be rescued, you may. I, however, am going to take my chances and escape right now." He licked my face, which I took as a canine oath of allegiance, and we descended the turret together.

As we stepped onto the main floor I was surprised that Elmer wasn't pounding on the basement door. He was, apparently, totally demoralized; I'm sure the sight of Buford's mangled body didn't help. I strapped on my gun belt, which was still on the table where Elmer and his brother had once sat guard, and peered out the front. I unpinned my marshal's badge and dropped it in my pocket. I flipped up my collar, raised my bandana over my nose, and tilted the brim of my hat over my eyes. "All right, Bad Boy, let's go."

We opened the front door and stepped boldly out of the house. The guards on the porch looked at us and I said, "My gosh, Larsen was right, you boys surely do smell!"

"Who the hell are you?"

"You better mind your manners, boy."

"And whatchya doin' with that dog?'

"You're supposed to be keeping guard, aren't you? Larsen hired me to knock you boys into shape. How'd that Armstrong man get in here?"

"Up that way," said one, pointing to the canyon wall.

"Who are you, mister?" said the other.

"I'm telling you once, and don't ever ask me again. Name's Durango— it gets around far enough without me spreadin' it. Now you keep a sharp eye out."

We didn't tarry for any further conversation.

At the gate through the picket fence, I bellowed an order to the guards, "Eyes front. Larsen's man Durango comin' through," and they let us pass without incident.

We went a little farther and then paused briefly to watch the trench diggers. To my right was a pile of filled bags waiting to be taken to a parapet. I lifted one over each shoulder, further hiding my face from view, and strode forward. Sweaty men with pickaxes and shovels barely gave us a glance. At one partially constructed parapet, a villain called out, "Hey, we could use some bags here," but I shouted back, "Mr. Larsen's orders: these go up front."

It was as easy as walking down a street in Monroe until we came to the canyon's mouth. Sentries stood on the high ground on either side of the opening, four others stood idly in our path, and a horseman rode down between them.

"Whatchya doin' with those bags up here!"

"Mr. Larsen's orders: supposed to seal the entrance."

"Seal the entrance? That'll take a helluva lot of bags. No one told me about it."

I dropped the bags I carried. "Name's Durango; Mr. Larsen just hired me—outta Texas. You mighta heard the name."

"Can't say I have."

"That's because most who hear it, don't live to talk about it."

"Mighty big talk—especially for a new man."

"Mr. Larsen asked me for that horse of yours too."

"What fer?"

"There'll be more fellas bringing up bags. He wants me to scout up ahead before it's all sealed up."

"But that's what I'm fer."

"Mr. Larsen reckons he found a better man."

"You?"

"None other—name's Durango."

"You don't scare me none."

"I don't mean to scare you none. We're working together, aren't we? I just want your horse, like Mr. Larsen says."

The horseman looked down into the canyon. "What's going on down there?"

I could guess. Elmer had broken out. They'd be coming this way soon. "Mister Larsen is probably chewin' their hides for not getting those bags up here faster. You better get off that horse and get down there and help 'em. Mr. Larsen was getting plumb crazy mad that he didn't know where Marshal Armstrong's men were. They're tough hombres, and I gotta track 'em down—*fast*. You're costing me time. Get down—*now*!"

"All right, all right," he said, dismounting. "Whatchya doin' with that dog? He goin' with ya?"

"He's a tracker," I said, stepping into the saddle. I touched the brim of my hat. "Name's Durango—you remember it, you hear? Adios."

We sprang up the canyon, my newly acquired horse and I, with Bad Boy keeping a good pace on my right flank. We went hell-bent for leather, because those sentries would soon be alerted and shots would come raining down on us. I cut a path southeast, towards the Trading Post, for as long as I thought the sentries could see me. But once a fold of land and a line of cottonwoods screened us, I cut southwest for Bloody Gulch, aiming for the farmsteads outside of town rather than the town proper; they were closer, which meant I could keep a faster pace. Not often, but occasionally, I looked back, expecting to see a distant cloud of dust kicked up by Larsen's gang in pursuit, but because I took advantage of every dip and coppice to keep myself hidden, my line of sight did not extend far.

I approached Miss Johnson's farmstead at a gallop and rode directly into her barn. Bad Boy trotted in and collapsed, panting and in dire need of water. I put the horse in a stall and directed Bad Boy to a half-filled water trough. He nodded in acknowledgement but still needed to catch his breath before he could even think about moving.

I, however, was still as spry as a young buck, and trotted to knock on Miss Johnson's front door. Given that she, like everyone else, had leave to return to her farm, I hoped I might find her returned to her homestead. The door opened, revealing that contumacious Confederate Beauregard.

"I should have known I'd find you here."

"Well, Yankee General, sir, I could be saying the same. Last I recollect you were in the arms of the enemy."

"And you, I see, hope to be in the arms of Miss Johnson."

"Well, that is a most ungallant thing to say, Yankee General, sir, seein' as I am here as a matter of duty."

"And what duty would that be?"

"Protecting this young lady from the ruffians you have recklessly directed this way."

"Have you seen them?"

"No, sir, but I don't reckon they set you free. You're an escaped prisoner of war."

"Where is Isabel?"

"She's in the kitchen, sir. We saw you charging and she immediately—charming young belle that she is—thought you might like some coffee."

"I'd be obliged for that, Major."

"And we also noticed, sir, a large black dog that looked as though it were reporting from the battlefield at Marathon."

"That would be Bad Boy."

Isabel appeared at Beauregard's elbow. "Why, Armstrong, are you calling Beauregard a bad boy?"

"I do not have the words at present, my dear, to describe my thoughts on Major Gillette. But I assure you, once I have them, he will hear them."

"Are you in trouble, Armstrong?" she said, her tone warm and sympathetic.

"Yes, Yankee General, sir," said Beauregard, all mockery and huckleberry, "just how big is your trouble? You were skedaddling like a Yank out of Manassas."

I ignored him, and said to Isabel, "Oh, nothing serious, my dear. I merely cut my way through Larsen's army of gunmen while Major Gillette was having tea."

"And that dog, Armstrong; did you bring a dog?"

"Yes, he's in your barn. He is the Bad Boy."

"But he must certainly have been loyal to follow you all this way."

"Yes, quite loyal, ma'am."

"Won't you come in? I have coffee on the hob."

"Yes, Isabel, thank you, but I must warn you; you could be in danger. I just escaped Larsen's men. They've made the Delingfold place a fortress; some may have followed me here."

"Then again," said Beauregard, looking out the window, "maybe not. If you're Larsen, maybe you're counting on a charge by some hotheaded Yankee General—a charge right down that canyon you've got all fixed up for him."

"Well, he might get a surprise then. Billy Jack signaled me. He's fetching a troop of U.S. Cavalry."

Beauregard was thoughtful for a moment; then he said: "Yankee General, sir, I reckon we've got business in town. Miss Isabel, I'd be obliged if you came with us. I don't expect pursuit, but it's possible."

She nodded and went to fetch a bag.

"General, you can leave your horse here. We'll take the wagon. You can load your Bad Boy in the back if you like."

"Are you giving me orders, Major?"

"Sir, there's something I need to tell you," he said, matter-of-fact. "I'll start by showing you this."

He handed me a folded sheet of paper on which was written in a firm, bold hand:

> In life, a man is a man and a woman is a woman;
> And in war, a soldier will honor his dead;
> For their love, a chapel provides for the wedding;
> And from gratitude, the soldier has a crypt for a bed.
>   —JMCD

"And what is this, Major, aside from a very poor excuse for poetry?"

"That, Yankee General, sir, came from Cousin Delingpole."

"Where'd you find it?"

"In the church, stuck in a Bible engraved with Cousin Delingpole's initials—and that Bible I found thrown on the floor. Larsen's boys had ransacked the church. I don't know what Yankees have against churches; used 'em for stables during the war, which seems a mite unchristian to me."

"So, what's it mean?"

"When I found it, I poked around that little church; and I'm pretty certain I know where the treasure is. I think that poem's a clue. And I'm thinking we should retrieve the treasure sooner than later."

"I know for a fact Larsen doesn't know where it is."

"I've no doubt of that, Yankee General, sir, but even a blind vulture can catch a worm occasionally. I'd rather not take the chance."

"Very well, Major, let's be off." Isabel returned, as if on cue, and I offered her my arm. "Lead the way."

CHAPTER TEN

In Which I Accept My Destiny as a Knight Errant

The three of us crowded together on the front seat, Isabel in the middle. I happily consented—indeed insisted—that Beauregard take the reins. Bad Boy jumped aboard. He was still panting, but I ordered him to regain his composure and keep watch behind us.

I meanwhile kept watch on Beauregard. I hoped that by making him wagon master I would ensure he kept his hands on the reins (which he did), and his remarks directed to the horses (which he did not). As the wagon wheels rolled on, so did Beauregard's honey-flavored tales of the Old South, as he reminisced to a wide-eyed Isabel about romantic soirées at graceful mansions, belles and beaux strolling arm in arm on immaculate plantation lawns beneath the soft Southern moonlight of a Richmond summer.

Now, Libbie, you know I appreciate the charm of Southern mansions as well as anyone—you might recall my serving as best man at the wedding of a Confederate officer, my old West Point classmate John Lea, at

Bassett Hall in Virginia during the war—but Beauregard laid it on as thick as jam on otherwise inedible hardtack.

He took her imagination dancing to the ballrooms of great manor houses. Then he pulled her heartstrings with piquant stories of the tragic aftermath: the pillared homes desecrated, the luxurious furnishings defaced, the graceful living vengefully stamped into cinders by the Yankee conqueror. He spoke of mansions in ruins; estates vandalized; masters dead in cold graves or crippled by saber cuts and bullets. He lamented the humbling of a high-minded aristocracy—the class of men from which sprang our nation's founders, the Jeffersons, Madisons, and Monroes—its few survivors financially bereft, their property, finances, and position in society reduced to ashes.

He talked about the women too—the tearful orphaned daughters and the proud widows, once mistresses of all they surveyed, who, under Reconstruction's harsh reign, struggled merely to survive. Even I was inclined to wipe away a tear, for, as you know, I always rather liked our Southern foes.

For a woman like Isabel, living on the frontier, far removed from antebellum Southern ballrooms and cultured men, the nostalgic, bittersweet glamour of all that Beauregard said was intensified. I recognized the excited glow in her eyes, because it had once been directed at me, and naturally I disapproved of her beguilement by Beauregard the Southern troubadour.

At last, however, his song of Southern sorrow came to its climax: "All that's left now is our honor, our self-respect, our conviction that the cause for which we strove was a worthy one, the same cause that drew our forefathers to Runnymede; the cause of Washington, whose image enlivened the great seal of our Confederacy; the cause of freedom and independence from a government we did not choose and did not want..."

"*That*, Major, is irrelevant. I grant you Lincoln was a Republican, not a Democrat, but he *was* elected president."

"Even so, sir, he had no right to interfere with our freedom, which must include the freedom to go our own way."

"The war is over, Major."

"So they say, sir."

"Still," said Isabel, "the South did have a worthy cause, or at least a refined, noble way of life, don't you think so, Marshal?"

"Yes, I suppose it had its points," I said, trying to tamp down her enthusiasm; to Beauregard I added, prosaically, "Watch out for those rocks, Major."

"Oh, I mean, it was all so wonderful, back in the day, wasn't it—the dresses, the parties, the beaux?"

"I will confess, Miss Isabel," said Beauregard, "it was quite a pleasant manner of life, for those who could enjoy it."

"And it's all so sad now," she added sympathetically.

"Well, yes, it is, Miss Isabel," Beauregard conceded, "but as the poet said, 'The old order changeth, yielding place to new, And God fulfils himself in many ways, Lest one good custom should corrupt the world.'"

"What a wonderful sentiment—and yet, tragic, isn't it? Is it from the Bible?"

"No, ma'am, Tennyson, an English poet."

"And you, Marshal, you were a Union General, weren't you? You fought against all that?"

"Not against that, ma'am, but for the Union."

"And you, Major Gillette, are you still against the Union?" she asked, all innocent.

"No, ma'am; I follow the noble example of the late Robert E. Lee; we must strive dutifully to make the best of things, and let the dead bury their dead."

"And you, Marshal? Are you still against the South?"

"I never was against *the South*, ma'am; I was ordered to prevent their secession; and after the war I kept the peace. But I assure you, ma'am, as a Democrat, I believed then, and believe now, that the South should be treated generously, decently, leniently. I knew too many good Southern men—and charming Southern ladies—to ever dislike Southerners as a class, but for me, ma'am, the choice was simple: I took a vow at West Point to defend the Union; I could not fight against it."

"And I, Miss Isabel," said Beauregard, "took a vow to defend my fellow Virginians; I could not fight against them."

"I'm so glad we're all united now."

"Yes, ma'am," I said, taking her hand, "all united now."

But Beauregard sensed an advantage: "And your people, Miss Isabel, surely they were Southerners? I cannot imagine that such charm could have developed north of the Mason-Dixon line."

She smiled bashfully—blast him!—and said, "Well, yes, in a manner of speaking. My parents were Tennesseans."

"And you, ma'am?"

"I was born in New Mexico."

"Well, that's South sure enough."

"My father didn't fight in the war. It was too far away, at least for the most part, and he had a family to support. He ran sheep for a while; then a dry goods store; he kept changing jobs, and we kept moving north, until we got here."

"No shame in that, ma'am. One thing I learned from the war—a man's got to look after his own."

I knew what "own" Beauregard was looking after, and I aimed for a tactical distraction. "Look out there, Major—you'll drive us into a ditch!"

"I've never wrecked a wagon yet, sir."

"Now about this treasure," I said, subtly changing the subject, "how do you know it actually exists? These hills are full of rumors of gold and silver waiting for any intrepid miner."

"Well, Yankee General, sir, we'll find out soon enough. Say a prayer I'm right—and that it's at the church."

⁋

We entered the church not through the front door, which was boarded up, but via a broken window. Beauregard threw open the sash and clambered in. I followed, carefully, and then offered my assistance to Miss Johnson. Bad Boy followed, jumping like a hunter, and I wondered if he might have a career with Miss Saint-Jean's Chinese acrobats.

It was a small church, but it had been vandalized in a big way. The pews were broken, dislodged, or flipped and sitting at awkward angles. Prayer books, hymnals, and bibles were torn and tattered, littering the floor. The altar was collapsed in the middle as if it had been punished by an ax. Visigoths in their prime could not have done any worse.

Beauregard cleared a spot with his boot and bade us look down. There was stone flooring that served as a border separating the elevated part of the church, where the altar was, from the wood floor beneath the pews. Each large stone square of this border had something carved into it. At first, I assumed each was a scene from the Bible. Beauregard's toe tapped on the inscription on one of the squares. It read: *Deo Vindice*.

"That mean anything to you, Yankee General, sir?"

"Well, Major, I assume it is the signature of the Italian who carved these stones."

"That's the motto of the Confederacy, sir. It means, roughly speaking, 'With God as Our Defender.'"

"We're not back to that again, are we, Major? I assume it means something different here."

"Don't be too sure, Yankee General, sir. I reckon that beneath that stone is a crypt."

"Well, that sounds quite eerie, but I thought our objective was buried treasure, not buried bones."

"I think, sir, that the crypt hides no human remains, but the remains of the Confederate gold."

"This is Montana, Major, not Richmond; and the war ended a dozen years ago."

"Past and present come together at this spot, Yankee General, sir. Beneath this stone is Delingpole's treasure."

"You're sure of that?"

"An educated guess, sir, based on that bit of poetry I showed you."

"I see."

"And, Yankee General, sir, there's a lot more to the story than that."

"So I surmise, Major. I trust you will explain."

"Happy to, sir, but maybe not now; now, I reckon, we need to see if I'm right."

He knelt down and brushed away dust and debris to reveal a few more details to the inscription. The words *Deo Vindice* were topped and underscored by wreaths. On each side were what looked like engraved crooks, like those used by the shepherds in Bethlehem. But as his fingers worked on these crooks like a sculptor molding immovable clay, *violá*, up they popped one after the other. He removed them from the stone and then used them as hooks on the wreaths, which folded upright, forming metal straps though which he could slip the crooks. He pulled, and the stone slowly separated itself from the floor.

"Major, let me help you."

Each of us, crook in hand, pulled—not violently; we didn't want to break the metal straps—but with firm, steady, manly pressure, until the stone came completely free, rising above a dusty shower of gravel and mortar. We carefully placed the stone to one side and peered into the dark vacancy.

"We'll need a torch," he said.

"What sort of treasure are we looking for, Major? What did you mean by 'Confederate gold'?"

"Just that, sir; at war's end, Cousin Delingpole had a secret mission. The Confederate Treasury Secretary, George Trenholm, told him to gather the Confederacy's gold—what had been saved from the mints at Charlotte, Dahlonega, and New Orleans—and spirit it somewhere safe; somewhere out West; somewhere the Confederacy might rally. Well, Cousin Delingpole did his part; he evaded every Yankee patrol. But there was no rally; there was no new Confederacy. There was only, in the end, a man without a country and gold without a cause. That's how Cousin Delingpole became the benevolent lord of Bloody Gulch."

"Am I to surmise, Major, that you were part of the mission?"

"Well, sir, I was his cousin—I knew about it. But the Confederate States of America had other work for me. Now about that torch, sir..."

There was no shortage of wood about, but it proved unnecessary. Amazingly, the villains had left the church's kerosene lamps undisturbed—so we each took one. I lit them from the box of matches I had kept during the siege (with which I might have had to set aflame our whiskey trench), and we each peered down into the darkness.

"Bad Boy," I called. "*Dropin downinzie, into the voidinzie, und let us knowinzie vether das ist ein safen holenzie.*"

He barked his version of "*Ja*" and dived into the dark. It was a short drop. He disappeared into the darkness, made a quick reconnaissance, and then returned into view wagging his tail.

"All right, Marshal. Shall I go first?"

"That would be my preference, Major," I said, taking Isabel's hand. "This being a church, we will pray for you; and if you don't return, we will guarantee you a Christian burial."

"I'm much obliged."

I took his lamp and he jumped into the darkness.

"Well, that part was easy," he said. "I'd reckon it's a ten-foot drop, sir." His hand reached up and I reached down, transferring custody of the lamp.

Our line of sight extended farther now, as Beauregard roamed about the crypt. "Come on down, Yankee General, sir. Isabel can come too. It looks safe enough."

I jumped first. After I landed, I had Isabel hand me the lamps and I set them on the ground. "Jump, my dear, and I'll catch you." I did—and then I stood there, as a sailor might with his mermaid, admiring her. Isabel represented all that was fair and good in Bloody Gulch; all of our adventures were, in the end, for her and the likes of her, I thought, so that such kind and handsome people—golden-haired, bronze-skinned, with shining blue eyes radiating our nation's future—could live in peace and harmony and prosperity.

"You can put me down, Marshal."

"I think I'd better not; it's a dirt floor, my dear, and quite dusty—and I could hold you for a very long time..."

"Put me down, Marshal."

"Very well, as you wish."

I placed her on her feet. Bad Boy growled.

"Settle down, boy. There's nothing to fear." I turned to Isabel and said, "A crazy, murderous, abusive miner kept him in the dark; he doesn't like it."

"He's not the only one," she said.

Bad Boy showed his teeth, and his growl became a bark.

"Shh now boy; you're safe here. You're with me."

"Do you think he sees something?" asked Isabel.

"There's nothing to see—except for that pile of luggage over there and those pickaxes and shovels, and that hammer and nails and cord wood. This hole is as deserted as...well, a crypt."

Bad Boy barked furiously, and then a voice came from above.

"Well, well, well, aren't you the happy couple?"

"Rachel?"

There she was, radiant in her own raven-haired way, but with an unmistakable six-shooter in her hand. "Yes, *General*; I see you've found the treasure."

"Well, not quite. Beauregard assumes it's down here, but..."

"I'm willing to assume he's right. Gus, ride off to Mr. Larsen. Tell him we've got it—*and* the general. We've got everything."

"Rachel, what are you talking about?"

"I've got some boys up here to help me. And you've helped me quite a lot too, General. Seth had you figured pretty well. He knew you weren't out here just to fight Indians. He knew what you were really after. What we all are."

"You mean to tell me you're in league with Seth Larsen?"

"Have been from the beginning; he knew you would be foolhardy enough to attack; he knew the Sioux would massacre your men; he knew, if I saved you, you would lead him to the treasure."

"But..."

"Don't try to figure it all out, Marshal. When you're an Indian captive and you see your chance with a man like Seth, you take it. The Indians run a hard school, and they taught me the violent bear it away. All right, boys, let's close 'em in until Seth gets here. Sweet dreams, General; at least I know I'm leaving you in good company."

Two burly cowpunchers lowered the stone back into place and we were trapped like rabbits in a stone-blocked rabbit hole—with hungry, squirrel-gun-toting jaspers sitting on top. At least we had our lamps.

"Well, sir," said Major Gillette, "it appears an unexpected card has been played against us."

"Yes, Major—it's as much a surprise to me as it is to you. I rescued that woman; and after all we've been through—I just can't believe she's working for Larsen."

"Well, sir…" he started, consolingly, but my anger was unstoppable.

"And I can't believe her gall in assuming my attack was foolhardy. Had I been supported, Major, as I should have been, by Benteen and Reno, we would have had quite a different outcome; but Reno, I tell you frankly, is incompetent, and Benteen, for whatever reason, has never warmed to me; in fact, he holds an unprofessional hatred towards me—jealousy, no doubt. Their duty, however, whatever their feelings, whatever their shortcomings, was clear: to support me in the attack. And I would like to know why, by heaven, they didn't. Their failure to support me turned a gallant charge into a trap—a trap beyond the agency of any Indian."

"You must forgive me, sir, but I am not familiar with this engagement, and Indians as we know are mighty clever—take Sergeant Billy Jack, for instance. Are we talking about a battle you fought out West?"

"Never mind that, but I have been betrayed, Major—and not just by Rachel."

"Well, sir, I hope you will not consider my next confession a betrayal."

"So, there's still more, is there?"

"Yes, sir, quite a bit more actually. I blush to concede that I've been less than forthright."

"Yes, Major, that has become apparent."

"I'm not *entirely* what I appear to be, Yankee General, sir. Oh, everything I've told you is true enough—but there's more to it than that."

"You're working for Larsen too."

"Actually, sir, I'm working for your own General Grant."

"You're what?"

"Well, you see, sir, old Colonel Mosby has become right friendly with the General—that is—President Grant, they both bein' Republicans and all now; and President Grant is well aware that many of these Indian agents might not be the most honorable of men, Larsen in particular. He wanted his own agent to investigate things. He asked Colonel Mosby, who recommended me, and here I am, sir, stuck with you in a cellar in Bloody Gulch, Montana."

This was such a momentous confession that it took me a while to fully comprehend it, but my mind clasped onto the essential fact: "Beauregard, you mean to say you are a Republican?"

"As I say, sir, a man has to look after his own."

"But I can scarcely believe it—a committed rebel like you."

"Still, a rebel, sir; maybe even more so than before."

"I'm at a loss, Major, I'm at a loss."

"Maybe not, sir. You see those chests in that corner. I wouldn't be a mite surprised if they're full of gold."

"But, if you're a federal agent, then the federal government means to retrieve it, yes?"

"Well, sir, not exactly. You see, my remit is to investigate Larsen and the murder of Cousin Delingpole; his secret mission is still a secret to the Yankee government."

If his earlier confession had stunned me, this one cofounded me further—for where now lay my duty; what, at this dramatic moment, was the proper course of action? On the one hand, as a United States cavalry officer, I assumed that, entrusted with this information, I should report it to my superiors, perhaps directly to Phil Sheridan. On the other hand, I was, officially, dead and in no position to report to anyone. Beauregard acting as a federal agent might have a duty to report the matter, but then again, what was the legal status of this gold, if it actually existed within those chests that Beauregard was illuminating with his lamp? Was it the property of the federal government? Or was it the property of the Englishman Delongpile, the Confederate officer who had acquired it and established this town with it? If the latter, was it then by rights Beauregard's on the basis of kinship and discovery? And if there was treasure within those chests, how were we to defend it from Larsen? But first we had to discover whether the treasure actually existed.

So, I put the question to Beauregard, "Major, are you going to open those chests, or are we just going to assume what's inside them?"

We examined the chests. There were six of them stowed like luggage in a railway station. One was conveniently without a padlock. Beauregard put his hand on it and said, "May I have the honor, sir?"

"Yes, Major, go ahead."

He flipped the chest open. I could not see its contents immediately because his body blocked my view, but when he turned around, he held up a gold coin.

"That's it?" I said. "That's the Delungpole treasure? A single coin?"

"No, sir, there's a few more where that came from, just enough to fill my pockets, which with your permission, I'll do, sir, in the interest of hiding the evidence. These other chests are heavy and have stout locks; their secrets will keep for a while." He handed me the coin. "But take a look at that, sir. Miss Isabel, you might recognize it."

"Why yes," she said as I held it up for her inspection, "these were the coins he used to pay for everything. The townsfolk accepted them—and so did Larsen because they were gold."

"So, let me see if I understand this, Major. This is formerly Confederate gold, now the legal currency of a Montana town, stamped with the image of an Englishman?"

"I reckon so, sir. I reckon that this was originally Confederate gold and that cousin Delingpole restamped the coins to hide their origin. The Confederacy never had any proper dies—so they might have looked like any other federal coin except for the mint marks. But he was mechanical like that; liked making things; so, making a die wouldn't have been beyond him. If I had to guess, all these chests will be the same. And if I had to guess, he probably had some sort of minting machine up at his estate, and destroyed it, not wanting to leave any evidence after he minted these coins."

"So, why the mine and the foundry?"

"To throw people off the scent—there's nothing there, I reckon. Larsen found nothing."

"Why, Major, this is fantastic."

"Isn't it, though?"

"But Marshal Armstrong," Isabel gasped intelligently, before turning and saying, "Major Gillette: what are we going to do?"

"Well, Miss Isabel, and beggin' the Yankee General's pardon, but if Rachel was a good spy, she's rather lacking when it comes to hostage-taking. We might be trapped here like squirrels at a barbecue, but she failed to disarm us. I'd reckon, sir, that means we could spring an ambush of our own."

"Indeed, we could, especially if we use these chests for cover. It could be a long wait, though."

"I've no inclination to wait, sir. I say we pay those guards a visit."

"Excellent suggestion: never sit and wait when you can act and do."

"Yes, I thought you'd like that, sir."

"But how?"

He held up his lamp to better illuminate what lay behind the chests, next to the axes and shovels, the hammers and boxes of nails, and the cord wood—a plank wall, about three yards square.

"One thing we learned from Mosby, sir, and General Stuart too—always have a way out. I'd wager, sir, that this here is a tunnel entrance. And if I had to guess, it'll lead us to some hidden place where we can pop up like gophers. If you'll join me, sir; I imagine it might be a little hard to shift, not having been used in a while."

There was a metal bar across the center of the planks, which, I now saw, was for opening this subterranean door. The two of us pulled, and as sure as my love for you burns strong, dearest Libbie, it opened to reveal a wood-planked tunnel, as fine as any miner could make. It was, however, unlit, and, of course, we had no idea if the tunnel was finished or where it might end. I knew what to do.

"Bad Boy! *Scoutinzie*!" I ordered, pointing down the tunnel.

He went off like a hare, and we waited with barely suppressed excitement for his return—and we didn't have to wait long. He came back bearing a small pine branch between his jaws.

"Of course," I said. "The outlet must be in the grove behind the farmyard—if you didn't want to be seen, if you wanted a convenient place to hide a horse—that's the logical spot."

"Quite industrious of Cousin Delingpole; must have taken him quite a while. Looks like he did a right good job too."

"No time to admire the craftsmanship, let's go. Major, you take the lead. Isabel, you follow. Bad Boy and I will bring up the rear, in case of enemy pursuit. Bring your lamps, and don't crowd."

Beauregard set us a good pace, scrambling like a lizard down the tunnel. Miss Johnson's pace was more like that of a graceful clipper ship, her bustle swaying gently to and fro as if borne on the waves of a salty ocean. Propriety bade me to tarry a bit, but Bad Boy pushed me with his snout, just as a mare prods an uncertain, long-legged colt to keep moving.

As a cavalryman, crawling is not my strong suit. In fact, I found the closed quarters of the tunnel shaft disquieting, to say the least. A cavalryman wants wide open spaces where he can maneuver. If it had not been for the calming effect of Isabel's rolling bustles, beckoning me like a beacon in the night, I confess I might have been a trifle agitated.

In the event, it was but a trice before Beauregard reached down and helped me extract myself from the hole, which opened at the far western corner of the grove where the underbrush was thickest.

"Well, Yankee General, sir, I'm feeling right prayerful—how about we take a pew?"

"I'm with you, Major. Isabel, you wait in your hotel room—there might be more hellfire in today's sermon than usual."

We trotted—in good order, but quickly, not wanting to be greeted by anyone—until we reached the church. Beauregard and I lined up our revolvers on the sill of the window where we had entered earlier. There were two guards sitting in chairs facing each other on either side of the crypt entrance. They were playing cards. Their revolvers were holstered.

"All right, boys!" I shouted. "Hands up—and don't touch those guns!" They were all obedience. "Now stand up nice and slow and ease your way over to the window."

Once they were within reach, Beauregard took their revolvers.

"Now you boys, head on back to those chairs," I said, and as they backed up, I moved in, followed by Beauregard. "Major, how about you prepare the crypt for these boys."

"Crypt?" said one of them.

"How the devil did you get out of there?" said the other.

"Let's just say you're not going to pull the same trick."

Beauregard slipped down the tunnel. I heard him hammering the escape hatch shut and shifting the treasure chests to block it.

"It won't be so bad. You can fill your pockets with Delingpoke treasure, but you won't be spending it."

"It's really down there? How big is it?"

"You'll see; you'll be its temporary guardians."

Beauregard called up. "All right, Yankee General, sir. Everything's all squared away. Even found a nice thick coil of rope. You can send 'em down, one at a time."

"You heard the man," I said. "Take the plunge." The first dropped down, and once he was hogtied I sent the second. When he was secured, I reached down, helped Beauregard up, and we replaced the stone.

"What now, sir?"

"I think, Major, in the spirit of your many confessions, and given that we are amidst the sanctified ruins of a church, I owe you a confession of my own: I am Colonel George Armstrong Custer, late of the Seventh Cavalry. If you had wondered how a frontier marshal could be such a master strategist and tactician, now you know. I tell you this because circumstances demand it. It is incumbent on me to operate incognito, for reasons too long to explain. But Rachel knows who I am; so apparently does Larsen; so does Miss Saint-Jean; and now so do you. That knowledge must not spread further. If Billy Jack brings the cavalry, I cannot be seen by them, and I must find a way to silence Larsen and Rachel."

"Well, Yankee General, sir, you could knock me over with a plume—straight from General Stuart's hat. *Custer*—that's a name to reckon with, sir, and I am honored, albeit astonished, to discover that my entire mission is tied up with Yankee generals."

"So, Major, without going into details, I hope you can appreciate the difficulties of my position."

"I can indeed, sir. You have your own secret mission."

"You could call it that. The entire world thinks I'm dead, Major. I cannot disabuse them until I find out who betrayed me; and until I can clear my name, I must lead the life of a knight errant, rescuing such women as I presumed Rachel to be, and Miss Johnson, and Miss Saint-Jean's entire troupe."

"I appreciate your confiding in me, sir, and as sure as Marse Robert is a saint in heaven, I'll be worthy of your trust. By my calculations, sir, Larsen will arrive here long before Billy Jack and the cavalry arrive at Cousin Delingpole's estate. In short, your every wish might be accomplished: the cavalry seizes the Delingpole place; Larsen comes here for our mutual, personal retribution; and Miss Rachel will likely be in tow as well. That gives us time, sir, for a quick council of war at the hotel parlor, and a spot of coffee."

The strategy we sketched out over coffee and biscuits was elegant in its simplicity, but would, we assumed, be perfectly lethal for Larsen and his band of cutthroats. I commanded Miss Saint-Jean to lock the girls in their rooms until the showdown was over. The Chinamen were posted as hotel guards. The engagement would be fought by just the two of us, the major and I.

We heard them before we saw them—a phalanx of perhaps twenty mounted men (Larsen was taking no chances)—their pounding hooves heralding their arrival. They brought their horses across the trench, left them at the hotel hitching rails, and exchanged sour glances with the Chinese. Then they strode over to the church. Beauregard was in the front bell tower, which gave him a view not only of the enemy as he approached, but down into the church, where that enemy would soon be. I was at the opposite end, in the choir loft behind the altar. Each of us had a Winchester along with our revolvers, and between us we had the entirety of the church interior covered.

The enemy filed in through the same window we had used. It would not be easy for them to escape. They gathered around the stone flooring, and Larsen bellowed to Rachel, "All right, where the hell are the guards?"

"I don't know, Seth, I left them here."

"Well, they sure as hell aren't here now. That's the stone, isn't it? You men, get it up."

"First man that moves gets a bullet," I called out.

"If not from him, then from me," added Beauregard.

"We've got you surrounded, Larsen. If you know what's good for you—and for your men—everyone will drop those gun belts. The game is over. President Grant himself knows what you're up to—there's no escape now."

"You think two of you can take me—with all these men?"

"Won't be two for long—we'll soon have a troop of cavalry. In the meantime, I reckon we can manage."

"Well, guess again—at 'em boys!"

The sound of gunfire in that enclosed space was deafening—and while they fired wildly, we made every shot count, and made certain not to harm Rachel. Given their advantage in numbers, we had to do a lot of ducking and rolling from one position to another, and the bell above Beauregard rang with ricocheting bullets, tolling for the dead. I spotted Larsen break for the window. I waited until he'd hoisted one heavy leg over the still. Then Beauregard and I nailed him with simultaneous clean shots. Larsen's corpse acted as a cork, plugging the enemy's sole escape route.

"Hold your fire, Marshal; we surrender."

"Best choice you boys ever made," I said. "Toss your weapons into the collection basket—the floor'll do for now, and then stand up with your hands held high; you too, Rachel."

Beauregard stepped down from the little bell tower and I leapt over the loft and onto the elevated platform that held the altar.

"All right, boys," I said, "you wanted to see the treasure—well, it's a mite dark down there, but you can do your best; lift the stone and drop right in."

Thus we had them all bottled up, save for the dead—Larsen and eight others—and Rachel, who I didn't think belonged in a hellhole with a dozen mangy murderers.

"Major, fetch Hercules and bring him here. He'll watch over the stone. Set two acrobats to guard the tunnel exit in the grove—just in case—and bring two others here to get these bodies out and buried. Leave one acrobat, and Fu Yu, as guards at the hotel. I'll meet you in the hotel parlor."

"Yes, sir."

"Rachel, I've been wondering what to do with you. I could turn you over to the cavalry—which is the real law around here—or I could send you back to the Indians or..."

"Please, Armstrong, you don't know how desperate I was."

"How desperate are you now?"

"I'll do anything. I made a mistake. I made a terrible mistake. I'm horribly sorry. Don't send me back to the Indians. Don't hand me over as a criminal to the cavalry. My daddy was a judge. What would he say? Oh, Armstrong, I'm so afraid."

"You looked pretty confident behind that gun—not like someone who reckoned they'd made a mistake. If you'd had your way, the major, Miss Isabel, and I would be dead, or maybe enslaved—Miss Saint-Jean's showgirls too. Not a very nice way to return their hospitality."

"General, you know what I've been through; a captive of the Boyanama Sioux—and then, in my desperation, to be connected with *that*"—she pointed at Larsen's corpse—"and to think that he was my only ticket to salvation."

"But you *had* been saved, Rachel; you'd been saved by me."

"For how long? Out here it's the strong and ruthless who survive; I thought that was Larsen."

"Sounds to me, Miss Rachel, that you've got your philosophy all wrong. But I reckon I know how to fix that." I kicked Larsen's corpse through the window. Then I said to Rachel, "Out you go."

$$\sim$$

I was savoring a stein of Alderney when Billy Jack appeared at the doorway.

"Sir, you're here!"

"Yes, quite observant of you, Sergeant. And you remember the major"—Beauregard raised his coffee cup in salute—"and Miss Rachel," who muttered something through the neckerchief with which we'd gagged her.

"Sir, the cavalry has occupied the Delingpole house. Larsen's men are captured or dead. And here?"

"Here we have the treasure, Sergeant, presently guarded by Larsen's men—who themselves are captured and disarmed. Larsen, by the way, is dead—and likely buried by now."

"Congratulations, sir. In French, *félicitations, mon général*; in Latin, *gratulatione imperatorem*..."

"That will do—and thank you, Sergeant. I need no further congratulations. The happy faces of the people of Bloody Gulch are reward enough. But I cannot tarry—duty calls me elsewhere."

"And me, sir?"

"You, Sergeant, have missed a great deal, but Major Beauregard will explain things in my absence. I do, however, have one more assignment for you. Please take Miss Rachel to your priest and tell him that her guardian wants her enrolled in an order of nuns—one that takes a vow of silence."

"Sir?"

"She is my ward, Sergeant, and I must do what I think is best for her. And do be careful." I motioned for Rachel to stand, revealing that her hands were bound. "I wish such precautions weren't necessary, but I fear they are."

"Sir," he said and saluted.

"On your way, Rachel. Billy Jack, Godspeed."

That left me alone with Beauregard.

"Well, sir, there's just one remaining item to clear up, and that's the treasure."

"I take it, Major, that you have a suggestion."

"I do indeed, sir. I reckon, we should have our prisoners pass those boxes up to us. They can only guess what's in them, and their testimony won't amount to much. We transfer the Delingpole treasure to Miss Saint-Jean—she's our finest business mind—with the proviso that she use the money for the betterment of Bloody Gulch. Otherwise she keeps it hidden."

"Sounds like a fine solution, Major."

"And Yankee General, sir, if I might add one more proviso: I suggest that as you ride through the West, righting wrongs and rescuing damsels, whenever you need money for your noble work, Miss Saint-Jean will be your banker, dispersing such monies as you require for as long as the Delingpole treasure exists."

"A capital idea, Major, and I accept your suggestion. And now," I said, taking a final swig of precious, cool Alderney, "I must be off. I will take Marshal Ney, Edward, and Bad Boy, and a couple of Winchesters and plenty of ammunition, if you don't mind. I have naught else of worldly value—and what more needs a man than his rifles, his ponies, and his dog?"

"You are married, sir, aren't you?"

"Yes—why do you ask?" But then it struck me: "Ah—you reckon that as a celebrated writer, I should describe this adventure in a long epistle to my wife, informing her of all we've achieved."

"That's an idea, sir. I'm sure she'd appreciate it."

"Such a letter exists, Major. I have been writing it as a contemporaneous account. I need only add a few parting thoughts and scenes, including the incidents of today. I will have this letter delivered to you—possibly via Bad Boy—if I might have your word that you will deliver it in person to my dearest Libbie."

"You have my word, sir."

"Well, then, there is nothing more to say but well done, Major. I will scribble the final pages of this letter by the light of my campfire tonight, and when next you hear from me, I trust it will be with further tales of glory."

And thus it was, my dear; and that is why that clever and mysterious man Beauregard Gillette brought you this package. Though he is a Republican, treat him kindly, for I had, as these pages attest, no greater friend in this dangerous adventure; together we lifted the Larsen tyranny and liberated the Delingplume treasure.

For now, my dear, I bid you adieu. But I will write again when I can. And please remember: if you have my staghounds Bleuch and Tuck, send them back with Beauregard. He will find me, and a man can never have too many horses and dogs.

Until we meet again, my dear, think of me in my flowing Chinese robes, bearing a marshal's star, and with you always on my arm.

Your devoted Autie